The

A

to

Rockaway

S W Hessel

CURVEBALL BOOKS

This is a work of fiction. Names, characters, organizations, places, events, and incidents are either products of the author's imagination or are used fictitiously.

Published by Curveball Books, London
SWHessel.com

GIRL FRIDAY
PRODUCTIONS

Edited and designed by Girl Friday Productions
www.girlfridayproductions.com

Design: Paul Barrett
Project management: Bethany Davis

Image credits: Shutterstock/Daniel D Malone; Shutterstock/elbud

ISBN (paperback): 978-1-8380093-0-4
ISBN (ebook): 978-1-8380093-1-1

First edition

For Harley

Prologue

Manhattan
Monday, December 8, 1980

For a split second, our eyes met. Neither of us saw it. The train rolled in fast and dragged Dan down under its wheels. My handsome young husband's face was replaced by a *SAMO IS DEAD* tag, graffitied on the train's side window. There would be no miracle escape, like in the movies, when the hero stands up and dusts himself off. No, my hero died under the A to Rockaway that evening.

Part One

Chapter One

CONNIE

After twenty years away, I returned for a fresh bite of this restless metropolis.

Earlier in the day, my mother had grudgingly said goodbye as I left our shared South London basement. I planned for my five-day trip to New York to be alcohol free, but after British Airways wedged me between arguing teens, my willpower took a knock over Ireland. The steward with the drinks cart misheard my order for just a tonic water and added a large measure of Gordon's. I didn't protest.

The never-ending immigration line and schlep from JFK to Manhattan didn't improve my mood. Then, at the Chelsea, the check-in clerk told me my room was still occupied. I left them with my yellow Samsonite carry-on and a blue-ribbon eye roll.

A minute's walk away from the hotel, at the Twenty-Third Street station, I saw him. He stood in the crowd hardly a car length away, with his head down. Moments later, we were both on a crammed C heading uptown. My intel on the guy came from a letter my mother had received a couple of months back. Sam Weston worked at Cosmic Computers, a block from the Chelsea. On my way in from JFK, I called his office and chitchatted with a rather helpful woman. After I told her I'd come in from England as a surprise, she replied that Sam usually left at six. She also let slip that he took the train from Twenty-Third Street. "We sometimes walk over together."

How old was this obliging woman? I wondered.

The train shuddered to a halt at Fiftieth, and Sam bent down to look out. His heart-shaped face topped with reddish-blond hair was reflected in the window. It was him, for sure. My God, he looked so much like Dan.

As the train moved off, I pushed the earphones of my Diamond Rio MP3 player deep into my ears. My head started to fill with Gabrielle's "Should I Stay." My Rio then clicked over to "Rise" as we thundered through the tunnels.

The tiled station signs whizzed past the window, and my mind flashed images of ten years growing up in New York. In the seventies, coming from London, I was already streetwise and enjoyed taking the subway on my own. We had the Guardian Angels here, of course—they were never much help. Whatever happened to those guys?

As I stepped off the train, my late husband's brother was by then in the turnstile. Slim and agile, he climbed the exit steps two at a time. I worried about our age gap. Hmm . . . but I could pass for ten years younger in the right light.

There it was—the Dakota. *Rosemary's Baby* pushed its way into my head. Sam paused at the iron gates to chitchat with the security guy. I decided to go up and introduce myself, but before I reached him, the breeze rustling the leaves of the elms in Strawberry Fields whispered, *He'll think you're some sort of stalker.* I turned and walked quickly back to the corner. My off-white Vivienne Westwood shirt clung tightly to my sticky armpits. So much for Dove original clean twenty-four-hour protection.

Rummaging in the tote bag my mother had lent me, I found one of her little helpers. The Coach tote had been Dad's last gift to Ma before he died. Swallowing the yellowish pill without water caused a yucky bitterness to bloom on my tongue. Fishing about in the bag for gum, I remembered my father always had a supply. "A stick of Wrigley's, Con. Spearmint or Juicy Fruit? Your choice, my girl."

It was in 1969, a month before my seventh birthday, when he didn't come home from one of his business trips. A double-decker bus with wonky brakes ran him down outside Victoria Station. He had worked as the European agent for Billy Weston's printing company. Dearest Billy came over to London, scooped us up, and brought us to live here at the Dakota. Ma and I had shared an attic the size of a closet, but an attic with a fabulous view of Central Park, if only from a single narrow window. During our first weekend, we met the rest of the Weston clan. Dan, an eight-year-old show-off, had tried to impress me with his magic tricks.

As the memory faded, I headed up to the gate after first slipping on my confidence-boosting Ray-Ban Clubmasters. Shit, Sam had already gone into the building. The guard let me through with just a nod. Had these people forgotten what happened here? I thought about poor Yoko upstairs.

As I climbed the few steps to the front office and pushed the door open, Ma's pill made my brain buzz in a super-relaxing way. No doubt my Dakota memories were waiting in line to torment me sometime soon.

Chapter Two

Monday, December 8, 1980

Our apartment was in a teensy part of the Dakota's roof space; it was initially intended for the staff who looked after Mr. and Mrs. Moneybags living below. Its location and low status meant that the elevators never made it that far up. Nobody realized, when the place was built, that the scrubby eyesore in front would transform into one of the most beautiful views in Manhattan. The tiny sink doubled as a washbasin, and we showered sideways in a shut-in cupboard thing, where we also dried our clothes.

The bed took up one whole end of the room. A bed I should've been sharing with my husband, not my mother. No way, though, could Mom find out I got hitched the week before. Apart from being shocked to hell, she would've blabbed to Dan's mother, Pam. Yes, Pam the Pamperer still mollycoddled her darling boy something rotten, even though she was eight months pregnant with another pair of twins, would you believe? Our wedding at city hall played out like a romantic movie. We grabbed two witnesses from the street. The couple from

Poughkeepsie said how honored they were. The promised diamond solitaire engagement ring remained on Dan's to-do list.

The loft's window allowed in only a tiny amount of the early-morning light and even less fresh air.

"Hey, Mom, this window is stuck—can you take a look?"

"We haven't the time for your dramatics this morning." At thirty-seven, Mom was in her prime. Her alluring auburn hair was still glossy and thick, like mine. An empty pack of Clairol Frost & Tip stashed in the garbage last week proved Mom had some help there, though.

She enjoyed the odd glass of Californian Chardonnay, but I'd never seen her tipsy.

"Mom, can I borrow some of your roll-on?"

"Yes, you should."

"Thanks. Hey, what do you mean?" Perhaps being two months pregnant made me stinkier, in some hormonal sort of way.

As the door banged behind my mother, a barfy wave surged. Having a baby was no fun. I barely managed to throw the toilet lid up before I threw up.

After rolling on a double dollop of Ultra Ban antiperspirant, "a lotion for more protection," I took a long sniff to confirm. No way did I want to stink out our new place in Hawaii. Dan had been on a short trip to Honolulu to check out his upcoming computer job and our apartment. I didn't want to get all naggy, but he'd told me zilch about it.

Dan's lovely Grandpa Billy and I had always been close. It was him I confided in with my news and also my worries about staying in the city. Dan's friends at the Chelsea, in particular, would be a problem. Billy understood immediately and suggested Hawaii. It was a place he knew well and where he had reliable business contacts.

Right now, it was time to start my day, the same way I had done since we moved here—breakfast with my mom and Dan's grandparents in the main apartment. As I headed downstairs, it dawned on me that my time here was almost over. New York had been a brilliant place to grow up, but now I needed to move on to the next stage of my life with my new husband.

Chapter Three

Wednesday, June 28, 2000

A familiar aroma of linseed mixed with Aqua Velva Ice Blue greeted me in the Dakota's lobby. Walt, the doorman, stood at attention behind the front desk with his white-gloved hands clasped together.

I took off my Ray-Bans with a flourish. "Walt, remember me?"

After a puzzled second or two, his face lit up. "Oh my, Miss Connie." He glided around the corner of the desk as if on casters. "Welcome back. How long has it been? Oh my, oh my, how lovely to see you again. How are you?"

"Very well, thanks. Lovely to see you, too." A web of broken veins surrounding his nose made me think about the three gins I'd had on the flight.

"Oh my, yes . . ." He looked me up and down before his eyes caught on my grubby pink Converse slip-ons.

A quick tote move covered my shame. "That young man who just walked in?"

"Master Samuel, or rather, Mr. Weston. He keeps correcting me. So much like his brother at that age."

"Yes, very much."

"Oh my, yes. I'm so sorry, Miss Connie, what was I thinking?" Walt's finger went into his shirt collar for a moment. The cotton was pristine white but worn through at the edges.

"Could you do me a favor? Please give Mr. er . . . Samuel this." I handed Walt a folded yellow Post-it Note. "My cell number."

"Very good. I'm sure he'll be in touch."

"Best if you don't mention our conversation to anyone else in the family."

"Yes, very good." Switching to a whisper, he drew closer. A waft of gingivitis found its way through the Aqua Velva. "Miss Connie, I may be speaking out of turn, but do take great care if you decide to get involved with the family again. Things are . . . How should I say it?" He lifted his eyebrows and nodded. "Yes, rather chaotic up there now."

My sunglass twirling, which I'd begun without realizing, ended when the Clubmasters jumped from my hand. They bounced off the front desk and wrapped themselves around one of Walt's immaculate black brogues. A ladylike curtsy to retrieve them put me a tad too close to his inseam. He flinched.

While we said our goodbyes in the doorway, a dumpy middle-aged woman dressed for much colder weather stormed through us. Her partly unbuttoned tweed jacket showed off an elaborate corset under a rough cotton shirt. A short, balding man stayed outside the door and gestured to her every so often through the glass.

"Mr. George Weston. Where is he, please?" the woman asked in a thick Eastern European accent, before turning to the bald guy and nodding.

"Let me call up to the apartment for you," said Walt. "Your name, please, ma'am?"

She turned, strode out the door, and stomped down the steps in her mannish burgundy oxfords. Her associate followed. Instead of returning to the sidewalk, they went through the inside gate into the open courtyard. I was ready to involve myself in new Weston family intrigue. Walt and I joined them. The once fabulous ornamental fountains were still in need of a refurb.

A memory of my first kiss flashed into my head. Dan and I had just returned from a special showing of *The Muppet Movie* at the Paris

Theatre. He was jumping around the fountains trying out a Kermit impression when his pepperminty lips surprised me.

The woman began shouting up to the apartments. "Mr. George Weston, you should know that you can't hide from us. What about our missionary?" She needed some deep breaths before continuing. "You come down now if you care about your family."

Walt returned to his station and called 911. He insisted I should leave. Wanting to know how it would all play out, I lingered across the road in the park. Within a couple of minutes, the pair came out and walked around the corner onto Seventy-First, where they climbed into the back of a Lincoln Town Car. As the limo drove off down Central Park West, both their heads turned and peered out at the Dakota. Who was "our missionary"? Those two didn't strike me as the sort to give up on stuff. Like me, in fact.

As I walked down to Columbus Circle, my plans started to take shape. A meetup with Sam Weston stood at number one on the list. I hoped he would call me later.

During the days before my trip, I'd daydreamed about my new life with my husband's brother. The fuzzy *New York Post* photo inside Walt's letter to Ma hadn't done him justice. Seeing Sam in the flesh sparked a much-cherished memory. On a warm summer evening in 1977, sixteen-year-old Dan was returning from his baseball game. He'd tied his shirt low around his hipster shorts, and his tanned muscle-y torso was all sweated up. It set off something new deep inside me. That lovely erotic sensation returned in a big way, while the memory played over and over again. As I pushed through the station turnstile, it was now Dan's younger brother in those low-slung shorts.

Chapter Four

Monday, December 8, 1980

Opening the door to the Westons' apartment, my nose started to fill up with the usual linseed and beeswax aromas. Dan's grandmother, Aileen, polished her surfaces to the max. The windows always got her special attention, and she Windexed them to the point the glass disappeared. They still didn't have a view of the park, though, much to her annoyance. "We should have paid the extra hundred thousand, Billy. You would have got it back tenfold." Aileen, a canny, wee, five-foot-five Scotty lady with bright, dyed red hair, was right every time.

Billy always got the blame for anything wrong, whether it was his fault or not. He didn't seem to mind, though.

Walking through the living room and toward the chitchat, I checked that everything was buffed and "up to snuff," as Billy tended to say. A ray of early-morning sunlight danced around on the window of the locked corner cupboard and tried to hypnotize me. Aileen's gleaming Waterford lead crystal glasses stood in their neat rows on the wooden shelves. "A dozen of every type and size you'd ever need, hen."

"Good morning," said Aileen when she spotted me in the doorway. She wore one of her many Pringle of Scotland pastel-colored cashmere twinsets and her favorite Clan Mackintosh tartan pleated skirt. Her little silver brooch contained a wee sprig of heather.

"Hi, guys." My upstairs before-breakfast barf had lifted my mood.

"Come and join us. Would you like some eggs today, hen?" The patterned pleats jigged on Aileen's knees as she fussed around me.

"Just Cocoa Krispies for me." Even after a decade, I still wondered why they didn't call them Coco Pops here?

"Constance, did you sleep well, my dear?" Billy's jolly red face made me smile.

"Like a top, old boy."

"Bright-eyed and bushy-tailed. Good show, old girl." Billy Weston was big boned and carried his two hundred and twenty-odd pounds without looking chubby. His remaining gray sides of hair bushed out today. Aileen would no doubt soon be wielding her wee silver-handled haircutting shears.

"Could we speak properly, please? It's nae eight o'clock yet."

"Ooh, pardon me, ma wee lassie." He sometimes used his hilarious Scottishy accent when his wife became testy.

Mom paused her toast buttering. "Oh, Connie, lovey, is your boyfriend calling in this morning?"

Husband, he's my husband, I wanted to say. "Not sure, but we are meeting up this afternoon. He's leaving work early."

Billy pulled a shocked face. "That's news to me, my dear."

"He said he had asked you personally, old boy."

"Yes, he did—just yanking your chain."

"I'm away back to my bed with the *Times*," said Aileen with a wee eye roll. "Please send Polly in when she arrives."

"Dan is finishing off the installation of the computers this morning," said Billy. "He's done a fine job. They are expensive things, but we're handling much more business. A computer will be taking over from you, if you're not careful, Evelyn, my dear."

"Not sure an Apple can quite do what I do for you, Billy." Mom gave him one of her awful winks.

"Mom, please, don't. Not at breakfast."

"One of these days, Evelyn, my dear . . ." Billy chipped in a wink of his own.

The front door shut with a bang. My husband was in the building.

"Hey, Dan." I left my Krispies for a moment to go and welcome him. A waft of his cologne hit my nose. He loved that Hai Karate—I was getting used to it.

"Hi, everyone." He had on his fab green Swedish parka jacket.

Mom clasped his arm as he passed her. "Lovey, aren't you warm in that coat?"

Dan grinned at her. "So, what's happening outside?"

"Something to do with John Lennon," said Mom. "He's in and out a lot. People keep asking him to sign stuff."

Pushing Aileen's plate aside to make space for my husband, I knocked her precious pearl-handled silver fruit knife onto the table. Billy leaned over, wiped the pocketknife, and folded the blade away.

Mom veered off into a topic she knew little about. "Things have warmed up for him now that he's recording again."

"Not sure about *Double Fantasy*." Dan knew everything about John Lennon. "Inspired by him sailing to Bermuda and having to take the wheel when the crew got sick during a storm."

"Sounds like marketing flannel," said Mom.

"You're an awful cynic, Evelyn, my dear," said Billy.

I touched Dan's wrist. "So, we're meeting up later, right?"

"Yes, I'll be all yours at three." He put his hand on mine. His gorgeously thick hair shone in the early-morning sun.

My hand went up to touch it. "I have to go. I'll be late for class."

A dribble of chocolatey milk from my spoon dropped on Dan's jacket sleeve. We both smiled at it for a second before I dabbed it away.

"I need to go to the store." Dan stroked my wrist. "Be back in ten, Grandpa."

"Okay, my boy. We're not leaving until nine o'clock, so plenty of time. You go and have a moment with your *girlfriend*."

"Let's go," I said, guiding Dan toward the door.

In the elevator, Dan grinned to himself as he scribbled something in his notebook. I tried to look, but he snapped it shut as the doors opened. "Oh, you go ahead, Con, I need a quick word with Walt."

"Okay, I should run." I blew him a kiss. "Catch you later." As far as it concerned my husband, I still attended school—I didn't, and for a good reason.

Cafe La Fortuna was closed Mondays, so I went to grab a coffee over by the Guggenheim.

Could my life be any better? I was eighteen years old and married to the most gorgeous guy ever. Next year our baby would arrive, and we'd be living away from all this city's distractions, in fabulous Hawaii.

Chapter Five

Wednesday, June 28, 2000

By 7:30 p.m., I should have been enjoying *Contact,* Susan Stroman's new play, at Lincoln Center. It promised "an evening of acrobatic swing dancing." Something to keep my jet lag at bay. But the tumbling and swinging had already begun without me, so I decided to return to the Chelsea.

While waiting for the check-in clerk to deal with a weird couple insisting on room 100, I recalled memories of the evenings and weekends Dan and I spent here. My husband's best buddy, Jack, had worked in the hotel as a busboy or bellhop or whatever. Though I never saw him bussing a table or hopping to a bell.

A well-thumbed memory of him popped up. Sitting at an upright piano, he had his graceful fingers poised above the keys. A striking Irish look of coal-black hair and milk-fair skin, coupled with his cuteness and soul-piercing blue eyes, created a trap for the careless. Many famous faces got entangled in Jack Beckett's web. He began to play "Piano Man," and his honeyed voice charmed me once again.

Once the couple had been dealt with, I asked the check-in clerk if he remembered Jack. He did, and we shared memories of his legendary stamina. His parties went on all night. He'd arrange breakfast "on the house" for survivors and always included the limo drivers. With his eyes welling up, the clerk told me Jack had died of AIDS-related complications in early 1992.

Later, in the elevator, I recalled Jack's seedier side, with its tequila-drinking competitions, late-night card games, and God knows what else. I went along to their "sessions," as Dan called them, on a couple of occasions. It was all pretty dull. Just boys letting off steam. Dan had a lot of common sense. Jack, on the other hand, could be unpredictable and never knew when to call it a night. Lucky for Dan, I was close by when he needed a shoulder to cry on after one of their massive liquor-fueled arguments about nothing.

My room on this visit skulked at the rear of the building. It retained the hotel's hallmark shabbiness, but on a much smaller scale than the swanky suites I recalled from my earlier Chelsea days.

The clingy plastic curtain flapped open as I showered and allowed me to check myself out in a small mirror above the half-size washbasin. Plenty of bloom remained on this rose.

I imagined being pregnant again. It could be just like before—me in New York expecting a baby.

Lying on the bed in my bathrobe, I pulled out a dog-eared Polaroid of Dan from my purse. "Taken by Andy himself, on his personal SX-70," my husband had told everyone, more than once. I propped him up on the nightstand against a bottle of Frog's Leap Zinfandel. A wine with "delightful aromas of summer-berry conserve combined with a touch of spice and fresh fruit flavors." It had been waiting for me in the room as compensation for the delayed check-in. In my jet-lagged fogginess, I'd opened the bottle and drunk half a glass before remembering my no-alcohol pledge.

A rasping, incontinent air conditioner made it difficult to hear the small TV, perched too high on the corner of a narrow six-drawer chest. I flipped through the channels and landed on *The Man Who Came to Dinner*, a black-and-white movie and a favorite of Dan's. We had enjoyed the stage play, back in 1980. Coincidently, a revival of it would preview on Friday evening. In my head, Sam Weston would be in the seat next to me.

Relaxing into a pleasant wooziness, I drifted back to when Dan and I made love for the first time. One of the hotel's long-term residents was away for the weekend, and her suite was free. By cutting my last class, I arrived early. The front desk clerk told me Dan had gone up with Jack. I dashed to the room and used my jaunty knock.

Jack shouted, "Hi, who's there?"

Hmm. He knew. To begin with, he barred entry, kidding me that Dan had someone with him. Then he wandered off, but not before winking at his best bud. It looked like they'd been playing cards. Three-card brag, no doubt. A game Jack had picked up from some English dude who lived in one of the better suites. Gambling brought out the worst in Dan, especially when he lost. But, judging from the pile of bills I spotted on the nightstand, his luck had been in. Two Rolling Rock beer bottles stood empty on the small round table next to the deck of grubby playing cards. Also sitting there was Dan's A5 Leuchtturm1917 notebook. "Think of it as my journal, Con, for my doodles and private shit."

He started to unbutton his shirt and invited me over to the bed. Within moments, I was on top of him, shedding my clothes. After some frantic fumbling, he groaned and finished before my T-shirt hit the carpet.

A few weeks later, a visit to the doctor's office confirmed things.

"Yes, Miss Williams, there is no doubt," said the physician.

I couldn't have been happier.

Almost twenty years later, I could hold on to that blissful old memory of expecting Dan's baby. I wanted a baby now, too. I relaxed back on my bed, turning the idea over and over until I dozed off.

Chapter Six

Strolling deeper into the park, I kept my hand tight over the top of my trusty Tod's canvas shoulder bag with its white Italian leather trim. According to Aileen, a wee thing in the *Times* last weekend warned about purse grabbing in the park. All appeared quiet today, the usual confused dudes stumbling around, but nobody threatening. They would take a dollar if you wanted them to have it but wouldn't grab at stuff. Central Park was so scuzzy these days. Not charming scuzzy, but icky, dirty scuzzy.

I quit school a week ago but decided to pretend like nothing had happened. One of the old lecturers who liked to lech over the prettier girls said my grades could be improved with a private session or two. As a married and pregnant woman, I told him to go fuck himself. What the hell? They wanted to hush things up. "Boys will be boys. You're an attractive young woman, Miss Williams." So it was: *fuck you all.* "For your information, my name is Mrs. Weston, thank you very much." Dan was unaware. I didn't want him causing bother when we were so close to leaving the city.

I bought a coffee and crossed back through Shakespeare Garden on my way to enjoy a spell on the Whisper Bench. The area was super overgrown, but the seat was spotless. The Weston family shared all their important stuff there, and as its newest member, I liked to check on it regularly.

For two people to use its powers, one sat at each end of the bench, and nobody else should be on it. You put the side of your head against the stone, and either you listened or went ahead and said what you wanted to say. It was here where Dan had asked me out on our first official date, and where, a few weeks ago, I had broken my news: "Dan, you're going to be a dad."

The way both people were positioned on the seat meant they didn't see any immediate reaction, and you had time to put on the suitable face. Dan had said nothing that day as we walked through the garden, which worried me. After a short while, though, he led me back up to the bench, and we returned to our positions. Then he asked me to marry him. "Yes. I will." My mind was soon in the world of Mr. and Mrs. Daniel Weston and their new baby—living away from the influence of his friend Jack. The best buddy who encouraged him to drink White Russians all night in random hotel rooms with a bunch of weirdos and to gamble our hard-earned money away.

Dear Billy had quickly understood my worries and come up with the idea of us moving to Honolulu. Dan had already been over to check it out. Thank God for Billy, and what's not to like about Hawaii.

Hanging around outside the Dakota when I got back from my walk was a strange-looking dude in a too-heavy-for-the-weather full-length coat. He carried a furry hat pressed up against a copy of *Double Fantasy*. As the guy came forward, his funky smell made me swerve by him and quickly walk through the gate.

"Hi, Walt. Did you spot the creepy guy outside in the fur hat?"

"Oh my, yes. According to the Lennons' nanny, he tried to shake hands with Master Sean. Strictly between us, of course, Miss Connie."

"Do you know if Mrs. Weston is home?" I lifted my bag onto the desk and rested my arms on top.

"Let me check the book. Hmm, no, Mrs. Weston went out about a half hour ago."

"Thanks, Walt. Catch you later."

Billy had said to take a few bits and bobs from the apartment for Hawaii. He knew we wouldn't snag anything valuable, only things they didn't use. Billy also mentioned, as Aileen could be overly attached to any "wee thing," to do the taking when she was out. He told me about when one of her Waterford crystal wineglasses went missing. She was convinced Polly had made off with it. To keep the peace, Billy told her he broke it. "Aileen, my dear, I panicked and hid the pieces in the garbage." But it was me who broke that glass. When I confessed this to Billy, he said, "I'll take the rap for you anytime, my dear." I loved that man.

Chapter Seven

I was dozing on the barely double-sized Chelsea bed when my Nokia cell started dancing on the nightstand. Dan's photo ended up on the carpet. It was 3:00 a.m. in London, too late for Ma.

"Hello," I said, re-propping the picture.

"So, hey, is this Connie?"

Jesus, he could have been Dan.

My eyes were on the photograph. "Yes, yes . . ."

"Yeah, hi, I'm Sam, Sam Weston. You left your number?"

"Yes. Thanks for returning my call." I searched for more to say and blinked back tears.

"So, hey, you're in the city, then?"

"Just arrived . . . Yes, from London—today."

"So, yeah, old Walt filled me in. He said you were married to my bro. I didn't even know, but hey, Con, you came to see us."

I loved that he called me Con. "Er, yes . . ." My gesticulating arm knocked the Frog's Leap onto the floor. The gurgling wine began to add to the pattern on the carpet.

"Are you still there? Are you okay, Con?"

"Yes, yes . . . Um, perhaps we could meet?" Why was I rubbing the carpet with the too-long hem of the curtain? "Are you free tomorrow?"

Sam was around the same age as Dan had been. The time had come for me to pick up my life where I'd been forced to leave off, nearly twenty years ago. He said he was due a personal day, so we agreed on one of Dan's favorite haunts, the Cafe La Fortuna on West Seventy-First, at eleven in the morning.

After we said our goodbyes, I tried to bury my face in a limp Chelsea pillow. With my mind buzzing between the two Weston brothers, I dozed off.

A little later, my jigging cell phone woke me again.

"Connie?"

"Hi, Ma, how are you?"

"How are you?"

"Wow, four thirty. You're up very early," I said, after finally making sense of the hands of my Kiki Picasso Swatch and doing the math.

"I didn't sleep a wink. Sunday can't come soon enough. Why don't you come home earlier, lovey?"

"Oh, Ma, please. I'm only here four days."

Following Dan's death in 1980, Ma and I returned to London to "get some space," as everyone called it. The understanding was that the Westons would welcome us back after a short break. Ma expected to be sent for within weeks, but then Pam had her twins, and soon after, when Billy died, it became clear they no longer wanted us. They packed up and FedExed all our stuff. With the help of a mortgage, we bought our cramped basement in Bermondsey, where we still live. At eighteen, I'd spent half my life in America. I should've been with my husband and our new baby in sunny Hawaii.

"Did you enjoy your theater?"

"Er, well . . ." I grabbed for a pillow and held it tight. "I got delayed and missed the start, so I decided to relax at the hotel."

"Constance, promise me you didn't go anywhere near *them*."

"Please, we've been over this too many times." I laid Dan's photo facedown before pouring myself a splash more of the Zinfandel. "How's everything else?"

"Auntie Betty popped by this evening. We shared a little drink."

"No, really, Ma." I downed a mouthful of wine.

"Why not come home? Your aunt will leave me alone then."

I tapped the nightstand with my glass a couple of times. "Oh, I have to go. Someone's at the door. I'll call you tomorrow."

"Tomorrow?"

"It's not midnight yet, here. You know what I mean. Later."

"Well, yes, later. Who's at the door at this hour?"

"Got to go. Love you. Bye."

I took a last swallow of wine and pulled myself under the staticky bed linen. Sam Weston was already in my head, and now my body wanted him, too.

Chapter Eight

Monday, December 8, 1980

My hands were deep into the cutlery drawer when the front door opened.

"Hello, is that you, Connie?" Aileen was back.

I threw all the utensils in my hand into an almost-full paper grocery bag. After dropping it to the floor, I silently closed the drawer and stood with my back to the counter.

"Yes, hi. I just need to . . ." Not wanting to get myself or Billy into any trouble, I bundled the swag outside the service door without mentioning a word. "Er . . . I'm here to freshen up."

"Would you like to share a chicken salad, hen? How about a wee glass of Chardonnay?"

"Yes, thanks."

I sat at the highly polished table and stared at the front page of the *New York Times* and then over to my reflection on the wood—did I look guilty?

"Now, where's Polly put my lovely wee sharp fruit knife?" Aileen asked the room. "The one I always use for tomatoes. It was here in the drawer at breakfast."

Oh, shit.

"Maybe she's put it somewhere else." The *Times* covered my lying face. I would return it later.

"My particular knife, you remember the one. My da gave it me when I joined the Girl Guides in Edinburgh. The knife with a lovely solid silver blade and pearl handle."

"It will turn up, for sure." I squared the pages of the paper.

"Anyway, sit yourself over here—let's eat." She pulled my chair out, then went back to the drawer for a further rummage. Before joining me at the table, she picked up a pair of her remaining Waterford wine-glasses. She placed one in front of me and took the bottle from the refrigerator. She drew out the half-in cork and poured us both a gener-ous slug. "I caught your mom drinking a wee glass of this with George when I came in last night. My son's pregnant wife would, no doubt, not approve."

I had my suspicions that something was going on between them.

"This all looks lovely—thanks, Aileen." Speaking of pregnancies, I'd only take tiny sips of the Chardonnay.

"So, my granddaughter is coming over this afternoon. Why can't you two stop all your nastiness? You were such firm friends until your hormones started up."

She had a go on this every so often. Between sixteen and seven-teen, Dan had grown hunkier before moving up to super gorgeous. We checked each other out. I spent all my time with Dan and stopped hanging out with Lou. She protested at first but realized she couldn't compete with her brother's increasing handsomeness. She switched to resenting us both, before ignoring me altogether.

"Someday we'll kiss and make up." I wouldn't be holding my breath.

"You two had so many plans. All those places you wanted to travel to. Your little plays. Yes, we loved those performances."

Yes, our plays were so much fun. Lou and Dan came up from Brooklyn to the Dakota almost every Sunday, and we would put on a performance of the *Dakota Soap*. A spicier version of *Mr. Rogers' Neighborhood*. Lou and I ran up our scripts while we waited for lunch.

Dolls and stuffed toys stood in for the residents and staff. We wrote so well together and came up with all sorts of plots and stuff. The Lennons appeared in every installment. An actual Beatles puppet played John, and a white rabbit with a floppy hat and dark glasses acted as Yoko. I later realized it was a Ringo puppet. A weird, frizzy, blue Gonk, which had come with me from England, stood in as Dan's dad. Nobody here had ever heard of Gonks. Billy loved the big old bald teddy bear we used for him. Aileen always made out not to be interested, but as soon as she spied the crazy coiffured Barbie wearing a kilt and bagpipes accessory, she leaned in.

"We had ideas of writing together. For TV and the movies."

"You two would be good, really good. A real shame, hen."

She was right, as always. We ate our lunch, sipped our wine, and made general chitchat.

"Time for me to go meet Dan," I said, making a plan to head back to the service stairs to pick up my haul. I could return the knife at breakfast, slipping it into the drawer when I got a spoon for my Cocoa Krispies.

The janitor entered the apartment, followed by his young son, who fastened himself to the guy's leg. The boy's mom worked for Aileen's neighbor across the hall.

"Hey, young man, how you doing?" As practice for being a mom, I decided to be more buddy-buddy with kids and their parents. "How old are you?"

Still holding his dad's leg, he tried to hide his face.

While his dad unscrewed a light bulb in Aileen's most treasured Tiffany lamp, she anxiously took a breath and held her hands up just in case. The guy managed to free the bulb and, with one quick movement of his wrist, put the replacement in. Aileen breathed out, lowered her hands, and turned away.

"He's five, five today," the man said. "We're taking him and his brother to see *Flash Gordon* at the movies. The boys are mad about the comic book."

"Yeah, Flash ah . . . um . . ." The boy attempted the theme tune.

"What's your name, sweetheart?" My list of words to try out included "sweetie," "pumpkin," "dear," and "darling." Not "lovey," though—that was too English and far too mom-ish.

He stepped forward and muttered a word. It sounded like "Jaden."

Aileen broke in. "There is some garbage outside if you're headed down." She rarely made general chitchat with the domestics.

As his father turned and nodded to Aileen, the boy stamped on my foot. I raised my hand but quickly lowered it. His small, dusty footprint stood out on my pristine pink Chucks—the little . . . sweetheart.

They let themselves out through the service entrance. As the door closed, the father picked up my grocery bag, and his son turned and pushed out his tongue. Damien from *The Omen* sprang to mind.

I planned to call Walt from the print shop and get him to retrieve my loot.

Ⓐ

Outside the building, John Lennon's limo swooped in and almost knocked me over. The fur-hatted, weird guy thrust his record forward for signing. Lennon ignored him and went on into the Dakota. The man's face took on a dark scowl as he mouthed, "Fuck you." His finger went up as I turned onto Central Park West.

Just in time, I spotted Lou coming up from the Seventy-Second Street station. I took advantage of the walk sign and diverted over to the park.

Chapter Nine

Why had I built this meetup with Sam into my life's most important event in twenty years? I needed calming down. The inch of Zinfandel left in the complimentary bottle looked tempting, but I didn't want a red, winey mouth at this hour. After trying some deep breathing for five minutes, I felt panicky and downed the wine anyway. A quick sluice with mouthwash took care of matters.

Was this whole thing a bad idea? Did Sam already have a girlfriend? He must have, looking like that.

Wearing my lucky Dakota blue Levi's boyfriend jeans with my freshly rinsed and dried Viv Westwood shirt, I headed for the door. Shit, I needed the bathroom again.

With ten minutes to spare, I turned the corner onto Seventy-First and spotted the Italian colors of Cafe La Fortuna's canopy. Close to the Dakota, it had been a regular haunt of John Lennon's. His photographs still decorated the otherwise naked brickwork.

After a quick freshen-up in the cramped restroom, I took a table with a clear view of the door and ordered a black Americano. The grumpy young server's pigtails swung about as she worked the levers on the old Gaggia machine—"Baby One More Time" played in my head and distracted the butterflies below.

Ten minutes after our agreed-upon time, Sam strolled past the narrow window and up to the door. He checked himself out in the glass—something his older brother had always done, too. I stood and gave an awkward wave as he made his way over. My God, talk about gorgeous. What was he thinking right now?

We shook hands—a lovely soft, dry hand, but unlike his brother's, on the small side.

"Hi, sorry to spring this on you." I sounded all high-pitched and squeaky.

His eyes were moving all over me. "Yeah, Connie? Is that what I call you?"

"Yeah, no one uses Constance."

"Hmm, no, Constance is a bit weird, but, yeah, why not?" His eyes did a final lap.

What was his rating out of ten?

"Five . . . uh, no, I'm ten minutes late. Sorry, Con."

"Er . . . No problem. Um, yes, seeing you yesterday reminded me so much of Dan."

"A little better looking, though, wouldn't you say?" He gripped his chin and showed me his profile before nodding at my almost empty cup. "A refill?"

"Yes, black coffee, please." The sun shone in through the window, and for a brief moment, a glowing halo surrounded his total gorgeousness. Sitting back down, I almost slipped off my chair. Shit, I should be back, living in this city.

"Hey, snap." He clicked his fingers and pointed at my red Nokia on the table. "You have the 8210."

Sam pulled a blue version halfway out of the pocket of his snug-fitting Levi 505s. My eyes rested there for a short while after he returned his cell. He caught me and went off to order the coffees, grinning. His Converse Weapon 86 Hi sneakers, the ones with indigo detailing and yellow laces, confirmed that this guy had style.

"She's bringing them over." He sat down opposite me. "Yeah, you leaving your number was weird. Walt said to call you, though."

"So pleased you did." I was in love with his smile . . . and those sneakers.

He ran a finger under one sleeve of his black Stüssy Eight-Ball tee. "Only the other day, I discovered that Dan owned one of the first Apple computers."

I leaned in to inhale. "Yes, your grandpa Billy bought it for him. Dan taught himself how to program it and modernized the family's print business." Did I sound boring?

"Yeah? My bro was so cool. The print shop almost went down after Grandpa died, but we still own the property. We do the odd job for old-time customers. Ant handles that kind of stuff."

"Oh, yes?" Wow, so he still worked there. I hadn't thought about Anthony since leaving New York in 1980. Perhaps I hadn't been very sympathetic back then.

"I visited the shop last week, the first time in ages." Sam yawned and ran his hands through his lustrous strawberry-blond hair as he put the chair on two legs and rested his knees against the tabletop. "Yeah, the family wants me to get more involved in the business now Dad is so out of it."

"Okay, nice."

My inner Ma voice taunted me. *Don't lean back like that, young man; you'll ruin the chair.*

"Yeah, they're doing almost nothing now." His eyes began to drift away. "Old Ant is on easy street."

"What about the awesome old clock in the office—like the one in the movie *It's a Wonderful Life*?"

"Oh yeah, love . . ." Now full-on staring over my shoulder, he nodded to someone behind me. "Um, that movie."

"Yes, the clock is in the Bailey Building and Loan. You see it during the run on the bank. When George and Mary are leaving for their honeymoon," I continued on, regardless.

He turned his attention back to me, a little at least. "Yeah, such a great movie."

"The one in Billy's office chimed all the time. When I used to go down to meet Dan, we always raced to be out of the door by the last bong of six." The thought brought back Billy's warm, smiling face.

"The thing is still ticking and bonging away. Suppose Ant must wind it."

I needed better anecdotes. "Ha, yes, the sort of thing Anthony would do." His snaggle-toothed mouth now flashed through my mind.

"You know old Ant? He's been with us forever. Well, I guess I'm his boss now." Sam tapped his fingers on the table and frowned. "Yeah, he'll be moving off easy street pret-ty soon now."

"Were you wearing Dan's Levi denim jacket yesterday?"

"Wow, good spot, Con. Found it in a locker down at the shop. His old Apple was in there, too." He fished around in his pocket and brought out a familiar brass key. "Appeared from out of nowhere last weekend. Someone suggested it might be for a locker at the print shop."

"Sounds intriguing."

"Yeah, intriguing. Pretty weird, too, how nobody opened the thing in twenty years."

"Pretty weird," I mimicked back, all playful.

As he stretched his arms above his head, some tufts of underarm hair became visible. His scent was Dan's. It took me by surprise. My attraction to Sam Weston dialed up to eleven.

"Are you okay?"

"Yes, sorry, please carry on. What else did you find?"

"Dan was heading off somewhere. His passport was in a bag along with clothes and stuff. Yeah, and a bundle of twenties, nearly five hundred bucks."

"Wow, yes, for our trip." Hmm . . . I didn't know he had a passport. He never mentioned I should get one. What was that about?

"Where were you going?"

"Honolulu." I ran my sweaty palms up and down my inner thigh.

"Nice . . ." He noticed as I dried my hands and swallowed. "So, yeah, Hawaii . . ."

A peep at my watch confirmed we'd already been talking for a quarter of an hour. Our conversation was bubbling away nicely. Sam seemed genuinely interested in me and the way I was connected to his brother. He must have done the math on my age, but hey, maybe he was one of those modern young guys who preferred more experienced women? I wondered if he would invite me up to the apartment.

Chapter Ten

Monday, December 8, 1980

The presses were humming to each other as I entered San Remo Print. Those machines never got tired of defiling truckloads of virgin white paper. An inky stink filled the air and made me giddy, but not in a barfy way.

Dan's best bud, Jack, came bounding down the steps toward me. He missed the last step and skidded to a stop, inches from my face. "Connie, hi, if you want Dan, he's doing some computer thing."

My supersmart husband looked after all the Apples here. His computer obsession had really paid off. Though, I remember being jealous of all the time he'd spent playing with his Apple when we first started dating.

"Hey." I forced a smile.

"I'm here to drop off a tape." Jack tapped the pocket of his too-smart-for-this-time-of-day jacket. He'd probably been to see one of his *special* friends. Why was Jack wearing Dan's new Vans #95 skateboard shoes? Only the other day, Dan had told me he was saving those for Hawaii.

"Isn't this out of your way? We're meeting up later." I stared at the shoes.

"I thought one of my famous mixtapes for his new Walkman might cheer up the old Danster. He's lost his mojo recently." Jack removed the hand-decorated cassette from his pocket, but his pianist's fingers hit a bum note. The thing slipped from his grasp and burst open on the floor.

I kept my hands behind my back. "Hmm, yes, lovely. What is up with the . . . the old Danster, and when did he last have his mojo?"

Jack collected his tape and shoved the pieces into his pocket. "Maybe something to do with him leaving the city and all his friends"—his milky skin turned pink—"to jet off to the middle of nowhere."

I caught him in a stare. "What do you mean?"

"Well, you've got yourself pregnant, and you're forcing him to move to the other side of the fucking planet. Is there more?"

"Wow, what's that to you?"

"I'm losing my best buddy since kindergarten. That's all."

"Did he tell you we got married last week?"

"Jesus, the fucking idiot," Jack said in a whisper. "Sorry, Con, I shouldn't have said any of that." He flashed his long eyelashes. "I'm going to miss you. My sis will, too."

I put on a frowny face. "So, you told her?"

"No, Dan swore me to secrecy. Can't you both stay in the city? I would be a spectacular uncle. We could set up one of those nursery things at the hotel."

Jack worked his magic, and my fists relaxed. "I'm sure we'll be back soon." We wouldn't.

"But why go all the damn way to Hawaii? Why not Jersey?"

"His grandfather found him a job in a computer place in Honolulu. There's an apartment and everything."

"Living over the shop isn't right for mom and baby, surely?"

"The weather is amazing there. And no violence." I rubbed my tummy. "I'm thinking about the future."

He nodded but stared blankly at the door.

With all his friends at the Chelsea, he didn't need my Dan. The old Danster was wasted on him.

"Okay, right, catch you later," he said.

"Yes, take care, Jack."

He half turned, fixing me with a stare. "Yes, you be sure to take care, too."

"Everything all right, Connie?" asked Anthony, who popped up from somewhere. He was the dorky guy who worked on the computers with Dan. His thick reddish hair dropped down over his ginger-haired, stubbly, acne-covered face. Gross snaggleteeth poked from his lips. Lips he kept on licking. I called him Licky Lips, but not to his spotty face.

"Yeah, I'm good. Why? Shouldn't I be?"

Mom always knew Dan's whereabouts, so I headed over to her station. Billy had set her up outside his office at the end of a corridor. Her 1940s, crappy, partly wood, mostly metal desk faced out to welcome visitors—or to keep an eye on what was going on, more like. It stood in a random checker pattern of worn-down, loop pile, downright nasty, black synthetic carpet tiles. Odd chairs that must've lost their mojos sometime in the 1960s completed the scene.

Before I got halfway down the corridor, I caught the sound of chatter and laughter coming from Billy's office. Mom was eavesdropping for sure.

"Hi, Mom."

She jumped. "Oh, Connie."

"Is Dan around?"

"He's installing the new girl's computer." She glanced up for my reaction, no doubt. "I'm popping down to get her Social Security details."

Sorry, Ma, worries about new girls have lost their power since I got married. "Tell him to hurry on up, could you?"

"Do you remember Burt?" Mom nodded toward the door.

"God, we haven't seen him in forever."

"He's in with Billy. George arrived a few minutes ago."

"Interesting." George was all about the money these days, with his hush-hush deals.

"Okay, Connie, I'll leave you to it. You'll find a copy of *Vanity Fair* and a *Women's Journal* from home. They're over in my top drawer if you fancy a flick through?"

"Thanks." Wow, *Women's Journal* from England, what was she thinking?

She picked up a natty pale-green leather purse and started on her way. Mom sniffed the air as she passed me and nodded. *Yes, Mom, I rolled it on thick.* I needed to know more about the new purse, but at that moment the goings-on in Billy's office were calling me. I positioned the 1960s purply swivel chair opposite the door and listened.

Billy came through loud and clear. "So we'll be in touch early next week, old man. We'll hang on to it and find a buyer. No sense in going down to one of those auction houses. We'll give you a fair deal."

"No need for the wife to get wind of this cash injection, eh?" Burt's volume level matched Billy's.

They laughed loudly and clinked glasses.

"Thanks, boys. I'll see myself out."

Before the door opened, I dashed over to Mom's desk and shuffled some papers.

Still facing into his office, Billy said, "We'll catch up next week, old man."

"Less of the old." A red-faced Burt carried on chuckling as he left the room. He spotted me. "Well, Connie, my girl, you're all grown up. Mighty fine you look, too. Are you still dating that no-good Weston boy? You need a reliable, mature man." He pointed at himself and laughed.

"Ha-ha, how are you, Burt?" My nose filled with the whiskey fumes coming off the purple-cheeked old boy.

His bloodshot eyes began to wander all over me. "I'm mighty well. Doing some business with the guys. Mighty nice to see the shop again, and the newfangled computers."

"Yeah, Dan is really into the computer thing."

"Billy tells me young Anthony Houseman is working here now. His stepmom is real sick. That boy is the only help she's got. He's the reliable type. Well, must keep moving, got stuff to do. Furnaces don't service themselves. Well, maybe one day, if computers . . . Well—"

"Great seeing you, Burt."

"Yes, you too, my girl." He took a step back and whispered something to himself before leaving.

Needing to know more about the *business* they were doing, I returned to my listening position.

"Burt receives the sale price, and we take a commission. You hear me on this?" Billy boomed out.

"Yes, you are . . ." Damn, why hadn't George inherited his dad's loud voice?

The chair got jammed on a tile as I moved it closer to the door. The heavy metal bit almost gashed my leg when it did a swivel without warning.

"We need to be fair, my boy. Remember, reputation is everything. Let's ask Dan to go along to Albertson's studio. They'll do a professional job, and we—"

"Don't let the boy leave it with them." When George got excited about money stuff, he spoke over people. "Ask him to wait. No need to mention . . ."

"Yes, of course, son."

George walked out of the office. "This could be a—" He stopped midsentence when our eyes met and gave me a smile. He was always friendly but didn't do chitchat, which suited me fine. Whenever we talked, he appeared bored, and his eyes skipped around, looking for better options. His son did the same.

Billy emerged with a massive grin on his face and hugged me. "Hey, Constance, my dear, are you wanting me?"

"I'm waiting for Dan. He's doing computer stuff with some new gal. Mom is reminding him about me."

"Oh yes, the attractive blonde. Er . . . she's not a patch on you, though."

"Thanks, Billy." I smiled and touched his arm.

"The tall one," said George, without looking up. He finished writing his note and wandered off to the restroom.

"We need Dan to do something before he stops for the day." Billy examined the contents of his wallet. "I'll give you the price of a good meal as compensation."

"So kind of you." My touch moved up to grip his forearm, and I switched to a whisper. "I'm trying to focus Dan on you-know-what. The sooner we're away from best buddies and random new girls, the better."

Chapter Eleven

Thursday, June 29, 2000

At Cafe La Fortuna, things had gotten busy, and our coffees were still somewhere on *Britney's* to-do list. Sam and I had been chatting about Hawaii, but neither of us knew much about the place. It was like I'd pressed play on a movie paused in December 1980, but the lead actor had been recast.

If we began dating, I could see myself getting close to the family again.

Sam stood. "Where's our damn coffee? That girl is—"

"No problem," I said in a whisper.

"Well, it will be if we don't get it soon." He sat, then got up again. "Miss, please . . ." He jabbed his finger in the air.

She replied with a finger of her own.

Oblivious, Sam fished out Dan's old silver peace dollar from his back pocket and started the thing moving through his fingers. Dan had found that coin behind my ear so many times.

I remembered Walt mentioning that things were "rather chaotic" in the apartment—time to find out what was going on. "Um . . . when

I was at the Dakota yesterday, an Eastern European woman barged in, shouting for your father."

"We heard the noise outside. The whole thing started Dad off. He talked on and on about weird shit. He kept calling me Dan. The denim jacket didn't help."

"What's wrong with him?"

"His doc thinks he's gotten, like dementia, I guess? He's only sixty-nine . . ." Sam paused. "Or fifty-nine? He's totally confused, any which way. One minute he sprained his ankle in the park walking my sister's stupid dog, the next he can't remember who anyone is."

"Gosh, how awful for you all."

"Gosh." He smiled. "Lou looked like she understood what that woman said. You know my older sis, right?"

"Oh, yes."

"Well, she moved back in when Dad started with his memory-loss thing. What a pain in the ass she is . . ."

The coffee arrived.

"About time, Miss, you—"

"Are so welcome, Sam." She flicked a pigtail.

Oh, yes, they had history.

"Bit—" He took a deep breath. "Yeah, there's another sister. Her name is Liza. She's only ten minutes older, but we ain't close."

Sipping, with my eyes raised over the cup, I expected the coffee to be warmer. "So, you, Lou, Liza, and your father are living in the apartment?"

"Yeah, also, this physio . . . a guy Liza brought in to massage Dad's foot after his accident. Scandinavian . . . a physiotherapist, is it? He's now Dad's full-time caregiver. His name is Jacob, and he's screwing my sis. The guy lives in our attic room with Liza—awesome view of the park."

"My mom and I lived up there." I thought about the double bed I had shared with my mother for ten years. It took up nearly all our space. "Did you know that my mom worked as your grandfather's personal assistant?"

"Yeah, no, they never talk about those days."

"Your grandma was very kind to us, but after Dan . . ."

"Dear Grammy passed a month ago. An accident, would you believe? Jacob found her. She fell in her bathroom. She never normally took her bath in the middle of the afternoon. One too many martinis at her lunchtime bridge party, they said." Gazing unfocused into space, he continued, "She did insist on having the marble floor. We would have been in trouble without her. She took the place of our mother. Grammy told us that Mom had spiraled down after Liza and I were born. Dan's accident, apparently, hit her hard."

"He was her darling boy."

Brittany stared over and began twiddling the end of one of her ridiculous braids.

"So yeah, Mom drowned herself in gin. Dead in less than a year. As Grammy said, 'She was a mother ruined.'"

"Did your grandmother ever mention my mom or me?"

He thought for a moment before taking a slurp of his coffee. "Nothing springs to mind."

Shit, it's like I never lived in the apartment and was never part of the family. But no point torturing myself with all that, when I needed to focus on now and the future. "So what do you do, Sam?"

"My main job is in a computer place downtown. I worked for them while I was in school. They wanted me to go full-time, so I ditched Columbia. The whole millennium-bug thing made us a pile of cash. I write code in my spare time. A buddy and I are writing a game for the new Nintendo. I should head on over to the Valley." His slender fingers were in his strawberry-blond hair again as he leaned back. "Yeah, *the* Silicon Valley."

"Wow, *Silicon Valley* sounds like an excellent move."

He was just like Dan. Same fantastic hair, too.

"After Dan died, nobody, other than your grandfather, wanted us here. Even he thought we should return to England for a few weeks until things settled. We arrived back in London before Christmas, then Billy passed in early 1981."

"Yeah, so, if Grandpa hadn't died, you'd have come back?"

"For sure. My mother and I are US citizens. It makes visiting easy, but this is the first time I've been back."

"What are you up to in little old England, Con?"

"We live in London, so loads to do. I teach visual art at a local college." How did I come across? Girlfriend material or more middle-aged maiden aunt trying too hard?

"I should come visit. Such a cool place."

I looked him in the eye. "Is anyone keeping you here?"

He glanced away. "Did you remarry?"

"Um, no."

"Any kids?"

"No, unfortunately not." I wanted one, though. *I plan on having one with you, Sam. We would live together at the Dakota—in the attic apartment.*

"Well, you're still young, so?" He reddened.

Jesus, was I scaring him? Were my thoughts leaking out somehow? "Are you up for a stroll in the park?" I needed more time to work out my next move.

"Good idea, Con. Let's do it."

The sun shone as we talked and walked. We sat up on the rocks and chatted about music and movies. I likely did most of the talking. A call to the concierge of the Chelsea snagged us two tickets for *The Man Who Came to Dinner*. We arranged to meet at the theater on Forty-Second Street at seven the following evening. As we said goodbye, he surprised me with a kiss. Unexpected or what? I mean it was just on the cheek, but still . . .

Savoring my Sam moments, I skipped down Broadway like a teenager with a first date on the books. My show-tune renditions of "Just Leave Everything to Me" and "It Takes a Woman" didn't receive a second glance. I loved this city.

Chapter Twelve

Monday, December 8, 1980

As Billy and I chitchatted together outside his office at the print shop, it hit me just how much I was going to miss this man. But my future lay with Dan and our baby in the superfriendly Aloha State.

"Not sure who's going to take care of the Apples when you leave us." Billy appeared unusually glum. "Dan says Anthony is a quick learner, but . . ."

"Burt told me his mom is very sick."

"Oh, you talked to Burt. Did he mention . . . ?"

"No, we just made small talk."

"Did you overhear anything?" Billy knew me too well. "Doesn't matter if you did. You're part of the family now."

At that moment, Dan and Mom wandered up the corridor, chatting and laughing.

"Hey, Con." Dan's gray San Remo Print sweatshirt was all sweated up.

Dan leaned over and planted one of his office kisses on my cheek. I inhaled deeply.

Billy broke the spell. "Can you come in for a second, my boy?"

"I'm finishing early, remember? Con and I are going out to do *stuff.*"

"What *stuff*, Daniel?" I could almost hear Mom's radar blipping.

He turned and grinned at his mother-in-law.

If only she knew. We planned to tell Mom everything on the day before we left for Honolulu.

"My boy, come with me." Billy led him into the office, then shut the door.

Mom picked up and twiddled a pen. "What are they up to?" She tapped her foot, drummed her fingers on the desktop, and stared at the closed door. She returned her purse to the safekeeping drawer. "What was Burt doing here, for starters?"

"Furnace cleaning?" I suggested.

"We do the servicing in the summer. We can't do without the heating now."

That green purse would go well with the Salvatore Ferragamo sling backs I had borrowed from Aileen.

Dan came out of Billy's office with a slim portfolio in his hand. "Hey, Con, I need to take this over to Albertson's on Forty-Sixth. Do you want to hang out here? I'll leave you my Walkman. You can make a start on *The Catcher in the Rye*, too, if you want. You'll love the guy, Holden." He pulled the book and the Sony from the pockets of his green parka separately. He flashed each before pushing them back and tossing me the coat.

So they were getting whatever it was Burt had brought in professionally photographed. "I could come along."

"No, best if you wait here," he said.

"We're meeting the guys at seven, remember?"

"Don't worry. I'll be back ages before."

Anthony slid in, blinked, and licked.

"Hey, Ant, can you finish off the last of the Apples in Carl's office?" Dan showed off his managerial potential.

"All done." Anthony stood taller for a moment. He tried a grin before covering his mouth and blushing.

Dan's eyes darted between us. "Now, don't you go seducing my girl with your sexy moves, you dirty dog."

"No, Dan. I'll . . . go back and sort Apple stuff . . ." He caught my eye, reddened, and covered another snaggle show.

"Well, I'll leave you two lovebirds to coo together. Now, remember, Ant, don't—"

"Daniel, don't tease the boy." Mom came over and gave Anthony a little squeeze.

"Yes, catch you later." Hugging his jacket, I detected Dan's top-secret notebook. But I would be respecting his privacy—no chance.

Dan ran back. "Oh, Con, sorry, can I?" He took the parka and removed his notebook from the pocket, along with the gloves I had bought him for winter. "Thanks, Con." He strode off, holding his secrets.

Anthony reminded me of a faithful old Labrador, the way he hung around Mom's desk. He even baked a chocolate cake for her birthday, with her name on the top in real icing. A weird guy. But the cake was super tasty.

Ⓐ

In the print shop's small kitchen, I found a can of Mountain Dew in the refrigerator. After I'd taken a couple of large gulps, Anthony came in and nodded. *Shit, was it his soda?* I smiled and left the room, slurping the drink. Needing Hawaii stuff, I decided to make a quick trip to Loehmann's on Seventh, and I headed for the front door. While trying to aim the empty can in the trash, I walked straight into Jack's sister, Josie.

She lifted and inspected the foot I'd just trodden on. "Are you and Dan leaving the city?"

"So, the word is out," I said to the back of her head as she checked for damage.

"Oh, Con, we'll be sorry when you go." She was shaky, but that might have been to do with her one-legged shoe dusting.

"You'll miss Dan, but—"

"No, you too, but Jack and Dan were best buddies in first grade—"

"So this will be the first time they've been parted, but we're all set."

She held me in a stare. "Is Dan ready, too?" Why did Josie and her brother think Dan had doubts?

"Yes, definitely. We are off to Hawaii after the holidays."

"Oh, that Anthony guy is over by the door." She did another check on her shoes.

"He's always around."

"Doesn't he freak you out?"

"My mom likes him."

"He's more like a stalker. You take care. Honolulu, you lucky girl."

"Billy arranged everything for us."

"I presume twin sis Louise isn't in the loop?"

"Nobody other than Billy, and now you and Jack. Likely others . . ."

Mom appeared with her coat on. "What's all this, girls?"

Josie helped me out with her cheerful tone. "Hello, Mrs. Williams."

"Your Jack was here earlier." Mom opened her lovely new purse and looked inside. "Is everything cool?" She snapped the bag closed, looked up, and smiled.

"Yes, really cool, thank you, Mrs. Williams." Josie wrapped her tongue around the words.

Mom gave her one of her frowny looks before turning to me. "Louise is coming to see you."

Dan's sister needed to be told the whole story, but not today. I spotted her arrival, and as she spoke with Anthony, I left through the side door with Josie as cover.

Ⓐ

Thirty minutes after returning from my shopping, I put a message on Dan's desk, slipped his jacket over my arm, and started for the door.

George burst out of Billy's office. "Connie." He paused for a breath. "Glad I caught you." He pulled out his Lefax organizer. Made from a beautiful, soft, dark-brown kid leather, it was a gift from my mom for his birthday. She couldn't resist stationery stuff, but he was a married man. Mom probably got some sort of sexy feeling every time he produced the lovely thing in front of her.

"Yes, how can I help?"

He opened it up and rubbed his fingers together under his nose. He removed five crisp twenty-dollar bills. "For you and Dan." He took a long sniff of the lovely leather as he returned it to his pocket.

"Thanks, George."

The Burt thing must have been big bucks. A hundred dollars was a huge handout for George. I wanted to know what could be so valuable.

I headed off to the West Fourth Street station, running the possibilities over in my mind and hoping that Dan had peeked into the portfolio.

Chapter Thirteen

Friday, June 30, 2000

With the flight home scheduled for the following night, my theater evening with Sam needed to be a success. We had chemistry for sure, but how close were we to entering the bedroom? I should have booked a longer stay. My low-rent room was a huge worry, but right now, I had to focus on an outfit. The few options from my yellow Samsonite carry-on lay like tumbleweeds on the unmade bed—none was Sam suitable. While re-ironing and folding, I recalled the subway ad for H&M's first store in the US. And it was only a short train ride away.

After half an hour in the place, all the patterns and colors started to make me dizzy, so I headed back to the hotel. Walking down Fifth, I pulled my only purchase out of its bag for a quick look. Shit, the blue top was the same as the one I'd bought in their London store a month ago.

Back at the Chelsea, a celebrity sighting distracted me. My eyes tracked Ethan Hawke across the lobby, and I missed a chance to duck Jack's sister as she stepped out of the elevator. With my foot holding the door, we both overdid the delight at seeing each other again. Josie had on blue cotton trousers and a candy-striped jacket with a white shirt underneath. Her lovely linen jacket made my brain buzz in a pleasant way.

I had no option but to let the elevator go when a security guy came to check on the beeping.

Josie held me in one of her trademark stares. "What are you up to tonight?"

"Well, I'm going to the theater with a friend." Anxious to change the subject, I said, "You look like you're on your way to something important."

"No, these are my work clothes." Her quiet ta-da released an odor. She'd likely skipped her morning shower.

"Mm, love the jacket."

A hint of Saint Laurent Rive Gauche tried hard.

"All from the new H and M on Fifth." She pointed her manicured index finger at my bag. "Oh, you popped by, too." Her garish purple nail varnish showed a couple of days' wear.

"Um, yes."

"What are you doing now, girl?" She scanned a nifty little gold-colored watch on the inside of her wrist. "Do you want to grab some lunch?"

"Well, I planned to take a nap before getting myself ready for later." Wow, how lame did that sound?

"Hey, you can nap in the afternoon when you're sixty-four and living at home in ye olde England. This is New York City, girl, the Big Juicy Apple."

"Why not come up to my room? I snagged some rather fine Zinfandel." There was a mix-up over my thank-you note for the complimentary bottle, and another two arrived when I was out with Sam.

"Hmm." She patted the face of her faux Gucci.

"Or we could meet somewhere in an hour or so?"

She glanced away, fiddled with her cell, then gave me her full attention. "Bring on the Zinfandel."

In the elevator, I kept out of armpit range.

As soon as we stepped through the door, her eyes got to work on the room. "I didn't realize we had one this small. Where exactly is this in the hotel?"

I shrugged. "Yeah, I know. I'm spending most of my time out and about. It's only a base." People said that sort of crap when they got stuck with the shittiest accommodation. I would need to get a few drinks inside Sam before we landed in here.

"Well, you got all the amenities." She nodded in turn at the bathroom, the TV, and the air conditioner.

"Sit down, I'll pour the vino."

She nodded again, this time at a pair of graying H&M undies. Grabbing them, I reassured her they were clean—they weren't.

"Okay, here we go." Giving her the only glass, I made do with the toothbrush mug.

The glass and plastic beaker came together with a clack. "Cheers, Connie, you're so fresh and youthful, girl."

"Cheers, babe, and you . . ." The minty taste surprised me. I made a mental note to order a bottle of Bollinger champagne and two proper glasses for later.

Josie frowned. "We last spoke that day at the print shop almost twenty years ago, do you remember?"

"I heard about Jack. How dreadful," I said.

"Yeah, the worst experience ever, watching him die like that. A lot of them who hung out with him had it. He had sex with them all, of course. He didn't want to think about the consequences—Jack thought he was invincible. Then one day, I caught sight of him in the bar and barely recognized him. He told me he had the flu and couldn't sleep. I realized at that moment."

"Jesus, Jose, how awful."

We drank down our wine and refilled.

"He lost so much weight, real quick, and faded in front of my eyes. They didn't want him at the hotel. Mom didn't want him at home, so I nursed him for the last few weeks at my place. He refused to go to the hospital. Dear Ant helped me, you remember Anthony? He came by every day, brought stuff in, and kept our spirits up. He even baked a cake for Jack's birthday—icing and everything. Nobody else came."

"Dan knew what went on, of course, but it wasn't his world."

"Yeah." Josie lifted an eyebrow. "My brother lived life fast. That's what people say, isn't it? Lived in the fast lane. He became bitter, though, at the end, going on and on about the unfairness. Completely his own fault, but hey."

"Well . . . yes." I couldn't find anything else to add and focused my eyes on the apartment building, which almost filled the view from the small window. Like James Stewart in *Rear Window*, obsessing over the residents in the block opposite his apartment, I was checking out some of my neighbors. The cute young guy directly across had given me plenty to think about when he exercised earlier. His skimpy translucent shorts were having another workout in my mind.

"I was all sympathy." Josie slurped her wine. "You know me."

"Well . . . of course." My turn to raise an eyebrow.

We drank a toast to Jack.

"So, Jose, what do you do here?"

"Last month I got a promotion to guest relations, hence the clothes." She took off her lovely linen jacket and inspected the material in front of the window before laying it by her side. "Someone spotted my potential."

"Who is this 'someone,' babe?"

"So, Con, what are you doing in the city after such a long time?"

"Er, well . . ."

"Let me guess. You visited the Dakota to check out the hotty. Did you?"

"Er, well . . ."

"You did."

"What makes you think that?"

"My spies are out."

"Spies, who—"

A knock on the door stopped the interrogation. Josie's aroma worked like smelling salts on my slight giddiness. I held the handle for a moment before opening the door a crack.

"Oh, hello, ma'am. Is Ms. Beckett with you?" asked a tallish woman in her late thirties, dressed in a smart dark-gray suit with an eye-catching aubergine necktie. She could have been Louise Weston's double.

"Josie, *someone* for you."

Josie came over, put her arm around the gal's slim waist, and gave her a sloppy kiss on the lips. "Con, this is Petra." She gave me a fluttery wink. "She's a friend. Got to go. Let's catch up before you head home. Hope you have a successful evening with the Weston boy."

"Weston man," I tried, but it was too late.

Sam was a full-grown man, and I was a woman, young for my age. "Wow, thirty-eight. You could pass for fifteen years younger," the receptionist at the optician's had said only the other day.

Josie's jacket lay abandoned on the bed. It fit perfectly. If she didn't retrieve it before, the lovely linen would be joining me tonight. A spritz of Clinique Happy in each underarm dealt with the Eau de Jose.

Why had I drunk all that wine? My eyes were puffing up for sure. I went out in search of the ice machine. This was likely my only chance with Sam, so I needed to look superhot.

Chapter Fourteen

Monday, December 8, 1980

This city, for sure, had a crazy, scary scuzziness, but what the hell did I care? I would soon be on my way to Hawaii with my gorgeous husband.

Skipping down the steps onto the Uptown side of the West Fourth Street station, I dug in my purse for a token. A Polaroid of Dan in among the bills made me smile. Some guy had snapped him at a Factory party a couple of weeks back.

Every so often, Dan's parka gave me a lovely nose full of his scent. In the pocket, my hand held his precious Walkman. "Don't flaunt it on the train, Con," he'd warned more than once. I put on the headphones and pressed play. *There you go, Dan, done without a flaunt.* Billy Joel's "Piano Man" filled my head and made my lips move.

A woman with a young child in a stroller beamed. "Billy Joel?" she mouthed, pointing to my ears.

After a half smile, I turned away, still performing.

Pushing my hands deep into the pockets, I came across a large key in the lining and pulled it out. A handwritten tab said *Courtyard door—NOT IN USE.* What had he been up to?

Two young girls dressed in matching pink tees started throwing a red-headed Little People doll between them—one of those with the big thumbs. Their mom nagged at them to stop, but they ignored her whiny voice. When one missed her catch, the damn doll got under my feet. I barely nudged the thing, but it found its way onto the tracks.

The mom grabbed hold of the girls, one wrist in each hand, and led them down the platform.

Ten-year-old Judy Gibson, already tall, with dark hair and a prim, round face, stood on the Downtown side opposite. Though her head was in one of her stamp books, the streetwise girl kept on checking all around. I remembered doing the same at her age, especially on the subway. She lived with her grandpa on the same street as Dan, in East Williamsburg. My level of small talk didn't go into finding out what happened to her mom and dad. Dan's did. He went on and on about this person and that person. As a train came out of the tunnel, she held her big ol' stamp bag tight to her flat chest.

The cars thundered in, parking an insane three-car-wide yellow, red, and blue tag bang in front of me. New York's subway was turning into an enormous art gallery. The train made some clicking, whirring noises before the doors clunked shut, and it rumbled off. I expected Judy to be gone, but there she was, chitchatting with a good-looking dude in tight-fitting 505s. The cute butt belonged to my husband. Tipping his head to one side, he ran one hand through his thick strawberry-blond hair, while in the fingers of the other, he began to roll his silver dollar.

Judy took a step closer to him, appearing unable to stop herself. Her shoulders lifted as she inhaled. Dan recognized his power for sure. Both ignored my waves—probably stuck into their stamp stuff. Dan got everyone keeping those boring bits of paper for her. My amusing little stamp stories never got much of a laugh. What the hell, Judy's big ol' stamp bag was gaping open, with her encouraging my husband to peek in at something. *Careful, Dan, she might throw you in and carry you off to have her stampy way with you.*

If she were a few years older, I would be on her case. Well on it.

Finally, Dan finished his chitchat and waved.

Dropping the headphones from my ears, I signaled to him to come over.

Suddenly, he shoved his stuff into Judy's stamp bag and, after a quick glance into the tunnel, climbed down onto the rails. Judy slid to the ground, hugging her big ol' bag and pointing.

What the hell was he doing? *What about the fucking trains, Dan?*

He stumbled back and forth a couple of times before stooping down. I fixed my eyes on him as I pushed and elbowed forward to get closer. Everyone was blocking my way. Why wouldn't they move?

People shouted for him to get off the tracks. What the hell? Others cheered him on.

"Piano Man" started to murmur through the headphones around my neck.

Dan was on his feet. He was the most gorgeous man I could imagine, and we were about to start an amazing new life together.

Billy Joel and I began the chorus as my eyes connected with Dan's.

The train screamed. The locked wheels sparked, and smoke poured from under the cars.

People froze and stared.

I dropped to my knees as the A to Rockaway destroyed my life.

The train slid to a stop halfway along the platform.

Inside the cars, people hammered on the doors and yelled.

Screams and shouts came from all corners of the station. The racket vibrated and echoed around in my skull.

Someone's arms went around me as everything faded.

Chapter Fifteen

Friday, June 30, 2000

Some forceful knocking and discreet calling out of "room service" woke me. The waiter came in and checked around for somewhere to put the Bollinger champagne and glasses. It all ended up on top of the air conditioner. Not ideal—two words that summed up my room. I asked him not to open the bottle and hoped five bucks would help him remember to freshen the ice at 9:30 p.m.

I primped and prepped while supping and sipping. A splash of Zinfandel helped keep my first-date nerves in check.

Outfitwise, I settled on a not-too-short, tight-fitting skirt and my new H&M top. My choice of shoes came down to the now much cleaner Converse slip-ons or a new pair of tabby kitten heels bought especially for the trip. The sleek kittens purred nicely with Josie's jacket. I hoped they'd loosen up over the evening.

The TV occupied my jitters for half an hour before I started out on my walk to the American Airlines Theatre on West Forty-Second Street.

Waiting outside the entrance to the circle, I distracted my growing need for the restroom with the neon and billboards. My eyes scanned the crowds for Sam's smiling face. The last bell rang—where the hell was he? My calls went to his voice mail, and my texts remained unanswered. Sam did not strike me as the sort of guy to stand a person up without a call or a text. My phone started vibrating. At last—but no, it showed as international.

"Constance, my lovely."

My heart sank. "Auntie Betty?"

"We're having a little drinky."

"Is Ma with you?"

She didn't take the receiver away from her mouth. "Evie, are you with me, lovely?" Then, after a pause, "No, not at the moment."

"I'll call before the flight home."

"Ladybird, ladybird, fly away home—"

"Okay, nice to talk," I said. "Got to go. Bye."

Ma was playing her Auntie Betty card and trying to make me suffer for leaving her.

What had happened to Sam? Why hadn't he shown? Had he stood me up? Why would he do that, without even a text? If there was a perfectly simple explanation, I wanted to know it.

I walked quickly to the Forty-Second Street station to take an Uptown C to the Dakota. My need for a restroom could wait.

Ⓐ

As the guard at the Dakota main gate nodded me through, the damn kittens began nipping.

Walt stood at his post in the front office. "Oh my, hello, Jos . . ." He reddened. "Oh my, Miss Connie, my apologies, I thought you were someone else."

"Hmm, yes, well." There was no time for chitchat. "I'm trying to find Sam, um . . . the young Mr. Weston. We arranged to see a show together. Is he upstairs, do you know? I don't need to see him or anything."

"One moment, Miss Connie, I'll check the book." He flicked a page back and forth. "Oh, yes, young Mr. Weston left here at 6:30 p.m. I'll call up to the apartment, though, in case we missed his return." He picked up the telephone and dialed. "Yes ma'am, sorry to . . . Yes . . . a visitor for young Mr. Weston." He fiddled with the cord. "Um . . . yes, a visitor for Master Samuel." After a short pause, he said, "Yes, thank you, sorry to trouble you. No message, thank you, ma'am." Walt hung up, clicked the button on the end of his pen, and positioned it ready. "Miss Connie, you no doubt gathered, the young Mr. Weston is not currently at home. Any message?"

"I'm not stalking him or anything . . ."

"No, no. Shall I send you a text message when he returns?"

"Thanks, Walt."

While he wrote down my number, I looked through the window in the door and spied Lou approaching. I stepped into the corner behind the door and busied myself with my cell. She didn't spot me. I took the opportunity to remove and rest my feet on the backs of the tormenting kittens. Ma wouldn't be happy. *You'll ruin those shoes,* she'd say.

"Good evening, ma'am," said Walt. "A letter arrived earlier for Mr. Weston. Please, may I give it to you?"

"Yes." Lou put her hand out, palm up.

He pushed the small white envelope onto the waiting hand. She ripped off the top and inspected the note.

"Walter, have you seen my brother this evening?"

"He went out at six thirty tonight, according to the book, and hasn't returned, ma'am."

"So your psychic powers can tell you what's in the book without looking?"

"Uh, no, ma'am."

It was time to reacquaint myself with Louise Weston. "I asked Walt about Sam."

Her head swiveled around. That girl in *The Exorcist* sprang to mind, but without the green vomit. "Josie? Hi, I thought we agreed not to . . . Oh, *you.*"

Lou's face looked a lot older than mine. We were almost the same age.

"What are you doing here, Constance? Have you anything to do with this?" She waved the letter in my face.

"Well, if it mentions Sam, we arranged to meet up at the theater an hour or so ago, but he didn't show."

"God, are you making a play for my little brother? Killed one off, now on to the next?"

"Is Sam in trouble?"

"Go away, this is nothing to do with you."

"Is it connected to the missionary?" The Eastern Europeans weren't going away without what they'd come for, and they'd been asking for George. "Yes, is it about your father's missionary *deal*?" I was going all in.

A visibly unsettled Lou signaled me to follow her up to the apartment.

We headed to the elevator, me wrestling my kittens back on, and my husband's twin sister smirking at my predicament.

Chapter Sixteen

Monday, December 8, 1980

Almost everyone at the print shop had gone home for the evening.

The big ol' clock started bonging—I counted seven. *I should be at the Chelsea with Dan.* What happened? Why was I lying on the leather couch in Billy's office wrapped in a scratchy dog blanket? I threw it off.

Anthony lurked in the open doorway.

Mom came in as my brain restarted. She touched my arm. I grabbed her hand and held on. "Dan, where's Dan? What happened to Dan?" My voice did not sound like mine—all screechy.

Dan's smiling face kept escaping from me. Everything was surrounded in a smoky haze with the words *SAMO IS DEAD* flashing up every so often.

She looked at me and full into my eyes before using her telephoning voice. "His mom is on her way there now, and she's called his father. We're trying to get hold of Billy and Aileen." My mother could do calm in the uncalmest of situations.

"I should be with my husband."

"You need to rest. What do you mean your *husband*? Does his mother know?"

I gripped Mom's hand tighter. "Let me see him."

"Later, lovey, later. Here, drink this down. Some of Billy's Cabernet."

"No, Mom . . ." A sharp pain shot through me as something twisted inside. I dropped the wine and held myself tight, trying to stop my body from shaking. I brought my hand up to examine it. Blood, my blood all over.

"Con, what's happening?"

"Mom, help me. *My baby.*"

She jumped into action. "Anthony, we need an ambulance. Go call 911." Mom looked me in the eye. "*You're pregnant.* My God, did Dan know?"

"What do you mean *did*?"

After a couple of minutes, an anxious-looking Anthony returned to the doorway. "They'll be here in five minutes."

I passed out.

Ⓐ

I awoke in the emergency room at Roosevelt Hospital on Fifty-Ninth, wearing only a thin gown.

"*Where are you, Mom?*"

The entrance doors banged, and voices, loud, panicked voices, filled the air.

Cracking the curtain of my cubicle revealed a man in a white coat dashing around, his stethoscope swinging. "We've got a gunshot, gunshot in the chest."

"When's it coming in?" asked someone else.

"Now," said white coat as he propped open both the doors. "He's a VIP."

Two uniformed cops carried a guy in on their shoulders. The man appeared to be unconscious. His blood was all over them. They put him on a gurney, and the waiting doctors wheeled him quickly into a back room. One of the cops mumbled something. The other shook his head. They began talking like they knew the guy.

As I closed my eyes, "All My Loving" started up on the hospital's public address system.

Later, Mom came in. She stroked my hand and kissed the side of my face.

My dreams of living in Hawaii with Dan and our baby were no more.

Mom held my hand and whispered, "John Lennon just died."

Chapter Seventeen

Friday, June 30, 2000

The apartment's comforting aroma of beeswax and linseed had been replaced with an odor of cigarette smoke and something no one would want to put their finger on. Lou led me through the hall, into the sitting room, where a small dog was perched on a chair, licking his private area.

Over in the dining room, the door to the corner cupboard hung open. A can of Mountain Dew stood next to a half-empty Waterford whiskey tumbler on the marble table. Someone had used the lead crystal for soda, and not a coaster in sight.

The reassuring ticktock of the grandfather clock had gone, its hands now stuck at a frowny twenty minutes to four.

An old man I sort of recognized as George Weston shuffled through this domestic disorder. A pretty girl, Sam's double, wandered in as well. "Is that the person who wanted Sam?"

"Yes, it is." Lou looked through me. "Liza, meet Constance. She's your older brother's widow."

"Oh, God . . . Hey, Jacob, this is my older brother's widow. Can you believe that?"

A dodgy-looking guy came out of the shadows and shaded his eyes from the light.

"Hi, please call me Connie."

"Huh." Jacob ignored my hand but held my gaze for a split second. He then shrugged and scratched himself somewhere down below before wandering off. He was tall, quite good-looking, in his midtwenties, with thick greasy hair.

A clinking noise announced the small dog trying to drink Mountain Dew from the Waterford up on the dining table. He dipped his large tongue in and out of the tumbler as it moved to the edge. The shag pile was in danger.

"Oh, the sweetheart . . . Is Pompom thirsty?" Liza nodded and cooed at the canine. "Jacob, some water for my Pompom."

The dog let out a yap as the glass disappeared from his view.

"Bring a cloth, too."

Lou and I stared at the mess, probably with the same thought. She then looked me in the eye. "Constance, what do you know about these people who took Sam?"

"Jesus, they took Sam?" What the hell, why would they do that? It was nothing to do with him. All the confusion in the family may endanger him—I would need to help them sort this out.

"Yes, maybe they jumped him on his way to your date night, Constance. Soon after you make an appearance, he goes missing. Is it a coincidence or what? Okay, so this is family business. Leave us now, please."

"Surely I can help. Are they threatening to hurt him? Should we call the NYPD?" If this was something to do with one of the Westons' dodgy deals, then Lou must be clued in.

"I assumed you knew something about this, but you obviously don't. We'll handle it from here. Goodbye, Constance." Lou walked to the door, presumably expecting me to follow.

I gripped the top of the dining table. I couldn't go back to my hotel room and sit around. "I can't—"

Without warning, George threw the study door open with some force and stood tapping his right foot, the one in a slipper. "Oh, Connie, there you are. Is Dan with you? Gregor and his lady friend came here shouting about Burt's treasure. Pops isn't going to be happy with them coming to the Dakota."

George was up to his confused eyeballs in this missionary thing. The mention of Burt rang a bell. I remembered the old boys talking about something on the day of the accident.

Liza came over and stood close to her father. "Daddy, what's all this about treasure?" She put her hand on his shoulder, but he shrugged it off.

"Who is this girl? What is she doing here, again? Connie, please send your mother in. We need to discuss tomorrow's calendar."

Liza opened and closed her mouth and sent me a scowl. I smiled, as I didn't want to antagonize these people.

"All right, Constance, you might be useful," Lou said. She still wouldn't focus her eyes on me. "The note says they are holding Sam. They will return him unharmed when they get satisfaction, whatever that means. Also, it says they sent letters and emails to my father. Daddy still has stuff delivered to his office at the print shop. Anthony handles most of that. He used to print out the emails and bring them up here, but for the past few months we received only spam and junk, so I told him not to bother."

"We could try to access his emails from here," said Liza. "We don't have his password, but perhaps Daddy might be able to tell us."

"Last time I asked him, he told me he didn't understand," said Jacob.

Why had this guy been trying to break into George's email? Regardless of how Lou was treating me, I felt protective of my family—a cuckoo was in the nest.

"All right, so we need to check Daddy's email. They appear to think we are deliberately holding back." Lou led Liza and me into the study.

Jacob, no doubt keen to be involved, joined us. "I'll take the laptop over to the desk."

"Maybe we can obtain a new password if we log in from his usual computer. There may be some security questions, but it might be worth a try." I sounded knowledgeable. Their eyes focused on me, and I liked it. These guys needed me. Aileen wasn't here now, but I could soon get this place back on track.

The Apple PowerBook G3 refused to power up.

"The battery might be dead. We'll need the power cord and the modem cable." I located both and showed each to my audience as I plugged them into the Apple and the appropriate wall sockets.

George wandered in. "What are you doing in Pop's study? He won't like you poking around."

"Father, we want to look at something on the computer," Lou said as she checked her cell for the umpteenth time.

"We don't use computers up here. They're at the shop. You'll need to speak to Daniel. Go down to San Remo Print on Bleecker and ask for him, or Billy's personal assistant, Mrs. Williams. Connie, dear, is your mother at work today?"

"Er, yes, she is."

Liza muttered something under her breath to Jacob.

"We installed a computer for you in the study here," I said.

"Oh, yes, very good, carry on, Connie," he said as he left the room.

"How come he recognizes you and none of us?" Liza asked.

George was kind after the accident. The marriage surprised them all, of course. The family's lawyers failed to cut me out of Dan's will, but he owned nothing.

"Right, let's power this baby up," said Jacob.

All the while, I tried to place the guy's accent, not Danish for sure.

"The screen is coming on. We'll need to dial into AOL," I said. "Let's hope the subscription is paid up."

"Most of the accounts are on ACH transfers," said Lou. "The lights would be out otherwise."

"Here we go." Liza stabbed at the monitor. "Click on the AOL program." Her finger left a greasy smear.

"Username and password?" asked Jacob. "Shit, we don't have either. We need the username to reset the password."

"George," I said as he returned into the room. "My mom just called and says a client needs to email you. Can you confirm the address where you want them to send it?"

"Address?"

"Yes, please."

"Oh, yes, the Dakota, New York City. John Lennon and such."

"No, your email, please."

"What's email?" George beamed, then a couple of moments later marched over to me. "Oh, Connie, yes, your mom needed my email. It's GeoWeston at AOL.com."

"We need the password, too," said Jacob in a whisper.

"George, is your password handy?" I asked, but I'd already made a mental note to change the login information when Jacob was elsewhere.

"Ask Aileen." He tapped the side of his nose.

Without missing a beat, I said, "She's out for the evening."

"Sorry to tell you, my dear, but she died last month," said George.

"I think 'askaileen' might be the password," said Liza.

"It works. We're in," said Jacob.

"Okay, Constance, this is family business. Please leave us. We'll find Sam—you don't need to worry. What is he to you anyway? You only met him a couple of days ago." Lou stood, ready to escort me off the premises.

"But . . . but . . ." I needed to think about my next move.

She tried to block my view of the laptop screen, but I managed to glimpse the AOL page. Some emails from a Gregor Ionesco appeared.

"Constance, dear, now tell me, did you ever write anything original on your own?" Lou moved me toward the door. "See you again, never."

I had no words at that moment, original or not, but she would see me again, very soon.

As I stood in the elevator, about to press the lobby button, George dashed out of the apartment. He pushed a familiar leather Lefax organizer into my hands. "Protect this, Connie. None of it makes sense to me now. They got rid of Aileen—I'm on borrowed time, so is Sam. Don't involve the police, whatever you do. You must ask Anthony, he's—"

A yapping Pompom charged out of the apartment and slid across the polished wood floor, almost disappearing between the banisters.

Liza appeared in the doorway. "Shit, Daddy, why did you let my Pompom out?" She started after the dog, who now ran toward George.

As the elevator doors closed, I gaped at the sight of Liza tripping on an abandoned slipper and falling headlong onto her redsable Pomeranian. He let out a muffled squeal and a quantity of Mountain Dew.

What the hell had I just witnessed? The once quick-witted gentle-man who was now unable to keep his slippers on. Not to mention the sleazy guy who was, for sure, up to no good.

Hell, the carpets hadn't even been vacuumed.

I held on tight to George's Lefax as the elevator descended. My fingers were crossed that it would help me track down and rescue Sam.

Chapter Eighteen

ANTHONY

Brooklyn
Monday, December 8, 1980

Two months ago, the duty officer at the Sixty-Second Precinct called me at three in the morning. He told me that they had arrested my stepmother in a bodega on Eighty-Sixth Street. Wearing only her nightgown, she had eaten her way through a promotional display of original banana-cream-flavor Twinkies. She swore at anybody who tried to stop her, using words I had no idea she knew. A week later, I found myself wiping her bottom in the cramped bathroom stall of our local McDonald's. The branch I used to visit almost daily. As a non-blood relative, I should not have been expected to perform such duties. With no other options available to me, I subcontracted her care to the nearby Shore View facility. A place where the janitors' preferred method of repair almost always involved duct tape.

"Thank you for finally settling your account, Mr. Houseman," said the clerk behind the reception desk as she counted the bills. "We'll expect future accounts to be paid in full and in advance."

"I am not a dishonest person."

"Pardon me, Mr. Houseman, did you say something?"

"Uh, sorry, nothing."

I put my head around the door of my stepmom's "Economy Plus" room. "Hi, Mom." As far as I could tell, the only extra in a "Plus" was a potted cactus plant—hers was dead. "How are you today?"

Without looking up, she gestured for me to come in. Her curtains were open, but the small basement window provided minimal light due to the garbage dumpster in the parking lot above. "You can remove my tray. The toast is dry."

This woman's husband, my father, had done one of his trademark disappearing acts a few months back. Some wise guys at an Atlantic City casino apparently objected to him using his homemade poker chips in a high-stakes game. My actual mom died of brain cancer before my first birthday. Amandi was Bhutanese, and she met my father on one of his hush-hush government missions to her country. It was love at first sight, according to Dad. They married on their return to the States in 1952, and I was born nine years later. He used to talk about her calmness and patience—traits I inherited *in spades*.

I grew up in Las Vegas in an environment steeped in forgery and fraud. My father's friend and my mentor, Winston Wentworth, ensured that I passed Counterfeiting 101 before my twelfth birthday. He and my father collaborated on numerous "projects," as they called them. I'd recently been forced into some fakery of my own. Winston's advice came to mind as I contemplated my current cash-flow embarrassment: "When counterfeiting banknotes, you must make sure all the serial numbers vary in each lot—or else you're in for big trouble, man. And don't pass those bills within a hundred miles of where you live."

I had no time to think about the moral implications of my actions. I just needed to get through this, and then I could put my life firmly back on track.

Chapter Nineteen

CONNIE

Manhattan
Saturday, July 1, 2000

The way things were at the Dakota made my brain spin, and I couldn't sleep. What the hell happened to Sam? Who was that Jacob guy? What was going on with George?

Yet another bottle of Zinfandel had mysteriously arrived in my room, so I poured myself a glass—purely for medicinal purposes. I leafed through George's Lefax, taking tiny sips. It contained three sections: contacts, calendar, and records of financial transactions. Shit, one page mentioned the "missionary" selling for $1.8 million. I dabbed away some drops of wine from the page. The sale was made in April 1981 to GI, almost three months after Billy's death. George traded in historical papers and collectibles, so it was likely something in that line. A note said that $900,000 had gone to BR. Earlier today, at the apartment, George had gotten excited about Gregor and what he referred to as Burt's treasure.

The day Dan died, Burt Raymond had turned up at the shop with something valuable. It must have been the missionary. So, Burt got a commission when they sold the thing to GI—Gregor Ionesco. George told me not to involve the cops but to call Anthony. That made some sense, as he had access to the print shop's emails and would be able to throw more light on this whole—no doubt dodgy—business deal. Anthony Houseman's number stared out at me from the book's contacts section. His spotty face and snaggle smile popped into my head. Did I need to involve him in this?

Sam was a grown man, a strong character. He would take a kidnapping in stride. Yes, he could charm them, no problem. If Lou couldn't get her act together, Sam needn't worry, because I was on the case. I wouldn't be returning to London until he was safe. The Bollinger would remain on standby for my Sam moment.

I bathed my damaged feet and swallowed one of Ma's "V" pills. On the way back to bed, I took pleasure in stuffing the kitten heels into the waste bin.

Ⓐ

A little after three thirty in the morning, my cell phone drummed on the nightstand and woke me up. Ma's voice came squawking out. "I'm picking you up at the airport tomorrow, lovey."

"No need, I bought a return for the train."

"Well, can't you—"

"I should use the ticket."

"If you're sure. We'll have a leg of lamb for our supper, and I'll do some of those potatoes you like. Auntie Betty won't be joining us."

A memory of my last birthday dinner started up in my brain. The night the roasted shanks ended up among the soft furnishings. I swallowed hard. "Are you okay, Ma?"

"I am on top of things. Especially now you're coming home."

From the mid-1990s, Ma's life had grown smaller. She fell out with everyone and stayed home much of the time. She banged on and on about how she should be living in New York. She began to focus all her attention on me. I was being smothered. She frightened me sometimes, mainly when Auntie Betty showed herself.

My finger hovered over the little red telephone button. "I have to go—see you tomorrow." I pressed the key and sighed. No way could I leave before knowing Sam was safe. Besides, all my plans rested on getting way past first base with him—I needed a home run.

A voice mail alert pinged. Joy, it was from Sam. Gorgeous, resourceful Sam must have gotten free. Maybe we could meet for lunch.

What the hell, the message turned out to be from the Eastern European woman. "Is this Con Weston? Samuel Weston is here with us. We need to speak with Mr. George Weston. Why will no one answer me? Contact boy's cell"—the unmistakable bongs of Billy's office clock chimed in—"if you want to see the boy again."

Why call him a boy? Fuck, I needed to get down to the print shop. I wondered whether to phone her back. I decided not to. They wouldn't be expecting me.

Slipping on Dan's green parka, I inhaled deeply, though his scent was long gone. To bring the jacket with me, I'd had to ditch a pair of shoes and two summer dresses. It had been such a comfort in my darkest times. Now it was coming along with me to rescue his brother.

Ⓐ

Half an hour later, at four, cabs were plentiful. Why couldn't London be more like New York? I asked the driver to drop me around the corner from the print shop. The potholed streets and abandoned storefronts took me back to 1980.

A black Lincoln Town Car parked across the street from San Remo Print looked out of place. The shop's neon sign sputtered *an emo* as I collected my thoughts in a doorway opposite. All of a sudden, a couple of guys dressed in dark clothing, together with the short Eastern European woman, came out of the street entrance of the shop. It looked like my hunch was right.

The woman slipped into one of the back seats of the Lincoln, while the men sat in the front. The limo purred toward me, so I crouched lower in among some stinky garbage cans. A dim light in what I remembered was Billy's office caught my eye. The courtyard key was still in the lining of the parka. It never occurred to me that it wouldn't still unlock the anonymous-looking door on West Fourth Street.

Standing on tiptoe, I lifted my head enough to peer in through a high back window. Sam was there, duct taped to the 1960s purply swivel chair. A surge of pleasure rushed to every part of my body. He laughed as he chitchatted with a tall, thin man in dark clothing. The guy pulled a cell from his pocket and put it to his ear. He shook the phone a couple of times and headed out of the room, no doubt in search of a signal. A light went on upstairs, so I knocked on the window. Sam jumped and looked over. Ignoring my aching toes, I moved in closer to the glass. My pleasure rush turned into a full-on flood as Sam's face lit up with his wide grin.

I reflected his beam and mouthed, "Don't worry, I'll sort this out."

He nodded toward a small table where an empty Snapple bottle and the remnants of a McDonald's sandwich lay.

Thank God, I had timed my trip so perfectly. Coincidence or what? Maybe fate was bringing us together.

The guard came downstairs and opened the outside door, the handset still glued to his ear. I signaled to Sam that I was leaving him but would be back. He understood at once—we already had a connection, for sure.

"Yeah, finally," the kidnapper said. Then, after a pause, "Yes, I tried to call them, but it went to bloody voice thing again. Here is good reception, so I will keep trying. Rosa says should be no problem to hold boy in shop. He's okay and not causing trouble." The guy hung up, took a cigarette from his pocket, lit up, and started another call. The aroma of Sobranie Black Russian wafted by me.

Over a minute passed before the next person he'd dialed picked up. "Yes, Samuel Weston is with us. We will exchange him for the missionary or five-million-dollars cashier's check, please."

He must have been talking to someone at the Dakota.

"You know very well, the missionary. I telephone again at ten o'clock in the morning. You arrange delivery, and we send Samuel Weston back without bits missing. Otherwise, we deliver first little piece. Ten, I call." The guy smiled as he hung up.

The thought of Sam losing any part of his gorgeous body sent a shiver through me. Lou would presumably be straight onto it now they had made contact.

As I got back to Sam, the dawn started to light the window glass, so I wrote in the dirt on the pane: *going for pleh*. He winked and beamed. I rubbed out the message with the side of my hand, waved, and wiped a tear. Yes, we definitely had a connection.

In the cab on the way back to the Chelsea, my tired brain tried to make sense of it all.

George's words kept repeating in my head: *You must ask Anthony. You must ask Anthony.*

Chapter Twenty

ANTHONY

Brooklyn and Manhattan
Monday, December 8, 1980

Dan Weston and I worked together taking care of the new Apple II Plus personal computers at his grandfather's print shop on Bleecker Street. Lucky Dan dated Con Williams, the most beautiful girl in the city.

For Pete's sake, a few nights ago, Dan surprised me by coming in through the back entrance of the shop. The old handbill press was in the middle of printing a run of twenty-dollar bills. He caught me red-, or, in this case, green-handed and threatened to bring in the feds if I didn't cut him in. After I failed to make him understand about the dangers of passing counterfeit bills in the city, he helped himself to a bundle of fifty. The Chelsea's registers were likely already choked with them.

I would have resigned my job at the shop but for Con. She needed me to look out for her.

Running late and with a wet foot, I headed to my locker for glue to fix my sneaker. Something didn't look right in there. An increasingly frantic search couldn't produce the black PVC bag containing my father's printing plates.

Dan's smirking face appeared around the door. "So, Ant, my man, how are things? Ugh, is that smell something to do with you?"

My early start to visit Mom and no hot water at home had conspired against me.

"Any overtime in the print room planned?" Even his laugh sounded sarcastic.

"Dan, I need those plates back. We'll be in big trouble—"

"Not *we*, Ant. I have nothing to do with your after-hours activities. Jack's coming down here later. We have a proposal for you." He headed off, spinning his silver dollar.

What did Con see in him?

My desktop was covered in yellow Post-it Notes. I checked one at random and went to investigate the accountant's malfunctioning computer keyboard. "There you go, Carl, all done. Ring Ding crumbs under the space bar . . . again. Can't you—" I gave up.

As usual, I was doing all the work. Dan was in the outer office, drooling over a new girl.

A little later, I was in the small kitchen, eating my Skippy peanut butter and jelly sandwich, when Dan and Jack arrived and stood together in the doorway.

"So, Ant, this is where you've been hiding," Dan said.

"I'm just—"

"Yuck, is it that sandwich, again?" Dan mimicked two fingers down his throat.

Nodding, I bit my tongue.

Dan shut the door, then whispered in my ear. "We've been thinking. It's time to ramp up production."

"Not possible." If I were a cartoon character, steam would be shooting out of my ears.

"Slow down, Ant, my man. Let us tell you about our proposal. We can all do great out of this if we work it right." Jack's perfectly proportioned face turned away. "Can't you cover your gross mouth when you do that licking?"

"Uh, no, I mean, yes. Sorry. I can't do anything without the banknote plates."

Dan smiled in his friend's direction. "They're safe. We'll bring them in for a run tomorrow evening. You continue to receive the cash you need, and we have some to play with. I've also got some expenses coming up."

"What expenses might those be?" Jack was playfully nudging his friend in the chest with his fist. "Is it something to do with that woman of yours?"

"Dan, will you be taking another trip to Honolulu?" I asked.

"Is that where you went a couple of weeks back?" Jack's long eyelashes fluttered.

"On business. Yes, Apple business." He reddened when he lied. I knew that, but his buddy since they were in first grade apparently didn't.

"Ant, yeah, we'll need to start as soon as everyone leaves tomorrow. We're working on a plan. We can use the Chelsea's accounts and payroll. You're going to be rich."

"Guys, you're nuts. We'll get caught."

"We'll *catch you* later." Dan headed out into the main office with Jack on his tail.

"What's this Honolulu business?" Jack asked.

I had to do something, but what? They had the plates. Winston's letter was also in that PVC bag—*the instructions addressed to me for printing and passing counterfeit currency.*

I needed to show them somehow that I would not be intimidated.

Ⓐ

Con's mom, Evie Williams, and I were firm friends. She worked at a desk in the corridor outside Billy Weston's office, and I swung by whenever I had a free moment. Today, lovely Con was there, too. Dan's arrival spoiled things.

As usual, he showed off in front of his girlfriend. "Hey, Ant, can you finish off the last of the Apples in Carl's office?" *Finish off*—I've done every new installation this month.

"All done." I tried not to smile.

"Now, don't you go seducing my girl with your sexy moves, you dirty dog." Dan's eyes darted between us.

"No, Dan. I'll . . . go back and sort . . . Apple stuff . . ." Why couldn't I stand up for myself?

"Well, I'll leave you two lovebirds to coo together. Now, remember, Ant, don't—"

"Daniel, don't tease the boy." Evie was a true ally.

I hung around for a short while with her and then patrolled the floor, checking the computers. All the time, I was agonizing over how to get the plates back.

I stopped in the kitchen for my afternoon soda but let Con have it. How could I resist that face?

I felt a need to be close to her as I formulated my plans. My mind started running conversations with her where I would tell her all about her no-good boyfriend and his best buddy.

When she left for the evening, I decided to follow.

Chapter Twenty-One

CONNIE

After my backspacing and rekeying, Anthony's number began to ring.

"This is Anthony Houseman. I can't take your call. Please leave a message."

Shit, why wasn't he there?

"Hi, it's Connie, Connie Weston. I'm in New York and need to speak to you urgently. Please call me as soon as you can. My cell is 44 7771 055551. This is urgent—life-and-death urgent."

My phone started buzzing and I picked up.

"Who were you speaking to?"

"Hi, Ma." This needed to be quick.

"I bought us a leg from Tesco, lovey."

"Wonderful."

"Oh, you sound tired. Did you sleep last night? What are you doing today? What's the weather like?"

"All fine. Call you later."

"Yes, how—"

A missed-call and voice mail message popped up.

"Anthony here. I'm up in Montauk for the weekend. How can I help?"

Thank God for redial.

He picked up on the first ring. "Hi, Connie?"

I didn't really know the guy. He definitely had a thing for me back then—probably just a crush.

"Hi, yes, sorry to contact you out of the blue." I told him about my visit to the Dakota, George giving me his notebook, and the people holding Sam at the print shop.

"Connie. Are you all right, yourself? Not in any danger?"

"I'm okay, thanks. I'm booked on a plane to London this evening, but I can't leave, not with all this going on."

"I'll be with you in about two hours. Let's meet in the lobby of your hotel."

"Around lunchtime. You're a godsend, Anthony. Bye for now."

"Goodbye."

Wow, did I say "godsend"? I needed to extend my stay and come up with a story for Ma. I changed my BA flight with a small charge, and the extra nights at the Chelsea got me a room upgrade. Apart from Sam's terrible situation, I was pleased to be staying longer. After moving my stuff, I headed to the Starbucks on Twenty-Third for a double espresso and a couple of croissants.

As I walked back to the hotel, the caffeine kicked in. I decided Lou couldn't be relied on. Lucky for Sam, I would do anything and everything necessary to release him. Together, Anthony and I would be able to plan and mount Sam's rescue. He could be free within hours.

Ⓐ

As I stood waiting in the lobby, a well-groomed, tall, and slender man came through the front doors, carrying flowers. It was Anthony reborn. His well-cut reddish hair was still thick, and his complexion smooth and healthy with no hint of acne. Dressed in tight-fitting Levi 505s and a light-blue linen shirt, he spotted me at once and came over.

He appeared young for his age. He must've been around forty—older than me. His Adidas sneakers were nothing special, but they were new and not cheap. When he grinned, it seemed a miracle had occurred. His snaggleteeth were gone. Neatened up to the max and wearing some fabulous Eau Sauvage cologne, he offered his small bouquet of red roses without trying to touch or kiss me.

I touched his arm. "Thanks for dropping everything and dashing down."

"Pleased I can be of help."

"I've extended my stay a week."

"Not involving the police was a good move," he said.

"Why is that?"

"All will become clear."

Keen to get Sam's rescue underway, I didn't ask for more details—although there was clearly more to this affair. "We should head to the print shop right now." Sam hadn't seemed in danger, but that was hours ago. I suddenly remembered what the guard had threatened and wanted to check Sam was still in one piece.

"Great idea, Con."

I gave him a quick frown for calling me "Con."

How had he known to come to the Chelsea? Had I mentioned the hotel in our call? I dropped the flowers at the front desk. With a small bow and an arm out, Anthony let me go first. As I passed by, he inhaled and held his breath for a moment—something to keep an eye on.

Anthony's 505s fit perfectly. I glimpsed the jean's rear label when he helped a young mother with a wonky-wheeled stroller. The leather panel confirmed a trim 32:32.

"Kind of you," I said, smiling.

After boarding the A for the short journey to the print shop, I told him more about what I'd found. "An entry in George's notebook mentions a sale of the missionary and a payment to BR. Must be Billy's friend Burt, don't you think?"

"Yes, Burt was down at the shop the day, uh . . ."

"The day Dan died. I'm fine."

Anthony glanced up, but his gleaming blue eyes still refused to lock with mine.

"Billy sent him off to the photographers with Burt's thing." Jesus, that was the last time I kissed my darling husband.

"Dan was almost certainly carrying the missionary." Anthony put his left hand under his chin and held on to his elbow with the right. "So they had photographs to work from."

"Maybe George used the photos to make a copy of it?"

He stroked his smooth chin. "Sounds plausible."

I did a little chin stroke of my own. "But why now?"

"Possibly the original buyers tried to sell and found a problem."

With Anthony's help, I got through the West Fourth Street station without a wobble. Perhaps he'd always had my best interests at heart?

Leading him through the courtyard to the rear of the shop, I was almost running. To my relief, Sam was still strapped to the chair, but with his back to us. Anthony told me he planned to climb the fire stairs on the adjacent property and enter the building through a door on the flat roof. He asked me to go to the door and keep the guard talking on some excuse of wanting a print job done. Meanwhile, Anthony would free Sam, and they would escape across the roof together.

I kept the guard talking for at least five minutes before my phone vibrated with Anthony's text: *Back on the roof but alone, meet you on the corner of Cornelia in five.*

Someone came up as I put my cell away.

"This is nothing to do with you, Constance. If you try to involve yourself in anything connected to the Westons, I'll make life difficult for you," said a man dressed entirely in black.

Pulling off his beanie, Jacob showed himself. Why was he wearing Sam's Converse Weapon 86 Hi sneakers?

"What the hell?" I swallowed hard as the taste of espresso came back in my throat. "Are you here to get Sam released?"

"If only it was that simple." He blocked my path. "They ain't going to free him without getting the missionary envelope." He stepped closer and ran a gloved finger down the side of my face. "I understand you have the old man's notebook."

"I'm not here alone." I moved forward.

He didn't try to stop me from walking away, but he shouted, "Feeble Mr. *Mouseman* won't be able to help you. Be very careful, Constance."

I walked to the corner before looking back. He'd gone. Facing into a doorway, I retched.

"Everything okay, Connie?" Anthony asked when he arrived.

"Yes, yes, I'm fine. Er . . . what happened with Sam?"

"He's convinced the gang will grab one of his sisters if he escapes. They told him the family was taking care of everything. They haven't hurt him, and he doesn't feel in any danger."

Sam's unselfishness made my spine tingle.

How did Jacob know the missionary was an envelope? He had likely come to the print shop to meet with the kidnappers. Did he even care about Sam? His grip on the family worried me. I was beginning to think that he might have been involved in Aileen's death.

Chapter Twenty-Two

ANTHONY

Many New Yorkers, like me, still had to ride the subway, regardless of its deplorable state. The whole system was a shameful disgrace, with new graffiti tags appearing daily, sprayed in layers onto every visible surface. Some people had started calling it art. I guessed viewing it as such lessened the urgency to clean it off.

On the platform at the West Fourth Street station, I used the crowd as cover to position myself a few feet away from the lovely Con. A short distance from her stood Jack. Would they speak to each other? Was she in on the guys' loony tunes scheme? I needed to remain in the shadows, but at the same time, keep them both under surveillance. Something else Winston had taught me.

Con appeared fixated on a girl over on the Downtown side and tripped on a redheaded doll that had been dropped. Next thing, the doll ended up on the tracks.

Not wanting Con to catch me gawking at her, and with my plan formulating, I maneuvered up close behind Jack.

A highly graffitied train approached the Downtown platform and rattled to a stop. When it pulled out, Dan was there, talking to Con's young girl. He was spinning his silver dollar in one hand—showing off as usual.

Dan's eyes were scanning around as they always did. He glanced over, full-on staring in my direction. It occurred to me that my position behind his buddy could be used to my advantage. Jack now stood right at the platform's edge. I lifted my arms and, pointing my palms forward, nodded to Dan. I added a little shoulder shrug. *Yes, Dan, I could push your best bud off a subway platform any time I liked.* He looked like he understood.

I glanced away to locate Con and then back to Dan. He suddenly stuffed what he was carrying into the girl's bag. He pulled some gloves from his back pockets before climbing down onto the tracks. *Dan, that was a massive overreaction.*

Con went wild, shouting and waving at him.

Jack joined in and tried to make himself heard over the racket. "What are you doing, bud? Get back on the fucking platform."

I moved away, keeping Con in view.

Dan appeared to stumble before regaining his balance. He was standing in the center of the express tracks when the train hurled itself into the station. The cars screamed as they came to a shuddering halt.

The A to Rockaway stopped not entirely at the platform, and the conductor didn't open the doors.

Jack dashed to the front of the train. He vomited.

Con's horrified expression was seared into my mind.

Pandemonium engulfed the station.

Con's mournful cry penetrated the hubbub. She needed my help.

"Out of my way, please, ma'am. Leave her to me, sir. Please, I have to look after my girl . . ."

The severed head of the red-haired doll caught my eye as Con fell unconscious into my arms.

She smelled so good.

Chapter Twenty-Three

CONNIE

Manhattan and Queens
Saturday, July 1, 2000

At the hotel, Anthony and I headed up to my new room with a couple of double-shot Americanos. He appeared a little shy at first but soon lounged on the bed with his sneakers off.

As Anthony puzzled over a note from housekeeping he found next to the rescued kittens, Jacob's threatening words popped into my head. *They ain't going to free him without getting the missionary envelope.* I caught Anthony in a stare. "So what happened to the missionary *envelope*? The kidnappers aren't going to release Sam unless they get it."

"Yes, you're right," Anthony said, but with no further comment. Did he already know it was an envelope?

Jacob's face had gotten wedged in my brain. Lucky for me, the side pocket of the Burberry was able to dispense help. Soon after swallowing a red tablet marked *60*, the awful man floated away.

We found an address and phone number for Burt in George's Lefax. I called the number, but the kid who answered didn't understand me and went to fetch his grandmother.

"Hello, yes, what can I do for you all?"

"We're trying to find someone who lived at your address. Do you know Mr. Raymond?"

"Oh, yes, that would be my uncle Burt. Yes, he used to live here. He gave us this place when he moved on down to Florida."

"Do you have a telephone number for him, by any chance?"

"Yes, but he died a couple of years ago. His wife still lives in Boca. She might be able to help you, but they only met and married in 1990, so for anything before, maybe not."

"My name is Connie Weston. We're trying to find out about something your uncle sold to George Weston back in 1981."

"Oh, yes, that would be his Hawaiian treasure. It bought him a new house in Boca, a young wife, and most likely an early passing. He had lots of fun, though."

"Do you know anything about the missionary envelope?"

"Yes, I'm looking at a picture on the wall right now. It's just an old envelope from Hawaii. Not much, really, apart from it gave him almost a million dollars and a ticket to Florida, and me, this apartment."

"Can we come and take a look later this afternoon?"

"Sure, by all means. We'll show you our prize." She told us her name was Mandy O'Connell and gave us directions.

With no time for rest, we hit the subway again and took an E to Forest Hills.

Anthony insisted I have the only free seat. I rested my head against the cold metal pole and dozed.

As we pulled into the station, he bent down and gently whispered, but perhaps a little too close to my ear, "We're here."

Ⓐ

The apartment was one of two on the first floor, with a small yard at the back. We entered through the open outside door.

I led us down a dingy, pine-scented passage. "What could be so precious about an envelope sent from a Hawaiian missionary?"

"Hmm. It could be some sort of document containing valuable information. Or perhaps something about the envelope itself?" Anthony speculated.

A woman opened the door of the second apartment as we were about to knock on the first. "I think you want me."

"Yes, we spoke earlier—I'm Connie, and this is Anthony."

"Hi, I'm Mandy, and this is young Rory, my grandson, who you were talking to on the telephone. Would you like coffee? Or how about a Long Island iced tea, if you fancy? I've just made a batch. It's my own special *light* recipe. Just right for drinking at this time of day."

"Mmm, lovely." I needed a tissue to dab a drop of drool. Citrusy things always made my mouth water. Even more so when they had liquor in them. I would've taken a coffee, but she started pouring the tea.

Mandy nodded toward Anthony. "And you, my darlin'?" Her eyes flashed up and down him like an X-ray scanner.

"Hmm . . . a glass of water, please."

"Rory, fetch an ice water from the refrigerator for the nice man."

"So this must be the famous philatelic cover." Anthony sounded like one of those appraisers on *Antiques Roadshow*. With both his arms raised to elbow height, fingers stretched out and twitching, he glided over to the chrome-framed picture on the wall. It hung a little crooked above a 1950s-style table stacked with papers.

Mandy, wearing too-tight mustard-colored slacks and a washed-out purple blouse, sidled across. "You're looking at our treasure." Her hand soon hovered too close to Anthony's butt.

"Wow, so this is the missionary envelope." I went over to check out the philatelic cover. I glared at Mandy, and she took control of her wandering hand.

"It's basically an addressed envelope with stamps on it that has been through the mail delivery system." Anthony continued to educate us.

Someone had written the cover's New York street address in a fancy script. Five dull, blue-colored stamps peppered its top. On each, *Hawaiian Postage* was printed in two lines and the value as both a number and a word. The four twos and one five added up to thirteen. Presumably thirteen *cents*, the mail rate from Hawaii in those days.

"The Honolulu postmark is difficult to . . . I can't make out the year." Almost licking his lips but not quite, Anthony moved into his hand-under-chin pose and squinted. "It looks like October fourth, 1850-something."

He came in closer. His breath ruffled my hair, and a waft of Dior cologne hit my nose. As I shifted to the other side of the table, Mandy stepped in sideways to fill the space. Her eyes were soon straying to our expert.

I coughed.

After a momentary pout, she came to join me but continued to speak to Anthony. "Getting this apartment was a blessing, I can tell you. I was twenty-six with two kids. My no-good husband, who abandoned us a couple of years before, tried and failed to reacquaint himself when he scented Burt's bonanza."

"So, these are the papers discovered with the envelope." I fingered the dusty heap. "Some are quite burnt."

"The prize was the envelope. They told Uncle Burt the rest had no value, but he kept them anyway. By all accounts, he found them all stuffed inside an old furnace in a building owned by the city. He pulled out the bundle and took it down to Billy at San Remo."

"Yes, of course," said Anthony. "The value is in the stamps. Like in the movie *Charade*." His breath steamed up the picture glass.

I nodded toward Anthony. "You said it might be about the envelope."

He beamed from my praise. "Hawaiian stamps of this vintage are some of the hardest to find. And being on a cover . . . Well, priceless."

I got an image of ten-year-old Judy Gibson, the stamp girl, chitchatting at the station with Dan on that day. My kind, dear husband always had time for her and had seemed genuinely interested in her hobby.

"My uncle wanted to keep things hush-hush. Billy made promises, then it went quiet for a few months after the tragedy with his grandson. Oh, my, were you Daniel's young wife?" Mandy covered her mouth. "Burt told me he'd met Daniel's girl the day he took the papers to the shop and . . . Oh, my. How awful."

The usual Dan thoughts rushed into my head, but now a smiling Sam bounced around in among them.

Mandy stroked Rory's hair, while Anthony continued to be bewitched by a photograph of an old envelope.

I broke first. "Something has blown up about this envelope, er, this cover, and we're trying to find out more about what happened back in 1981. We think George sold it on."

"During the months when it went quiet, did you feel the cover might have been lost?" asked Anthony, tapping his chin.

"Well, yes, Uncle Burt resigned himself to it being gone. He trusted Billy, so he went along with things. My uncle thought it might be worth a few thousand. A lot for him, but not earth-shattering. Then, in April 1981, George telephoned. He told Burt he had found a buyer and wanted him to come to the Dakota apartment to tell them the story and write it down for, oh . . . what's the thing again?"

My brain was of no help. "Um—"

"Provenance?" our specialist suggested.

"Yes, thank you, so with this prov . . . *providence*, they did a deal, and nearly a million bucks came Uncle Burt's way. He swore us to secrecy. Apparently, there had been a problem retrieving the envelope after Dan's um . . . passing . . . and some restoration work was required."

Anthony rubbed his chin. "Yes, of course."

"Burt flew off to Florida, and we moved into this apartment. We heard nothing else about it until you telephoned today."

"Well, thank you, that gives us a good deal to go on." Anthony started digging into the dusty heap.

"I'll fetch us some more tea. Do you need more water, my darlin'?"

"I'm all set, thanks." The darlin' focused on his documents.

Mandy and I, both with straws in our mouths, looked on. Every so often, Anthony lifted a sheet up for a crafty sniff.

"You can take them with you if you like," said Mandy. "If you come across another million . . . please tell me," she added, laughing.

"Yes, we should take them," Anthony said. "It may help us. Thank you. Could we also borrow the photograph?"

"Why not? Burt left it here when he moved. Yes, take it."

"We'll be sure to let you know if we find more treasure," I said.

"A contribution to Rory's college fund would be useful." She continued to laugh through her straw.

Mandy and I slurped our teas and chatted some more, while Anthony and a less-than-helpful Rory collected the hundred or so sheets of paper.

"Rory, go find a grocery bag for the nice man."

"Thank you." Anthony beamed his now perfect smile. "Con, we should be on our way."

For some reason, I sent him another little scowl for the "Con," and his lovely grin faded.

"Thanks again, Mandy. We'll be in touch," he said.

"Come along anytime, handsome."

Anthony's smile came back strong.

"Bye, Rory," I said, waving to him.

He threw a paper airplane, which hit me on my thigh.

Mandy put a hand on each of his shoulders. "Rory, do you have some more of those papers?"

"No."

"Rory?"

"The nice man can take them." He shook free from his grandmother and picked up the plane and a half-dozen others he pulled from under the couch.

"Thank you, Rory." Anthony gave the boy a fatherly pat on the head before adding the airplanes to the grocery bag.

We said goodbye to Mandy and her grandson at the door and walked quickly back to the station.

Sam was relying on me—I wouldn't let him down.

Chapter Twenty-Four

ANTHONY

Manhattan
Monday, December 8, 1980

Almost everyone had left for the evening when we arrived back at San Remo. I headed for Billy's office, carrying the unconscious Con.

As I walked up the corridor, Evie looked up. "My God, Anthony, what's happened?"

With Evie's help, we laid Con on Billy's couch and covered her lower half with a blanket.

"Dan's been involved in a terrible accident at the station. He climbed down onto the tracks. Jack was on the platform—perhaps it was a stunt. The train couldn't stop in time."

"What—why would he do such a stupid thing?"

"Not sure. My priority was to bring Con back here, to safety."

"Thank God you were there. Did you see it all?"

"I will never forget it. As I said, Jack—"

"I don't trust that boy."

"Keep an eye on her, will you? I'll call Dan's mom and Billy. Oh, Jesus, they're going to be devastated."

Show-off Dan overreacted to my little joke. He surely understood I would never have pushed Jack. Something started to nag my brain as I paced around in front of the open door.

Was Dan's accident my fault?

Con came around as Evie returned. I kept out of sight but observed them from the doorway. Con needed her mom to confirm what had occurred.

"I should be with my husband," Con said.

They got married?—she was too young. Who knew? Not Jack, for sure.

Con doubled over. Blood began running down her leg.

"Con, what's happening?" Evie held her daughter.

"Mom, help me. *My baby.*"

A baby—I guess that's why she married him.

"Anthony, we need an ambulance. Go call 911." Evie snapped into action.

Within ten minutes, Con was taken to the emergency room with her mom. As no one had answered the telephone at the Dakota apartment, I set off to break the dreadful news to Dan's doting grandparents.

Outside the Dakota building, a weird guy was hiding what looked like a record album in the flower planter by the boundary wall. All the time, he fiddled with something in the pocket of his heavy fur-collared over-coat. The thing had a metal handle—I needed to call the cops.

In the front office, I found Louise Weston using the telephone.

Jay Hastings, dressed in his Dakota uniform and immaculate white shirt, was the concierge on duty.

Louise covered the mouthpiece. "Anthony, what are you doing here? Where is everyone? Jesus, is it Grandpa Billy?" She hung up.

"Can we go upstairs?" I nodded in the direction of Hastings. "I need to tell you something."

Without saying a word, she gestured with her hand, and we headed to the elevator.

"I have terrible news, but not about your grandfather. It's about Daniel . . . He's dead . . . Killed on the subway."

"Jesus Christ. A mugging?"

"No, a train ran him down."

Louise didn't cry. "Fuck, how the hell—"

I'd never seen her cry. "Not sure, um . . . Connie saw it all. Jack Beckett was there, too."

"Yes, of course. That boy is such a bad influence on my brother."

I nodded.

She led me into the kitchen.

I poured her some of the brandy that Aileen had always kept for emergencies. Louise didn't invite me to take a glass, but I gulped a discreet mouthful before handing it to her.

"Also, um . . . Connie was taken ill."

"I guess she would be if she witnessed that. We don't get on now, but I can understand—"

"I think she started to miscarry."

"What?"

"She was pregnant." *Why did I tell her that?*

"Fucking pregnant—did Dan know?"

"Ah . . ."

"Did he commit suicide?"

"Hmm . . . I can't say." *What could I say? "I wanted to show Dan that I might push his best buddy in front of a train if he didn't stop blackmailing me?"*

Ⓐ

Neither Billy nor Aileen had arrived back when I left the apartment around ten forty-five that night. As I descended in the elevator, a loud bang startled me. A gunshot, then four more in rapid succession.

Hastings was tending to a man on the floor as I entered the front office. A green Dakota-issue uniform jacket covered the guy's upper body. Hastings called 911, all the time tugging at the damp sleeves of his blood-soaked white shirt.

I recognized the guy's eyeglasses. What the . . . John Lennon lay on the floor. I attempted to say something helpful, but nothing came out.

The cops arrived in minutes and didn't wait for the ambulance. They carried Lennon out to their patrol car and laid him on the back seat.

Why hadn't I called the cops earlier?

I spotted what looked like a gun. *It was a gun.*

If Louise Weston hadn't been making a call . . . Yes, if she hadn't been using that telephone, I could, no, I would have stopped John Lennon from being shot. Why hadn't I done that?

I found myself down at Roosevelt Hospital, where Lennon's fans were gathering and where Con had been brought earlier.

Dan was dead.

Con, likely, had lost her baby.

The crowd started to sing "Imagine." A guy in a white coat came out and announced that John Lennon had just died.

The appalling events of December eighth, 1980, would gnaw at me for years to come.

Chapter Twenty-Five

CONNIE

Manhattan
Saturday, July 1, 2000

Anthony insisted we examine the papers together and invited himself to my room. My cell showed four missed calls from my mother. Taking a deep breath, I dialed with the hope she wouldn't pick up. She did.

"Hello, Ma. How are you?"

"I'm fine, lovey—can't wait to see you."

"Listen, I'm on the road to the airport, and ahead of us is a major pileup." Why the hell did I say that?

"Oh, my God. You're not involved, are you?"

"No, I'm caught in a massive gridlock and may miss my flight. I tried to call BA, but they didn't pick up."

"Let me phone them."

"No, please, I'll handle everything."

"Let me know as soon as you can, Connie. Why did this happen when you were on the way home?"

"I'll update you when—" I hung up.

Anthony took the back off Burt's picture frame. "Wow, there are four photos in here. The cover's front and back, and the same for a letter. Look, here, at the cross-out on one side of the letter. My guess is those frugal missionaries reused their old stationery."

"Oh, yes. I see. How interesting."

"If you look at the back of the envelope in this photo here, it's clearly handmade from one of the used sheets." The front of his Levi's twitched. Why was I looking there? "Some of this stuff is the correspondence from other letters. They're from the same source. On the whole, boring, mundane messages, but the crossed-out writing is more interesting. I'm going to take it back with me and try to piece together a narrative. Is that all right with you, Con"—he shook his head—"uh, Connie?"

"God, yes, please do."

He piled up the papers. "You seem distracted."

"I just need some sleep. Let's continue this in the morning."

He left the room to go and enjoy his papers. I tugged my mind back to Sam and began to think about how we would build a life together. He's such a considerate man—he'd make a great dad for our two or maybe three kids.

I'd also started to appreciate Anthony's good nature. Was I so shallow that this was only now his teeth had been fixed and his spots healed?

I needed a little something to take the edge off the day and headed to the bathroom. An opened bottle of Frog's Leap sat on the vanity, but after pouring a drop, I stopped—no more alcohol today. Instead, I rinsed my mouth with Listerine, which looked the same as at home but had a different minty taste.

I sent Ma a text: *BA working on getting me a flight tomorrow evening.*

Ⓐ

About an hour into some restless sleep on the top of the bed, my cell came to life. I tried to ignore the thing, but it kept on starting up again and again.

"Yes."

"Yes, Auntie Betty here, my lovely. *Ladybird, ladybird, come fly away home.*" Her slurring and nursery rhyming were bad signs. "Why aren't you flying home?"

I picked up the glass and the bottle from the bathroom and sat on the edge of my bed.

"Your mother is disappointed in you, Constance. You've been lying—lying about the accident on the freeway. Come home tomorrow, or else she's taking that cat of yours—"

"Please stop." Shit, Mom had set her Auntie Betty on me.

"Yes, taking your Simon to the vet. If you aren't going to be around, she doesn't want to deal with Simon filling up the kitty litter with all his stinking shit. *Pussycat, pussycat, where have you been?*"

"Please stop." I poured and drank half a glass without thinking.

"Please stop," she mimicked. "No, you stop."

"Ma, listen to me."

"Hey, diddle diddle, the cat did a piddle—"

"Please don't hurt Simon." I couldn't cope when she started on like this.

"Cry, Baby Bunting, Daddy's gone a-hunting."

"Ma, where are you?" Auntie Betty had taken her over. I sniffed, drank, and topped up.

"No, Constance, she's sad. *Simple Simon met a pieman going to the vet.*"

"Please—"

"Inconsolably sad, she is, my lovely. *Ding, dong, bell, pussy's in the well.*"

"I'll call back in the morning."

"All too late. Why can't you be arsed to come home? You found a New York buck you want to fuck, eh?"

"No, that's not fair." I tipped the last of the Zinfandel into my glass.

"What's not fair, Constance, are all those nights out. At your school disco, was it? Jiving, and rubbing yourself up against those boys, seducing them with your fading womanly wiles? Yes, your toy boys from school, lured to your mother's basement."

"It is a college. We'd been to a concert, and the guy was thirty-five."

"Yes, you were lusting after the young lads. *Little Boy Blue, come blow your horn.* She has to live with your stinking boy toys whizzing and jizzing all over her basement, the smell of sex reeking the place out. She suffers in silence while you're poked and pleasured."

"This isn't fair."

"What about her, is it fair on her? What does she have to live for, eh? She might as well jump off Waterloo Bridge. Simon put down at the vet's, and off to the bridge. Or Simon in a garbage bag and both of them off the damn bridge together. Yes, bugger the vet's bill. In a bag and off the fucking bridge. Do you understand what I'm saying, lady?"

I hoped poor Simon had made himself scarce. There was a lot of banging and crashing in the background. "What's happening?"

"I'm smashing the place up, my lovely. If you can't be arsed to come back, I'm—"

The line went dead.

I thought things had improved since my birthday. Over the past five years, Ma had threatened to kill herself many times, but this was the first time she'd included Simon in one of her sick fantasies. It had occurred to me frequently that if I could permanently banish Auntie Betty, then the *old Mom* would return.

For now, we needed time apart. Perhaps I'd go ahead and make my trip to New York a permanent deal.

Chapter Twenty-Six

My breathing picked up speed as I descended the steep stone steps to our tiny basement flat. Something I had planned would no doubt upset my mother.

My gorgeous ginger-and-white cat purred and weaved himself around my legs. "Hello, darling. Are you ready for your supper, Simon?" I kept on walking as his back-and-forth motion started to turn me on.

"Connie, is that you, lovey?"

"Yes. Hi, Ma." I made a try at perky.

"Come on through. Dinner's on the table."

Was my arrival home so predictable that everything could be laid out? With its two side leaves in place, the monstrosity of a dining table overwhelmed the room even more than usual.

"Wow, roast lamb on a Tuesday evening. Are you trying to fatten me up?"

Simon went over to his bowl for a lick or two of milk before sniffing the air and sneezing. How did his tongue reach over his nose like that? He jumped up and settled himself on the ledge above the radiator.

Our claustrophobic basement was a hellish place, where Ma and I spent too much time together. Once upon a time, I'd had ambitions. In my midtwenties, after finishing a creative writing course, I started a novel. My working on it most evenings and weekends appeared to annoy my mother.

"Can't you leave your computer thing alone for once? Let's have a proper conversation."

Eighteen months in, and almost done, I arrived home to be told by Ma that earlier in the day she had been distracted by a telephone call while filling her bath. The water somehow got into my bedroom, soaking my laptop and Post-it Notes. Ma went into detail about her rescue attempt, then dropped a ball of multicolored mush into my hands. At the repair shop, the guy showed me the marks on the keyboard and suggested somebody had stabbed it with a knife or meat skewer. The hard disk suffered a couple of punctures, and nothing could be retrieved.

Ma denied all knowledge. "Are you accusing your mother? More likely the shop wanted to sell you a new computer."

In a different world, Lou and I might have achieved something amazing together.

"Happy birthday." Ma licked her lips. "Pour the wine, lovey."

"I'm sure we're drinking too much." Almost three-quarters of the bottle of Merlot fit into our two favorite glasses. It was my thirty-eighth birthday, and like most other evenings, I drank at home with my mother. "Did you enjoy your lunch with your friend Beryl?"

"Didn't go in the end. All she does is moan on about her ailments. She never asks me about my legs. She's all about her bits and bobs down below. My veins never get a look-in."

"Yes, it is awful when people don't listen."

"What, lovey?"

"Nothing."

Ma spotted my added eye roll and soured. "Speak up, so I can hear you. You're always muttering. You're a teacher, for Christ's sake. Enunciate, woman, enunciate."

She had let herself go over the past few months. She had worn the same sweat-stained supermarket loungewear all week. When I thought of how well turned out she used to be in our New York days, it made me sad to see her now.

"You should go out a bit more, Ma. The whole of London is on your doorstep, with all the art, theater, and cinema."

I couldn't have gotten through the early eighties without my mother—she was so kind to me. I hoped the old Ma was still in there. An aroma of congealing lamb fat started to make my stomach churn. I took a medicinal slug of wine.

"And cheers to you, Connie." She shot me one of her scowls. "I actually did go out today, to buy your effing birthday dinner." Her hands went palms up to present her work.

Simon lifted his head and blinked.

"Sorry, Ma, I didn't mean to be ungrateful."

She handed me a creased envelope. "Here's your card."

"Thank you." I pulled it out and stared at the tag line: *I know you're my daughter, but you're still a bitch.* "A little offensive, perhaps?"

"Is it, lovey?"

I deposited it facedown on the sideboard and caught sight of myself in the oval mirror on the wall. With a smiley pout, I could pass for twenty-eight, for sure.

Ma leaned over the table, forked a chunk of lamb into her mouth, and began chewing. Her jaw clicked in time with the 1940s mantel clock.

"What about you, lovey?" She spoke while moving a lump of gristle around her teeth with her tongue before a couple of fingers went in to retrieve it. She took a peep and popped it back in. "You aren't doing a great deal in this magnificent city." She swallowed hard, and from the expression on her face, appeared to regret it. "It's all on your doorstep, too."

She had a point. I came in from work and flopped in front of the TV most nights. The students seemed less interested in me these days. Something to do with them staying the same age and me not.

"So, you wore that outfit to the supermarket today?"

She checked herself out and nodded. "So no birthday shindig with your school colleagues tonight?" She tilted her head and fixed me with

a stare before pushing another forkful into her clickety mouth. A dribble of grease escaped and ran down her baggy drawstring pants.

"Ma, I need to get away for a break."

"No, you don't. You're too old to go off gallivanting. Your place is
here with your mother. What if I have one of my dos?"

"Ma, really? You only ever had one *do*, as you call it. The night you
polished off two bottles of BOGOF price-buster Chianti in under an
hour. You slipped under the table and banged your head when you
got up."

"Don't attack me. Top me up."

I leaned over and started pouring. "Okay, but shouldn't you—"

"All the way." She placed a finger on the side of the rim. "We're
celebrating your birthday."

"I'm thinking about taking a trip to New York."

Simon lifted his head and looked at me before switching to Ma.

"No, our time there ended badly, and they don't want us back." Her
wine sloshed out on the floor as she gesticulated.

"By *they*, you mean the Westons?"

"Who the hell else? You won't be able to resist them. Do you want
to start up the Weston thing again? Without me this time, eh?" She
moved the glass between her hands, licking her winey fingers.

"Ma, please, I don't plan to go anywhere near the Dakota." I did,
of course. I'd read stuff in a couple of letters to Ma from Walt. He
mentioned George's twins had turned nineteen, and the son was the
image of my Dan. In the last letter, he included a clipping of a recent
article from the *New York Post*: *Son of Prominent Upper West Side
Businessman in Student Hangout Drug Bust.*

I had been obsessing over the picture of Sam Weston ever since.

The computer place where he worked was on West Twenty-Second
Street, so I arranged to stay at the Chelsea.

Ma and I were destroying each other. She would be better off without me here. I wanted to live in America again. My salvation now lay in
reconnecting with my past. Through Sam Weston, I could effectively
take up from where I'd been forced to leave off.

"I can't stop you, Connie, but remember, you were only a girl in
1980. You're a middle-aged woman now—thirty-eight years old today.

New York is a city for young people. You'll be lonely." She looked into the mirror and arranged her hair. "I should come with you."

Shit, she rarely wanted to go to the supermarket, never mind fly across the Atlantic. "Well, yes, but—"

"But what? Don't you want your old mother with you?"

Simon attempted to turn around on the ledge but lost his foothold and dropped to the carpet with a short meow. Ma and I paused and watched him stride off toward the door.

I locked her in a stare. "Come along, then, we can go on a mother-daughter trip. What do you say?" This was a big gamble.

"Not sure I can fly with my legs. Do you have to go? Oh, yes, my passport has expired. I'll need to go to the embassy. Hasn't yours expired, too?"

"I'll check." I'd renewed it last year. "Come with me, Ma."

"No, lovey, who'll take care of Simon? You know I can't cope without you."

"We can keep in touch. You can use the cell phone I bought you last Christmas. We can send text messages."

"I'm not happy, Connie. You're so selfish sometimes. Look what I've done for you. Caring for you after Daniel's accident and handling the business with that baby you stole. Do you hate me?"

Simon started meowing.

She promised me she would never throw the baby at me again. It was a couple of months after the miscarriage and Dan's death, almost twenty years ago. We had just bought our place here, and I thought the poor little mite had been abandoned outside the butcher's. I didn't know it was customary for mothers to leave their strollers outside shops when they went in to buy stuff. "Come on, Ma. Please don't go down this route again."

"No, you come on." She gulped down her wine and emptied the remains of the bottle into her glass. "Open another. Let's celebrate."

Still meowing, Simon now scratched at the linoleum around the door.

"Let's watch a film." A couple I had picked up from the Blockbuster lay on the sideboard. "Here we are, *Angela's Ashes* and the classic *Days of Wine and Roses*, starring Jack Lemmon. You like Jack Lemmon."

"Jack who? Never heard of him. No films tonight. We are having fun on your birthday."

"Let's have a restful evening—"

"You're so selfish." She guzzled down her wine.

I opened the door, and Simon shot out.

"You leaving me, already?" She grasped the protruding bone in the lamb shank with her thumb and forefinger, then waved the meat around. "What am I supposed to do with this, eh?"

Grabbing my cardigan, I followed Simon without looking back.

Chapter Twenty-Seven

ANTHONY

I visited the San Remo print shop every Tuesday to check on things and collect mail. Occasionally, an old-time client requested me to do some work for them—legitimate stuff, on the whole. I rarely had to call for any help. I lived my life on autopilot, avoiding social gatherings whenever possible. My few friends gave up inviting me to their summer cookouts and the like. I preferred my own company.

Early in January 1981, my father reappeared after Winston brokered a truce with the Mafia guys. He arrived in time to save me from myself. After that dreadful day, I had gone into a steep decline. My father helped to restore my sanity. Regrettably, he fell afoul of the mob again when a pair of rogue aces found their way into his hand during a high-stakes poker game. My father had completed a particularly complicated project for George Weston before he disappeared once more.

George made promises to return the printing plates his son stole, but they perhaps proved too useful for keeping me on the hook. A couple of years back, my old mentor, Winston, remarked that my skills now surpassed those of my father and likely him, too. George paid me well for my services, but he remained my blackmailer.

In my too-small Bensonhurst apartment, there was a stench of burning plastic coming up from my neighbor below. The smell, together with the empty cold-remedy bottles in the garbage, added up to stove-top crystal meth—something else to worry about.

I made my usual breakfast of coffee and toast. As I layered up the Skippy peanut butter and jelly, the phone rang.

"Hello, Anthony Houseman speaking."

"Hello, Anthony Houseman. Evie Williams here."

"Evie, *hi, how are you?*"

"I got your number from Walt. I need your help. Connie will be visiting New York at the end of June."

"Oh, yes?" Incredible news.

"Yes, I think she's interested in the Weston boy."

"Oh, yes?" Why was I surprised? Would a nineteen-year-old boy be interested in her, though?

"Could you keep an eye on her for me? That boy's been in trouble with drugs, and she's far too old for him. Let's try to stop anything before it starts. You understand what I'm saying. We must stop her making a damn fool of herself."

"Yes, I agree. I will protect her from that boy, have no worries."

"She'll be staying at the Chelsea—would you believe? Checking in on the twenty-eighth of June."

"Got it."

"I'll call you before . . . I need to put the lamb in the oven. I'm making Con a birthday dinner. Bye, for now."

She didn't need to tell me about Con's birthday. I wrote her a card every year. They were all in a drawer in my bedroom.

My vibrating cell phone started to move across the counter toward the cold toast.

"Hello."

"Ant, I need to see you. Come up to the Dakota this evening and bring the papers with you. I presume they're ready."

"Jacob, I need my—"

"All in good time. I'll return those items when everything goes through. I know you wouldn't try anything, but I ain't stupid, man. Make it five thirty."

Now that Con was coming back, I wanted it all done and out of the way. I needed to retrieve my property. Jacob had somehow gotten his hands on my printing plates—and the letter addressed to me implicating Winston. Why hadn't I pressed George to return them before Jacob began controlling things?

Anyway, I had to prepare for Con's visit and make sure she wasn't drawn back into that family again—I would protect her.

I needed to book a haircut, a manicure, and a quick checkup at the dentist's office. Getting my teeth fixed had taken up the first five years of the nineties. George's payments got put to good use.

Perhaps Con would stay on in the city for a while? Knowing she was interested in art, I made a quick note to check out the summer exhibitions at MoMA, the Whitney, and the Guggenheim.

Chapter Twenty-Eight

CONNIE

After wandering around the block a couple of times, I found myself on a well-trodden path to the Ship Inn. With the hope they had forgotten the night of Ma's birthday celebration, I pushed open the door to the lounge and made my way through a smoky fog to the bar.

"Glass of Merlot, please."

"Large one?" asked the barman, who didn't recognize me, which was good.

"Yes, please." Out of the corner of my eye, I spotted John Stephens, the pub's owner, in the shadows.

He slunk over. "Connie, it has been a while."

I lifted my glass, took some slow sips, then lowered it a fraction. "How are you doing, Mr. Stevens?"

"Fine, thanks. We redecorated the function room after your shindig."

"I see you got the old newspaper reframed, too." I nodded at a yellowing copy of the *Polynesian* in its new position.

"That paper is part of our family's history, came all the way from Hawaii, it did. Sent by my namesake ancestor, a hundred and fifty years back."

"I remember you mentioning it before." Many times.

"Survived all those years, so thank the Lord Almighty, the bottle of Bailey's someone in your party threw at it didn't seep under the glass."

Ma blamed Auntie Betty.

"I did offer to pay for—"

"Pete told me. My son isn't here now, in case—"

"I'm just here for a drink. To get out of the house, you know?"

"He's working away, up north, a long way from here. His new girlfriend is very nice, by all accounts. She's young, around the same age as him."

I gazed around, hoping he'd leave me. Then, much to my relief, Gilbert and Tom, our neighbors from the upstairs flat, walked in. Pointing in their direction, I gathered up my bag. "Catch you later."

The landlord watched me for a short while before returning to his shadowy lair.

"Hey, Connie," said Tom, beaming. "How are you?"

"Hi there. Good to see you."

He was in his early thirties and Gilbert around twenty years his senior. They were about the same height and build, which allowed them to share their clothes. Tonight, Tom wore gray chinos with a rather elegant blue-striped shirt. A burgundy pullover hugged his shoulders. Gilbert had on similar trousers but in a dark blue with a pastel-pink shirt. Unusually, he was without his beloved Balenciaga cashmere bomber jacket.

"We were both concerned," said Tom. "Quite the melee coming from your basement this evening. Simon came up to see us, bless him. We've left him in our sitting room. He made a beeline for Gilbert's bomber and settled himself down."

"Yes, Ma is a little tired and emotional tonight. She needed some space to relax on her own."

"We heard a lot of crashing and banging," said Tom. "Let's hope things aren't awry down there."

"All will be fine." There would be tidying up to do later.

"Can we tempt you, Connie, dear?" said Gilbert, tapping my almost empty glass with an immaculately manicured nail. "A small libation, perhaps?"

"You can, kind sir. Merlot, please."

"Coming right up, me lady," he said. They were always so generous and jolly. They worked from home. A stream of middle-aged men visited them at all hours.

"So, sweetie, today's your birthday," said Tom. "We got one of your cards with our mail today. I dropped it in, to your mother."

My index finger went to my lips.

"Of course. Gilbert loves a birthday bash, but not me—keep quiet, then nobody is counting. You're still all right, though, Con. You're in full bloom."

"Thanks, Tom."

Gilbert returned, balancing two reds and a pint of lager between his fingers. "Here we go."

"Thanks, you two."

"Cheers and happy birthday," said Gilbert.

Tom tried a shush.

"Cheers, guys." I clinked both their glasses. Perhaps a little too exuberantly. The landlord's eyes flashed on me, but he didn't move.

We chitchatted about the house, the state of the stairway, and the need for repainting the outside woodwork. Simon's toilet habits came up. I prayed for the well-being of Gilbert's Balenciaga.

"Your mother tells us you're taking a trip," Tom said.

"When did she tell you?"

"Ooh, must have been the day before yesterday. Yes, it was bin day."

"Did she mention where I was going?"

"New York," said Gilbert, "indubitably, the Big Apple."

"Well, yes, I am. At the end of—"

"June, end of June, beginning of July." He sat upright as if waiting to be tested further.

"Right again. So, everybody is aware of my plans."

"Well, a little vacation is just what you need, sweetie," said Tom. "Find yourself a fit, hunky American."

"Careful," said Gilbert, "you're getting Con and me all hot and horny."

"Enough, already." Though I couldn't wait to check out Sam Weston. As he shared the same genes as Dan, it figured Sam would be into me, too. I could pass for ten or even fifteen years younger in the right light.

"And young, of course." Tom continued his reverie.

"What? Oh, yes, a young, fit, American hunk."

We left the pub at the same time, but they went off up into town for a preview screening of *Mission: Impossible 2*.

A bottle bounced and broke not far behind me. I walked faster.

Simon dashed up as I gingerly opened the basement door. Shit, broken glass crunched under my feet. "Be careful, Simon." I pushed him back outside. "Ma, are you okay?"

In the parlor, she sprawled unladylike on the couch with her legs akimbo. I wasted a sneer before covering her embarrassment with Simon's second-best blanket.

After sweeping up the worst of the glass, I removed the lamb shanks from in among the sofa cushions. On my way back from disposing of the garbage, I collected Simon from the rear step. Pushing my nose into his fur and breathing deeply, I caught a whiff of Gilbert's lovely Aramis cologne. I shifted Simon to my shoulder, and we both went off to bed.

A while after falling asleep, the sound of someone stumbling around in the other room woke me. Everything went quiet before a thump on my door made me jump.

"Hello, Ma, are you okay?"

"Hello yourself, you selfish bitch."

Simon's ears pricked up. He lifted his head.

"Ma, is that you?"

"No, my lovely, it's your auntie Betty."

Simon sprang from the bed and started to climb the curtains. He then got on the windowsill and scratched like a crazy cat on the glass. I walked over and released him. He shot off up the fire escape, no doubt in search of Gilbert's cashmere.

After grabbing a handful of tissues from the box on my child-sized dressing table, I buried my face in them and thought of Simon. "I want to sleep now."

"What's that? You playing with yourself? Fiddling away, while you think about those American boys? Are you? Finished with the lads from your school now? I expect you—"

"I work at a college."

"Yes, and now you're adding the young Weston boy into your stinking orgy." She was bashing the door with what sounded like a bottle. "Let me in, Constance, or I'll smash my way in."

"Wait, wait."

"No, you wait, you slut. Do you need to dry yourself off? Hide your vibrating bunny thingy."

Ma had been in my drawers. There was zero privacy in the place. I had a lock put on my bedroom last December, but the key went missing. It popped up a week later, in the pocket of a coat I hadn't worn for six months.

"I'm coming over, hang on." I thought of Simon relaxing into the cashmere.

Moments after I unlocked the door, her head appeared from around the edge. She grinned and ran her tongue along her lips. "Here's Betty."

"Are you all right?"

"Are you all right?" she repeated.

"Let's move back into the parlor."

She outmaneuvered me and slipped past. Next thing, she grabbed a handful of my personal items and threw them at me with force. My faithful old Vibratex Rabbit Pearl glanced off my forehead, switching itself on. It began dancing around the rug in front of us.

I snared the Rabbit, which refused to turn off. "Let's just . . ."

"Fucking disgusting, Constance. Yes, you are. How does your mother put up with all your sexual shenanigans? She tries to sleep in her room while you're in here moaning and grunting. These walls are paper-thin." She bashed the wall with the bottle, leaving a dent. "You, pleasuring yourself when none of your boys is around to do you, eh?" She swiped everything off the top of my nightstand to make space for the still-half-full bottle of Tesco Chilean Merlot, then turned and threw a punch, which missed me.

I picked up the bottle by the neck. Sloshing the wine around, I lured her out of my bedroom and into the parlor. She grabbed a bottle of Bailey's Irish Cream from the sideboard and took a five-second pull, before passing it to me. I pretended to drink.

A frantic knocking on the back door stopped us for a moment. "Is everything okay in there? Connie, Mrs. Williams, are you two *all right*?" Tom said, his voice wavering.

"Yes, absolutely fine, thanks," I said.

"My God, now we have one of those damn pansies from upstairs poking his thing in where it isn't wanted." She made a thrusting action with her hips and the Bailey's bottle.

"Should we call the constabulary, Connie?" Tom asked. "Have things gone completely awry?"

"Yes, totally awry, but no need for reinforcements—I'm handling things, thank you."

"So, you're offering hand jobs to the nancy boys now, too, you filthy whore."

"Okay, Connie, I'll leave you to settle things," said Tom. "By the way, Simon is up with us."

Maneuvering Ma into her bedroom, I shouted, "Thanks."

Getting my life back on track in New York with the help of Sam Weston was now my number one priority—bring it on.

Chapter Twenty-Nine

ANTHONY

Manhattan
Tuesday, May 30, 2000

I arrived at the Dakota two hours early for my meeting with Jacob, ostensibly to check on George. My blackmailer of twenty years had paid me well, and we had a good working relationship, but he had controlled my life. Earlier this year he had finally agreed to destroy the plates along with the letter incriminating Winston and me. It soon became apparent that he never got around to it, when I heard that Jacob had stolen it all from the study safe along with the deed to the Dakota apartment.

I took the elevator up.

The Pomeranian ran to greet me and danced around my new sneakers. They would be back in their box this evening until Con's visit.

"Hello?" An aroma of linseed and beeswax greeted me as I entered through the open door. Aileen was obviously back from her trip.

She popped her head around the dining room door. "Oh, Anthony, come in. Will you take a wee glass of something?"

"No, thank you. Oh, maybe a glass of ice water, please."

"Coming up."

She splashed some of the water onto my sneakers but appeared not to notice.

"Is Mr. Weston here?"

"Yes, he's in his study. What's going on? I had no idea George was in this state. I've booked a consultation for him with a specialist recommended by Mrs. Van de Coot, on Friday this week. Jacob's got too much control. I suspect he's overmedicating George, and that's what's causing his memory problems."

"Yes, I think that's a good move."

Aileen was now on it, at least. The letter from the Mayo Clinic, confirming a diagnosis of early-onset dementia, was my work. The whole Jacob thing had gone too far. It occurred to me that if we could get George sufficiently *compos mentis*, Jacob's power would crumble. With Con on the horizon, I needed to sort all this out. My priorities had changed.

"I'm away to my bath now. My son will be pleased to see someone. Not sure he'll recognize you, though." Aileen scurried off.

George and I sat together for about half an hour, but he didn't seem keen to talk. A noise coming from the dining room broke the peacefulness, and I went to investigate.

Jacob stood at the table, knife in hand. A plate of graham crackers, a jar of Nutella, and a can of Mountain Dew were gathered around him. "Hey, Ant, the mortgage company has been on my back. Have you brought the power-of-attorney documents?"

"Yes." I pulled them from my satchel and laid them over his crackers.

"Careful, Ant. Remember, I hold something of yours."

A shriek came from somewhere at the other end of the apartment.

"We need to check on that." I waited at the door for Jacob.

"Yes, I think you should," he said, smiling.

I dashed down the corridor and into Aileen's bedroom. "Aileen, are you okay?"

Blood was oozing from under the en suite door. I managed to push it open a little way.

Jacob came in behind me. "Looks like there's been a wee accident."

Stooping to check on the naked Aileen, I stared up at Jacob. "Call 911."

He pulled out his cell. "Is she alive?"

"Call an ambulance, now, or I will." I opened my cell.

He dialed. I took her pulse.

Aileen was already dead.

Chapter Thirty

CONNIE

Manhattan and Brooklyn
Sunday, July 2, 2000

I woke up at dawn, confused by my new room. An image of Judy's big ol' stamp bag barged into my brain as I tried to focus on my watch. Yes, before Dan went to cross the track, he slipped something into that bag. He'd been to the photographer's, so he must have been carrying the genuine missionary envelope. When everything had settled down after the accident, and there was no sign of the envelope, George had assumed it was lost. He had photographs and Burt to tell his story.

It was too early to speak to Anthony.

I managed to read twenty pages of my book, Donna Tartt's *The Secret History*, before dozing off. The sun blazing on my eyelids woke me at seven, and I fired off a text to Anthony to ask him to call. My cell lit up almost at once.

"Hey, how are you today?"

"It's your mother. Hope you aren't too disappointed. I'm using the old rotary phone. Auntie Betty had an accident with the lovely new one. I found it in the sink, smashed to pieces and reeking of Bailey's. What did you say to her?"

"How are you, Ma?"

"Fine, I cleaned up the mess." A first.

"Is Simon safe?"

"He never came to his bowl this morning. He made himself scarce after someone threw Pinot Grigio over him. From the dusty bottle we got from that awful woman who did the curtains, remember her?"

That someone being you. "Oh, poor Simon." He was likely upstairs, snuggled into some cashmere. I put Ma on speakerphone and started writing a text to Gilbert to confirm.

"Your room is in quite a state. You'll need to buy a new lamp, and some of your clothes are in next door's bin. I discovered something nasty on them."

"Shit, Ma, what the hell happened?"

"So which flight are you booked on this evening?"

"Let me get back to you in an hour." My cell showed a missed call from Anthony.

"But reassure me, you're returning today?"

"Let me call you in an hour or so."

"Constance?"

"In an hour, bye."

Anthony's line was busy. Who the hell was he talking to?

He picked up on my umpteenth try and launched straight into his thing. "These papers are fascinating. The letters are all mundane: *We've converted so-and-so. The weather is this and that.* But on the reverse of each letter, a story builds into something entirely different."

"Before you go into that, I know what happened to the envelope."

"Dan put it into that girl's bag."

"How long have you known?" I walked into my luxurious bathroom to examine my face in the gigantic mirror above the his-and-hers washbasins. *Shit, where did that zit come from?*

"I worked it out last night. The fact that George made and sold a copy, believing the original was lost, accounts for all the hush-hush Burt's niece mentioned. The original cover surfaced a few weeks ago on Dials' website, the star lot in a prestigious auction of rare American stamps."

"We need to speak to Judy."

"Louise Weston works for Dials Auction House," said Anthony.

I pressed on the pimple hard with the handle end of my toothbrush. "Yow, fuck."

"Uh . . . yes, she's been working at their main office for years. All George's dealings gave her an in back in the late eighties. We should speak to her, but I guess there's a client secrecy thing?"

I wondered if Lou had continued with her writing. She'd had such grand plans to be a dramatist—at least she didn't have a mother to thwart her. "It might be easier to talk to Judy directly, if we can find her. I'm still not on the best terms with Lou."

My spot, now expanded and red, made me look like a drinker.

"Perhaps we can track her down. Any ideas?" asked Anthony.

"She lived close to George Weston's old apartment in East Williamsburg in 1980, with her grandfather. He must have been seventy then, so he's likely not around. Judy will be about thirty. She might still be living there. Let's go and check the place out. We could meet up outside the Morgan Avenue station in Brooklyn?"

"Um, yes, that will be fine."

"You sound unsure?"

"Well, Connie, I took a room here, at the Chelsea."

"Okay, well, yes . . . The lobby then . . . at nine?"

"Great. See you soon."

What the hell was Anthony's game? Did he still have a thing for me after all this time, or what?

I dabbed my nose until the spot and redness started to fade, then got to work on my makeup. This would need ongoing maintenance.

As I typed a hopeful text to Sam, I spotted something under the door. It was an unaddressed envelope containing a faxed grainy image of Ma entering our Bermondsey basement. It included a tagline: *A C C I D E N T S H A P P E N.* Must be something to do with Jacob, but how? Would that associate in London be prepared to do more than take a picture? I would need to warn Ma somehow, but without spooking her.

Why did Jacob see me as such a threat?

(A)

We were soon off the train and walking along some familiar streets. Anthony went on about his papers, while I thought about what to do about Ma. Should I mention the fax? I needed to tell her that I was staying longer. Sam was still my main worry. Why hadn't I heard anything?

"I have to make a call to my mom. We can grab a quick coffee." There was a cutesy place on the corner. "I can meet you inside in five. Let me see if she answers."

"Okay, yes, whatever you need to do. Has Sam been in touch?"

"No, we have to find out what's going on."

"I'll call the Dakota now," Anthony said, pulling out his cell.

I dialed Ma's home number. She picked up on the first ring. I nodded to Anthony, and he walked away toward the coffee shop.

"Hello."

"Ma, is that you?"

"No, dear, Auntie Betty."

"I can't talk to you. I need to speak to my mother. I can explain what's going on, but only to her. Ma, are you there?" I inadvertently squeezed my spot. The concealer was surely off the nose.

After a short pause: "Lovey, are you coming home?"

"Ma, listen to me. I visited the Westons."

"What? You promised me."

"Well, yes, but I bumped into Sam Weston on the subway."

"How do you mean bumped into him?"

"He is the image of Dan. I followed him."

"He led you to the Dakota. What a surprise. So you visited the apartment. They welcomed you in with open arms?"

"No, but some Eastern Europeans kidnapped Sam because of a valuable envelope George sold twenty years ago."

"God, yes, I recall the deal made them all a pile of cash. The sale was after we'd returned to London. Burt Raymond was made as rich as Croesus."

"I need to stay a few days to make sure Sam is okay. Anthony is helping me. You remember wonderful Anthony?"

"Of course. Yes, he called me earlier to tell me not to worry. He's watching out for you. Like he used to do."

"What, he called you?" What the hell was going on? One conversation with Anthony, and all was fine. "So you're all right with me staying here a while longer?"

"If you must. Simon's back, in case you were worried."

"Wonderful. Give him a big kiss from me."

"Yes, a young man knocked on the door this morning. He said Simon ran out in front of his car—nearly caused an accident. He said poor Simon was a little stunned, but soon came round when he picked him up. Not sure how the man knew to bring him back here."

"What did the young guy look like?"

"He wasn't anyone I'd seen before—nice looking. You'd have given him a once-over."

I didn't want to start a quarrel. "Let me know if Simon has any ill effects or if that guy is hanging around."

"He's too young for you."

"Yeah, yeah. Let's catch up later."

"Make sure you do. Bye."

The guy must've been connected to Jacob. Probably took the photograph.

As I entered the small artisan shop, Anthony signaled he was getting me coffee. By the time I sat down and sorted myself out, an Americano stood in front of me.

"Is everything okay? You look worried," Anthony said, on it as always.

"No, I'm fine . . . thanks for the coffee. Yes, my mother seemed remarkably calm." I didn't want to go into the Jacob thing with him right now.

"Did she mention my call?"

"Uh, yes, it did come up."

"Sorry, Connie. Your mother and I used to be close when we worked together at the print shop. We watched out for each other. She was concerned about you getting involved with the Westons on your trip here. She called me a few weeks ago to ask me to keep an eye out for you but didn't have my cell number, so she couldn't reach me."

"Keeping an eye out or stalking, more like," I said in a jokey tone. I had him down as a bit of a stalker, but perhaps we could all be guilty of that on occasions.

"No, I wanted to ensure you were okay."

"What else didn't you tell me?"

"Well, I never went to Montauk, and I moved into the Chelsea the day before you checked in. I do still work for the Westons, and I had nothing to do with Sam's kidnapping. He did tell me not to free him yesterday. In case you think otherwise."

"Wow. So, you're my protector."

"Yes, that's it."

My mother and Anthony had plotted this together. Regardless of the outcome with Sam, I would not be returning to live with my mother long term. I was an American citizen. Hell, I could wait tables if necessary until I got a license to teach here. Sam and I could make plans together.

I picked up and hugged the oversized cup. "So you spoke to someone at the Dakota?"

"Louise told me to butt out and hung up."

Taking a last sip of coffee, I stood up. "Okay, well, let's get on with this now we're here. Judy's apartment is down the street opposite. We can swing by the Dakota straight afterward. I need to know if Sam is safe."

Chapter Thirty-One

ANTHONY

Brooklyn

As we approached Judy's grandfather's apartment, Con kept looking in the windows of the buildings and flexing her nose. I almost said something reassuring about the massive spot but decided against it.

I pushed the top buzzer on a panel to the right of a peeling blue-painted door.

A young voice came on the intercom. "Hello, who is it . . . please?"

"Hi, is Judy Gibson there?" I asked.

"Judy Robinson is here."

She probably got married. "Could we speak to her, please?"

"Mommy isn't very well at the moment."

"Is your daddy at home?" Con asked.

"No, my daddy went out for a KFC family bucket, two years ago last Easter, but didn't come home. We ended up eating boring pasta."

"Oh, that's a pity. What's your name?" I asked.

"Wendy. My name is Wendy Robinson."

"How old are you, Wendy?" Con continued.

"I'm eight years old."

"Is your mommy okay? Does she need a doctor?" I reminded Con of my caring side.

"No, she has the flu."

Con came in close. She smelled so good. "My name is Connie. Dan and I used to bring her stamps. We're old friends."

"Oh, stamps, yes, we have been looking at lots of stamps. Mommy gave them to me. I'm a stamp collector. A phil . . . philata . . . thingy."

I jumped in. "A philatelist."

Con gave me an admiring nod.

"Yes, one of those. Wait, here's my mommy."

"Hello." Her mom began and ended with a sniff.

"Is that Judy?"

"Who wants to know?"

"She's your stamp buddy—Connie," Wendy said in a loud whisper.

"Connie, wow, come on up." Her buzzing us in was unnecessary as the door-close mechanism required attention—I took a quick look. Someone had wedged a penny inside. Con looked intrigued as I levered the coin out with my always-with-me multitool pen.

The small landings on the way up to the fourth floor gave us a welcome breather. Con needed the break more than me. Evie's heads-up had given me time for an intensive month in the gym.

An attractive, youngish woman with a truly red nose came out to meet us at the open door. Her daughter rushed up to her side and lightly gripped her waist.

"Better not come too close, I have the flu." She nodded in the direction of Con's nose. "Oh, you're suffering, too."

"No, no, just an annoying pimple. Down to my youthful complexion."

"Yes, of course." Judy showed us into a recently renovated living room with a high-quality real-wood floor and a strong odor of tomcat. A new plasma television took center stage. She switched off the TV but left the VHS playing. Wendy tutted, dashed over, stopped the player, and ejected the *Toy Story 2* tape. She replaced the cassette in the box before filing it next to *Toy Story*, on the shelf behind. I immediately warmed to this young girl.

Both Con and I headed to the comfortable-looking sofa by the window from opposite sides of the low designer coffee table. Showing our synchronicity, we sat down at the exact same moment.

"Kind of you to let us in," I said. Judy had retained her trim figure. She was a few years younger than Con, of course.

"I remember you." Judy tapped her finger on her chin. "Licky . . . er, Anthony?" She appeared mortified.

Con reddened, too, as I looked between them. "I always knew what people had called me behind my back." Well, that was the reason I'd had all the expensive and time-consuming dental work done, after all.

"God, Anthony. Please forgive me."

"Nothing to forgive. You did me a favor in the long run." I trotted out my stock response.

"I guess you'd like to talk about the envelope," Judy said, deftly changing the subject.

"So Dan did put it in your bag?" There was no other possible explanation, in my view.

"Yes, he sure did. After that terrible day, I didn't open my stamp bag up again until my daughter Wendy here pulled everything out of the cupboard a few months ago. She immediately fell in love with the stamps. We spent hours working through them all and came across the last package Dan gave me. Well, yes, the envelope was different."

Wendy looked like she wanted to sit with us, so Con moved up a little closer. Some lovely framed photographs of Brooklyn in winter were propped against the wall.

"Old Hawaiian stamps, nothing special. I decided to raise a little cash for Wendy so she could start collecting herself. I took the envelope, together with a few other stamps inherited from my grandpa, to Dials Auction House, hoping for a few hundred dollars. Dan's sister, Louise, worked there, but they told me she'd gone on vacation. The disrespectful guy said they didn't handle small stuff, but when he saw the envelope, he did a one eighty, called it the find of the decade. Where had it come from? How long had I owned it? I explained that my friend had collected stamps for me some twenty years ago. He said he would arrange for an appraisal and thought the envelope would go in their next high-value auction. He wouldn't be pushed on the estimate but did call me the following day to recommend a four-million-dollar reserve.

I couldn't take the thing back, knowing its worth. All that money, well, yes, tempting."

Con licked her lips. "Shit . . . four million dollars."

I couldn't help smiling at her reaction. "Rather surprising Louise didn't catch on."

"Well, she did when she returned from her vacation and some sick days. She came here a few weeks ago. By that time, the catalog was done and out to everyone. To make a long story short, she wanted the envelope. She said she would make my life difficult if I didn't withdraw it from the sale. I didn't want any fuss, so I asked Dials to take it out. They weren't happy, of course. Louise made me promise not to mention her name. They even offered to guarantee me at least five million."

"Shit!" Con's latest exclamation coincided with the arrival of a tortoiseshell Maine coon. The feline ambled across the room and jumped up on Wendy's lap.

"This is my cat, Tigger." Wendy hugged, then stroked him from head to tail. "He's in *Winnie the Pooh and the Blustery Day*."

"He's lovely." Con leaned over for a quick fondle. "I've got a cat in London."

Wendy glanced up and smiled. "Cats are nice."

"So, you got the cover back?" I asked.

The feline strode over Con and came to snuggle down on my lap. All three females beamed at me. I basked in the moment.

"Yes, after I picked up the envelope from the auction office, a car door opened on the street outside, and Louise gestured for me to get in. As her chauffeur started off, she took the cover and checked it over for a couple of minutes. She then instructed the driver to pull to the curb, and they dumped me."

"That was magnanimous of you, Judy," I said, tickling the tortoiseshell into purring ecstasy. Their eyes focused on me again.

"Dan obviously meant to retrieve it. I don't need praise."

"Did you receive a good price for your other stamps?" I asked.

"Yes, they put them in an earlier sale. We did rather well. We got twenty-five thousand dollars. Can you believe it? Wendy and I went on a short vacation and made a property investment."

We exchanged details and wished her well. When I turned at the door to prevent Tigger from following us out, Judy picked up the feline and hid her blushes in the cat's ample fur. She must have been check-ing me out. The gym had really paid off.

We started down the narrow stairs. A flight down, Con whispered, "Judy fancies you."

"You imagine things." I felt elated for a moment but didn't want Con to think I had eyes for anyone but her. "Anyhow, let's get going. We should go straight to the Dakota. We know Louise has the cover. Sam may be free by now if she's handed it over."

Con had already picked up her pace. The boy was clearly upper-most in her thoughts. Somehow, though, I was optimistic my patience and determination would win out in the end.

Chapter Thirty-Two

CONNIE

Manhattan

In the Dakota apartment, things were going to the dogs—literally. Paw prints surrounded a half-empty, lidless jar of Nutella in the middle of the table. And someone had wedged a packet of graham crackers under one of the shelves in the open corner cupboard. A godawful smell suggested Pompom had missed his walk in the park—or worse.

It made me sad, particularly as Aileen's standards had always been so high. I would have liked to have seen the wee lady again.

"So, you connected with an old acquaintance. What do you want from us now, Constance?" Lou stepped around the source of the odor. "Liza, where are you? Come and clean up after your disgusting shih tzu."

I was going to correct her but decided against it. "Listen, we found out what happened to the missionary cover."

"Well done for finding it, Nancy Drew. Actually, you didn't, did you? The cover, as you rightly call it, was stolen but is now back with the family." Her grandstanding was interrupted as she watched her father enter and leave the room. "Uh . . . Yes, the philatelic cover's whereabouts came to light when that woman, our ex-neighbor in Brooklyn, attempted to pass it off as her own property. To add to the insult, she tried to do this at my own office."

"Didn't she hand it over when you asked her?"

"Yes indeed, she did. You've been a busy bee."

"So is Sam free? Did *you* hand it over?"

Lou's face gave nothing away.

"Or if not, are they prepared to agree to an exchange?" asked Anthony. "Do they trust you?"

"Anthony, like Constance, you're not part of this family. Let me remind you that you're a hired hand. From what I understand, we own you. So keep your nose out of it."

He stared down at his sneakers. I wondered what she meant by "own." I didn't like Lou's tone. Anthony didn't deserve to be treated like that. Why was he still working for them after all this time?

"Hey, hold on, Lou," I said. "We busted our guts trying to help this family." I tried to catch her in one of my stares.

"And who asked you to do that, Constance? Taken a fancy to another of my pretty young brothers and—"

At that moment George shuffled in. His unfastened robe showed off more than anybody would want to see. He stepped over the Pompom excrement without appearing to notice it. "Hello, hello, we have visitors. Ask Polly to arrange some tea. Or are we in the cocktail hour? Who's for a Sloe Comfortable Screw? Or would you prefer a lovely dry martini, eh, Connie?" His wink reminded me of Billy's.

"Daddy, please, fasten yourself up, for Christ's sake. Jacob, come and take my father."

"Oh, vas are you doing in here, Mr. Veston? Come vith me. We are going to do your meds." Jacob was attempting some B-movie accent.

"Anthony is up here, from the print shop. He and Connie are on important business. I need to be in the thing." George began to circle the droppings. "I need to be in the hoop, ah no, in the loop." His bare foot scored a direct hit in the center of Pompom's doings. "Yes, I need to be in the poop." He shook his foot and laughed. "Somebody deal with this."

We stared. I caught Anthony's smile in the gilt mirror.

"Jesus, Daddy." An agitated Lou paced around. "Please, Jacob, now."

"Catch you later, Connie," George said. He winked again as Jacob wiped the doo from his toes with one of Aileen's best white Irish linen double-damask table napkins.

"Constance and Anthony, we are done here—you can leave us." Lou waited by the door until we took the hint.

As we made our way out through the lobby, Walt called us over. "Mr. Samuel returned earlier but went out again. I know you were worried about him."

"Did you speak to him?" Anthony asked.

"No, he didn't come to say hello. He looked like he was in a hurry. Anyway, that will put your mind at rest, no doubt."

This seemed odd. Why hadn't he been touch? "Please ask him to call me."

As Anthony and I made our way out front, I fired off a text message: *Hey, Walt tells me you're free. Let's meet. Con X.*

Anthony and I got on, and we had worked well together. But now I needed to focus. "Okay, are we done for the day?" Perhaps I could hang around and wait for Sam if I could shake off Anthony.

"I'm coming in your direction. Remember?"

"Oh yes, of course you are, but you can leave me now. You might like some time to yourself? Hmm . . . I need to pick up—"

"Aren't you interested in the documents we got yesterday?" He looked so disappointed. "Those papers contain something interesting and valuable that's been waiting in Hawaii for almost one hundred and fifty years."

"How can you be sure?"

"Well, give me ten minutes of your time."

"Okay, yes."

Anthony had calming powers over my mother, and I might need those when she heard of my plan to stay longer.

"Great, I promise to keep it short. I'm sure you're anxious to meet up with Sam."

He read my mind.

Chapter Thirty-Three

ANTHONY

Within seconds of the door closing, I uncorked a bottle of Con's favorite wine and presented the label after taking a quick sniff—mmm, summer berries. "Connie, would you like a glass?"

"Oh yes, just a drop, please."

For Pete's sake, the tiny glasses the room-service waiter supplied were making me look cheap.

Eager to begin, I ushered her into the comfortable armchair and told her what I'd discovered. "In 1840s Hawaii, the crew of a ship called the *Spec* traded opium for gold. One hundred thousand dollars in gold coins, to be precise. The metal itself must be worth a couple of million today. The coins might be ten times that figure or more, all sorts of dates and types, with some real rarities."

"Wow, tell me more." Con leaned forward. Her glass was already empty, so I gave her a refill.

"The ship sank after they completed the transaction. It broke up in the Kaulakahi Channel, somewhere off the coast of Honolulu. Two of the crew survived. One of them is mentioned in a report about the wreck and the hiding of the gold. A James Joy from London, England. All this is in the crossed-out writing on the back of the letters—"

"Remind me, why was it crossed out?" Con checked her cell, not for the first time.

I needed to convince her about my treasure hunt idea before that Weston boy reappeared on the scene. "The paper had been reused for correspondence with the mission's headquarters in New York. Here on the other side is a report about, oh . . . let's see . . . here we go, *prostitution in Honolulu*. Hmm . . . well, we're more interested in the back. In fact, a couple of the crucial pages are missing."

"As in all good treasure tales, eh?" She beamed one of her lovely warm smiles.

"Well, yes, one or both missing pages may contain a map, referred to in detail on a preceding page. The original document is likely four or five pages in all and contains an agreement to give an amount of gold in exchange for saving James Joy's soul. Joy had killed the other survivor, by accident or otherwise. Possibly after an argument about the treasure."

"Yes, as you do." Con kept checking her cell. Had the boy been in touch yet?

"It's either an elaborate hoax or a huge cache of gold."

"If not a hoax, what makes you think something might still be waiting to be uncovered?"

"Yes, an excellent question, Con—uh, sorry, Connie. I did some digging. Well, not actual digging. That'll come later. What I read suggests they buried the coins in a protective chest with two separate padlocks. The mission retained one key, and Joy lodged the other with his lawyer. They agreed that when news came to the mission of James Joy's death, his lawyer would deliver the key. At that point, whoever ran things would pray for his soul and use both keys to release the gold, which would become the property of the mission. I can't find any record of this occurring, or of their funds increasing at any time since."

"Wow, yes, thorough work indeed, Anthony." She put her empty glass down on the small side table with a clunk.

I was about to get the wine but was distracted by my notes. "Yes, I'm researching what happened to this James Joy, but so far, I've found no trace of him. We should also find out who he killed. The missionaries' reuse of the paper indicates the whole episode was soon forgotten."

I picked up one of the photos of the cover we had gotten from Burt's niece and settled down on my haunches, close to Con. She didn't shy away, which I took as a positive. "Something is visible on the inside of the cover, through a tear in the back. It's a map, I'm sure. We should try to examine and photograph the insides of the actual cover before we go."

"Are you suggesting a trip to Honolulu?"

"Yes, exactly."

Con looked a little teary. "Anthony, do you mind if we continue all this tomorrow? I need an early night."

I was losing her. She needed more convincing. There was no point in trying now—her thoughts were no doubt saturated with the Weston boy.

"Let's continue this in the morning."

"Thanks." She headed quickly toward the door.

"Sleep well."

Of course, talking about visiting Honolulu like that, it must have brought back memories of Dan, and all their plans.

How could I have been so insensitive?

Chapter Thirty-Four

CONNIE

When Anthony mentioned a trip to Hawaii, I had to leave his room. The usual memories of Dan poured into my head. Holding on to the clearest image of my husband I'd conjured up in twenty years, I flopped facedown onto the bed. Burying my head in a pillow, I felt closer to him than ever. Then something weird happened. After I blinked, Dan turned into Sam, and however hard I tried, my husband now eluded me. All of a sudden, Sam was speaking his older brother's words: "Con, the apartment is on a quiet street with loads of trees. We've got everything we need. The three of us will be so cozy there. And the sunshine, Con. Honolulu is sunny all the time—you're going to totally love it."

After half an hour or so, I was back on my feet, thinking about the future. Sam would surely be up for a treasure hunt. Within a few days, I could finally be in Hawaii with my gorgeous Weston man.

Why hadn't Sam been in touch? I fired off another text message: *Hi again. Hope you're okay. I'm free for the rest of the evening. Con X.*

Did I seem overly keen? Hell, I needed to start things moving again before Lou and Liza poisoned him against me. I kept wondering how Jacob fit into it all. He was the sort of guy who would arrange the execution of someone's pet cat to *send them a message.*

I needed an adequately sized glass of wine. What was all that with Anthony's thimble-sized glasses? With only one top-up.

I paced around the room for an hour, checking my cell every other minute.

Then at fifteen minutes before midnight, a text arrived from an unknown number: *I am safe. Now vacationing in the Hamptons with my girlfriend. Keep in touch. Sam.*

A new cell phone I could believe, but the message didn't add up—not even a kiss. This, combined with Lou's reluctance to confirm his release, and Walt seeing but not speaking to him, worried me. What the hell—I needed Anthony, and, ignoring the hour, I called him. He picked up on the first ring.

"Hi, Connie, are you okay?"

"Yes, yes. I need to go over something with you. I'll be there in five."

"Okay, great."

Slipping on Dan's parka and my comfortable Converse sneakers, I headed up to his room.

In the corridor, my cell started up. "Hello."

"Con, lovey, how are things? Is Anthony taking care of you?"

"On my way to his room now."

"Wonderful news. He tells me the business is all cleared up, and the boy's gone off with his girlfriend—nice he's got a girl." How did Anthony know the contents of the text? Did he send it?

"How's Simon?" I battled on. I thought of Jacob's hired assassin.

"Yes, he's fine, lovey. He's laid out on your bed. Now it's dry. He's missing you. Anthony tells me you managed to book a flight for Saturday. I want to apologize for my behavior. My doctor gave me a new prescription today."

"Great. Call you later. Love you. Bye."

"Enjoy—"

I hung up and bashed on Anthony's door.

Chapter Thirty-Five

ANTHONY

Monday, July 3, 2000

Con's mom called as I tried to squeeze on my sneakers without first undoing the laces. I'd already made a quick change from pajamas into something more appropriate to receive her daughter. Staying calm, I quickly updated Evie on the latest situation.

After finishing up the call, I checked myself in the full-length mirror in the bathroom.

Had Con heard from the boy, too? Was this now my chance with her? Some frantic knocking interrupted my deliberations. I applied a generous spritz of my citrusy cologne and headed to the door.

Con remained in the doorway. "I'm convinced Sam isn't free." Her hand went up to cover her nose for a moment.

"What makes you say that? I got a text from him just now telling me he and his girlfriend are vacationing in the Hamptons."

"Yes, I got that, too, but the message came from a different number, and it definitely wasn't something Sam would have written." She looked quizzical. "Come on, surely you didn't believe it?"

"You're right. Sorry, I'm so caught up in my treasure escapade, it never occurred to me that someone could be duping us. We need to return to the print shop and fast." Pulling on my jacket, I returned to the door. "Please, after you."

Ⓐ

I spotted a Lincoln Town Car parked on the street as we made our way to the yard at the rear of the building.

Several lights were on in the print shop. After unlocking and opening the back door, I slammed it shut again. *"Gas."*

"Shit, what about Sam?" She tried to push me aside.

Holding her struggling arms, I said, "I'm going in, please don't follow me."

"Be careful. But hurry—*find him quickly.*"

"Keep the door closed and stand well back." After some deep breaths, I placed a handkerchief over my nose and entered. Pulling up blinds and opening windows, I moved toward where we had last seen the boy.

There he was, unconscious on the floor but still tethered to the now overturned swivel chair.

The next moment, Con was at my side. "Shit, Anthony, is he . . ."

I found his pulse. "He's alive. Connie, leave now. The place might blow at any moment."

"You can't carry him by yourself." For Pete's sake, her arms were already hugging his upper body. "Let's put him between us."

As we neared the door, his breathing got stronger, and he came around fast once outside. The boy reeked of urine and worse.

Con kissed him on the cheek before stepping back for what appeared a deep breath. "Shit, what the hell, Sam? Thank God, you're all right."

A loud panting, groaning noise grew louder. As I turned, a short, stocky, ashen-faced woman, gasping for air, stumbled through us and collapsed against the wall.

I called the trinity of emergency services before going back in to open all the doors and windows. The bodies of two of the kidnappers languished in the meeting room. The water supply in the offices was turned off and they'd likely switched the gas line on, mistaking it for the water main. The pilot light lit the furnace, but the vents were shut. The kidnappers most probably died of carbon monoxide poisoning. Lucky for Sam, the heating shut off because it was a warm night. Gas from the supply then appeared to have started leaking into the building. The fail-safe device was disconnected for a service. After securing the tap, I headed back out.

Con was stroking the boy's arm. "We need to get you checked out at the hospital." She'd evidently gotten used to the stench.

"No, I'm fine now. Just need a shower. Wow, you saved my life, Con."

She was beaming brightly. "Anthony is the real hero here." I got a little of her glow.

"I really need to clean up. Take me away from here."

Con and the boy took a cab to the hotel, while the short woman disappeared into the early morning.

I planned to edit down the events for the cops. Whatever happened here, we'd take care of it ourselves.

Chapter Thirty-Six

CONNIE

Even with the windows down and me wafting, the driver had caught Sam's stinkiness by the time we got to the Chelsea. A twenty-dollar tip kept things from getting stickier.

Back in my room, the hotel guy iced the Bollinger while Sam showered.

Sam, now restored to fragrant gorgeousness, appeared as laid back as ever and none the worse for his ordeal. We both flopped onto my bed, completely neglecting the champagne, and slept until nine thirty.

As I prepared to do some shopping, a text arrived from Anthony telling me he was finished with the cops. He was heading back to the hotel and would stop by my room in an hour, after showering.

Floating on a blissful cloud, I moved between stores, gathering up clothes and toiletries for Sam. I caught myself in a fitting-room mirror in the Levi's store. All the rushing around had given me a glow, and a slight tousling made me look hot.

Outside my room, I took a moment to calm my breathing. Then, at the sight of Sam lounging on the bed in his bathrobe, a sexy tingle started up between my legs. He popped the cork on the Bollinger, and we drank a toast to freedom. We were on our second glass when Anthony's knock interrupted a show-and-tell I was conducting with my purchases. I pushed the one-size-smaller 505s and a tight-fitting blue tee back into the bag, making sure the sexy undershorts he hadn't seen yet sat on top. Sam gathered himself up and perched on the edge of the bed.

With a fresh glass of bubbly in hand, I answered the door and handed it to Anthony.

"To us," he said, raising his glass.

The champagne made me a little woozy. "What's going on, Ant, man?" I giggled.

Sam was full-on smirking.

Anthony managed a weak smile before telling us what had happened after we left. "The cops appeared okay with the story. I know the lieutenant—he lives on the same block as me." Anthony went quiet as his eyes settled on the Levi's bag in my hand.

I scrunched up the top and handed it to Sam. "Here are the clothes you asked me to buy." He took them and gave me a wink, unnoticed by Anthony.

Sam then went over what had occurred the previous evening at the print shop. "They received a call from the family in the afternoon. Rosa and the guards talked of leaving early. She came in and told me they would be freeing me soon."

"Did anybody arrive?"

"Yeah, no, I can't remember. The gas may have already knocked us all out."

"So the envelope could still be at the Dakota," I said.

Sam took a sneaky peek into the shopping bag. His face reddened. He had no doubt spotted the minibriefs. A pair of plum microbriefs from the same store nestled in my tote—a little too much for now.

"Are you okay, Sam?" Anthony asked, appearing keen to share the moment.

Sam slowly dropped the bag to the floor by the side of the bed. "Yeah, must be the hot shower."

Anthony kept switching his gaze between Sam and me. "Yes, the family is up to something. What about the text message we both received from you, Sam?"

"What text?"

"Hang on." After a couple of taps, I handed him my cell. He scrolled through the message before checking the number.

"Yeah, it came from one of Dad's cells, but he can't work a phone anymore. It's either Lou, Liza, or most likely, Jacob."

"Your father told me he felt in danger when he gave me his notebook."

"Liza and Jacob are cooking something up, I'm sure."

"Jacob threatened me the other day, outside the print shop." I reached over into the nightstand drawer. "This was under my door yesterday." I handed the fax to Anthony. "A picture of my mother taken a couple of days ago."

They looked at each other for a moment before Anthony spoke. "Yes, we've been worried about Jacob."

"And not to mention, he's my sister's boyfriend."

"Hmm, yes, that, too," said Anthony. "We're onto him, Connie. I'll make sure neither you nor your mom is harmed."

"When you say *onto him* . . . ?"

"No, nothing to worry about. I need to go up to the Dakota and report in on the print shop debacle." Anthony reddened and ran a finger around his collar.

"I'll come with you, shall I?"

"No, Con, you stay here with Sam. Right, I'm going," Anthony said. "I would like to examine the cover if they have it. I'm sure there's a treasure map on the inside."

My anticipation of being left alone with a semi-naked Sam set a number of events running in my head. And they all had the same happy finish.

Sam stopped twiddling with the cord on his robe and sat up. "Wow, a treasure map, sounds cool."

"Yes, something Anthony's working on," I said, like a mom speaking up for her kid. "We think the envelope is made from the map."

"Wow, I wouldn't mind a little bit of treasure hunting."

Anthony started to leave us. "You'll be surprised. We're going to find a horde of gold quarter eagles, half eagles, and eagles."

Alone again, Sam relaxed into his previous pose. "You and old Ant are getting along well?"

"You think? He's been a blessing during the past few days. He's calmed my mom, too."

"Do you think there might be . . . you know . . . between you guys?"

"God, no, I mean . . . well, possibly. Do I like him in that sort of way? He's more like an older brother."

"Yeah, cool."

"Sam, you were so brave to stay in the print shop like that, refusing to be rescued." I fixed him in my most radiant stare.

"I'm tempted to take the credit. Ant suggested if I didn't feel in mortal danger, I should stay put. He said he'd take care of things."

"Wow, a small detail Anthony forgot to mention."

"Ant did apologize to me while you arranged the cab. I'm a bit of a coward, to be honest."

"Anthony said you refused to leave to protect your sisters."

"Good old Ant. He's plainly in love with you."

"You reckon? He likes the idea of being my protector. I'm not aware of anything sexy from him, though." I didn't want to think about Ant's feelings right now.

"Yeah, so, what about from me, Con?"

"Well . . . yes, for sure." My whole body blushed. My tingle switched up to a tremble.

"I'm totally into that you were married to my bro—I find you so . . ." Sam released the cord on his robe and let one side drop over the edge of the bed. He beckoned me in. Shit, was I ready for this? God, yes, I sure was. I yanked off the Hotel Chelsea signature bed cover—no point in exposing the fancy embroidery to risk. Climbing on top of him, I started to remove the last of my clothes. An image of Dan appeared in my head for a brief moment before Sam kissed me. Clearly getting overexcited, he was done before I had released my H&M push-up. He finished as fast as his brother had, all those years ago, but unlike Dan, he failed to score a home run—disappointing or what?

"Hey, sorry, Con," he said, with a nervous shrug, refastening his robe. "I usually—"

"Again later, perhaps?" I said, keen not to break the mood.

We lay on the bed together holding hands and fell asleep, our heads touching. My mind buzzed with anticipation for a rematch—the sooner the better.

Ⓐ

A scrawled note propped up against the Bollinger bottle greeted me when I woke at three thirty in the afternoon. *Gone up to the Dakota—S x.* A kiss, at least. My cell phone showed a missed call and text from Anthony along with another message from someone else. Anthony's text read: *Still waiting for Louise. Jacob came in wearing a hooded sweatshirt.* The other message read: *What's going on, are you seducing my brother?*

Ha-ha. I thought. *Too late, Lou, job done.*

My call to Anthony went straight to his voice mail. After leaving a message, I freshened up in the shower.

While drying myself off, I shut my eyes to enjoy again Sam's smooth, youthful body and every detail of our brief lovemaking. A familiar jaunty knock cut short my daydreaming. Wearing Sam's discarded bathrobe, I enjoyed a second or two of *Eau de Sam* before answering the door.

Chapter Thirty-Seven

ANTHONY

The boy's reappearance made things difficult for me. Con would need convincing I was the better man for her.

I took a deep breath outside her door and knocked.

She answered in her bathrobe. "Anthony, hi, come in." The sunlight bouncing off the television screen enhanced her radiance. The boy's odor hit my nose, as if to remind me of the task ahead.

"Would you like me to come back later?"

"No, no, as long as you don't mind seeing me in this state?"

I didn't mind at all. "I bumped into the b . . . uh . . . Sam on the street. He said he would check in at home and go to bed for a couple of hours."

"Okay, right. So, he's not coming back this evening?"

"He didn't say."

"Huh."

Mm, perhaps things weren't going so well? "Louise showed no curiosity about what happened, even when I told her about Sam. When I mentioned you, she demanded your cell number so she could text you."

"Yes, I got that. Did Jacob have the denim jacket?"

"I'm assuming so. He's almost the same height and build as Sam. His hair is totally different, but if he wore a hooded sweatshirt under that distinctive jacket, then Walt may well have been duped."

"Who else were they trying to fool? Not only Walt, for sure. We should ask him if anyone else inquired."

"Yes, I did."

"Wow, well done." Con beamed.

I felt a tingle where my tail would be if I had one. "Walt told me Louise asked. That was before she met with us." I reclined on the unmade bed and was pleased when Con joined me, sitting at my feet.

Con stared at my sneakers, which I quickly removed. "Do you think Lou sent someone to deliver the cover?"

"And whoever it was didn't hand it over. Then pretended Sam had been released." I stretched my free arm and yawned.

She reciprocated, revealing her wine-stained mouth. "Maybe they hung onto the envelope."

"Yes, a possibility. Whoever it was didn't care"—I delicately plucked a long fiber from the pillow—"about him." I scrutinized my rival's lustrous strawberry-blond strand. An image of the two of them cavorting on the bed crashed into my head. As I jumped to my feet, I rolled and crushed the abomination between my fingers before discarding it among the sex-soiled linen.

"Or they didn't see him?" Con said.

"Hmm . . . Yes, Connie, whichever way you look at this, it is calculating and devious."

The sex would have been meaningless to him. *Wham, bam, thank you, ma'am.* I shoved both feet into my sneakers at once and stomped around, forcing them on.

"Do you think we should alert Sam?"

"He's aware not everyone wants the best for him." At that moment, I didn't care much what happened to him. "He told me he would be in touch tomorrow morning."

The boy was the flavor of the moment, but it wouldn't last. I took some deep breaths. I needed to get over this.

"Anthony, are you okay?"

"Yes, yes. Don't worry about me, please."

"Should we warn Judy about Gregor?" Con had already moved on.

"No, let's leave her out of this. We need to examine the cover. Let's try to photograph the inside." I pulled out my Motorola cell. "These phones will, surely, contain cameras someday soon."

Con reached into her bag and extracted a Ricoh RDC-1. "Here you go. The battery is fully charged."

"Thank you, that should do nicely." I turned my thoughts into positive territory. I was in touch with Billy's old contact in Honolulu, and he was arranging things there while I checked on flights. We just needed a photograph. Then Con and I would be treasure hunting very soon.

"Let's meet up in the morning and head over to the Dakota."

In a perfect world, Sam wouldn't be coming along with us, but it was now clearer than ever, he was the necessary bait.

"Okay, I'll let you return to your wine."

She carried a half-full glass into the bathroom. "No, after today's celebrations, I'm firmly on the club soda from now on."

I didn't see her empty it down the sink.

Chapter Thirty-Eight

CONNIE

Tuesday, July 4, 2000

Back when we lived in the city, Ma and I always celebrated Fourth of July with the Westons. We usually had a meal at Billy's favorite restaurant of the moment. The last time was in 1980, and we all went over to the East River to view the Macy's fireworks in the evening.

Today, Anthony and I made our way to meet Sam at the model-sailboat pond in Central Park. It was early, so we climbed up on the rocks to enjoy some hazy sunshine and drink our Americanos.

All the time, I was replaying the previous day's events. Though my warm glow had cooled after not hearing from Sam.

Anthony furrowed his brow, opened and closed his mouth a couple of times. "So, Connie, uh . . . is anyone missing you at home . . . other than your mom, of course?" A direct question from the master of subtlety.

"Yes, Simon will be missing me like crazy."

"Oh, right."

"Yes, he's been with me for two years now. He's such a sweetheart."

"Where did you meet?"

"He came to our basement one night and sort of moved in."

"So, you're living together?"

"Yes, he lives with Ma and me. She's taking care of him."

"When you say *taking care*—"

"Yeah, feeding him and generally making sure he's happy." My face began to break into a grin.

"Your mom didn't mention you were seeing anyone."

"I'm not. Simon is my beautiful ginger-and-white cat."

Anthony took a deep breath and chuckled to himself.

"What about you?"

"No. I don't even have a significant animal. After my stepmom passed, I threw myself into my work. I wanted to travel, but George kept giving me projects requiring my personal attention. To be honest, I felt uncomfortable about what he asked me to do, but he'd helped me financially with Mom—"

"How do you mean, uncomfortable?"

Anthony pointed to a figure in the distance. "Oh, look, Sam's here, we better go meet him."

Sam looked hunkier than ever in his new tighter-fit 505s, baggy white *Frankie Says Relax* tee, and yellow-laced Converse. "Jacob is hiding the envelope—in his room, taped under his mattress."

Anthony snorted. "Obvious place, the man's an amateur."

I beamed at my two guys. "Lou must assume the envelope is either with Gregor or the cops."

"Ant, you're right about the map." Sam gave a little nod.

Anthony nodded back and started to bounce from foot to foot.

"I went to grab my camera."

"You didn't grab the cover?"

"Yeah, hmm . . . no. Should I have? I thought . . . Yes, I should have. Shit, sorry, guys."

"Never mind, we know where it is." I kept things positive.

"You say you took your camera up? Did you take a photo?" Anthony was excited again.

"No, I bumped into Jacob when I got back up to the apartment. I told him I'd seen a bald eagle flying around the park and thought I might be able to take a photograph from up in the attic."

"Did he suspect anything?" Anthony continued his questioning.

"Yeah, well, no, I'm not sure. Jacob isn't very bright, and his street smarts don't make up for his zero intelligence. What the hell does Liza see in him?"

"A big dick?" Shit, did I say that out loud?

They both gaped.

Anthony grinned. "Sam, please, go on."

"So, uh, yes." Sam stopped talking, turned away, and ran a hand through his hair. Perhaps he thought we had some private joke going on. He pulled a side of his tee out at the front to partly hide his crotch area.

Anthony, distracted by this, looked away when he caught Sam's eye. "Um, yes, we need a photo of the insides of the cover."

"Do you reckon Jacob understands its value?" I asked.

"Only with Liza's help." A preoccupied Sam pushed a part of his shirt into one of the pockets of his Levi's. "They're likely working out how to sell it."

"I'm certain Gregor isn't going to give up," said Anthony. "Without a doubt, he's making further plans. Do you know if Liza and Jacob are going to be out today?"

"They were talking about going to the fireworks later. Oh, yeah, and Lou mentioned lunch, but they weren't sure Dad would be fit enough."

"Sam, why don't you offer to take care of him while the others go out?" Anthony was in planning mode.

"Good idea." I couldn't keep my eyes off Sam but needed to be careful not to freeze out Anthony. "I'm now wondering if Liza realizes Jacob has the envelope. She wouldn't allow a priceless artifact to be stuffed under the mattress, surely?"

"You could be right. Maybe he plans to take off on his own," Anthony said. "We can stay in the area. Sam, you return to the Dakota and text us when they've gone out. We can buy some proper supplies to help dismantle the multimillion-dollar cover."

"Yeah, I'll text you." Sam still appeared troubled by the way Anthony and I bounced off each other today. He turned more than once to check on us as he walked toward the Dakota.

Had I detected a little jealousy? I needed to dial up my womanly wiles.

Sam seemed keen to be a part of Anthony's treasure hunt. A trip to Hawaii could be my best chance of keeping close to him. My initial emotional reaction to visiting the islands had been soothed considerably by the thought of Sam joining us. But now, as soon as I pictured myself with Sam, Anthony popped up between us.

Chapter Thirty-Nine

ANTHONY

Con and I had made our purchases and were back in the park eating pretzels when a text came through from Sam. He was taking charge of George, while Lou treated Liza and Jacob to lunch at Delmonico's.

Unusually, the front desk at the Dakota was unmanned when we arrived. We continued on up to the apartment, where we found the door ajar. Pompom bounced in and out of the hallway with one of George's slippers clamped in his tiny jaws. Stepping over the Pomeranian, we went in.

An unfamiliar and pungent spicy cologne hung in the air. "Hello," I said. "Hello there?"

The voices in the living room fell silent.

Walking around the corner, we almost tripped over Sam, who was unconscious and sprawled out on the dining room's parquet floor. Con immediately stooped to check on him. As Gregor trained his pistol on George's temple, the dog raced into the room, still carrying the slipper. George set off in pursuit of his mule. A seemingly powerless Gregor started to follow them around the room. Somehow the comedy of this spectacle disempowered the gunman, temporarily at least.

Meanwhile, Con tried to rouse the boy, all the time stroking his hair. Was that really necessary?

"Enough of this madness," said a panting Gregor, who now switched his aim to alternating between Con and the boy. "Leave him alone, young lady. He'll be fine. Did you believe I was going to give up? You hand over my cover, or he gets a bullet in the head. You all get a bullet in the head."

Gregor wanted his property back. I was sure this matter could be sorted out without it escalating if I took control. I filled Gregor in on George's mental state and explained about the envelope. "Sir, let me go upstairs and retrieve the cover for you, right now."

"I wasn't born the day before . . . today? Er, yesterday?"

"Sir, you are holding George, the boy, and my girlfriend." I caught Con's raised eyebrow. "You also have a gun. I'm not going to try anything."

Pompom took his cue to reenter the room, still biting on the slipper. He rushed over to the patriarch and dropped the fur-lined mule in front of him. George strode forward, again ignoring the pistol, and reconnected with his missing slipper en route. "Connie, my dear, our good friend wants his prize. Please ask your mother to bring the missionary cover from the safe, without delay."

Gregor scanned the room with a worried expression. "What, who else is here?"

"Nobody. As I mentioned, he isn't well."

"Chop-chop, Connie, let's not keep this important client waiting."

Con gave the boy's head a final stroke before standing. "Let me go up."

Gregor returned the gun to its holster under his arm. "Yes, this Connie fetches my cover."

"Do you have everything?" I clicked my tongue.

Con tapped her pocket. She looked remarkably composed. Together, Con and I could achieve anything.

Chapter Forty

CONNIE

I took the elevator up as far as I could before climbing the remaining stairs to the top floor. My heart never had to pump this hard when we lived here.

As I was about to curse at the locked door, the emergency key popped into my head. We kept it tucked away in the small alcove at the head of the staircase. What the hell, it was still in there. Wow, *Dial M for Murder* or what?

After letting myself in and stepping around the unmade bed, I lifted the mattress—yuck. My Ricoh warmed up as I checked out the contents of the plastic sleeve hidden there. As I ran my nail along the stuck-down edges of the envelope, the thing changed back to a sheet of paper. Anthony was right—the map was plain to see. After some gentle flattening, I took a couple of shots with and without the flash. Shiny gold coins started tumbling around in my head.

While attempting to put the cover back into its protective sleeve, I heard voices outside.

"I locked this." Jacob's accent was now downright Queens.

"Someone is in the apartment," said Liza.

Jacob pushed the door open. "What the fuck?"

"So how come you guys have this?" I waved the plastic. "Did you leave Sam to die when you failed to deliver it?" The front of the cover was clearly visible. "Did you kill those people at the print shop?"

"What the fuck?" said Liza as she stared in turn at me, the envelope, and finally at her boyfriend.

"Liza, in the apartment downstairs, your brother is unconscious, and Gregor has a gun to your father's head. He wants this." I shook the sleeve.

"Fuck, Jay, how come you didn't—"

"Uh . . ." He managed only a weak shrug.

"What did you think, Jay?" Liza scurried around like a caged gerbil in the apartment's tiny amount of free floor space. "Whatever, we can't get away with . . . er . . . that." She stopped moving and nodded at the cover.

"Listen to your girlfriend . . ."

"Fuck" was all he could manage.

"What about our original plan?" Liza asked.

I locked eyes with the rodent. "Which was what?"

"Nothing to concern you, Constance." The poor mouse wanted so much to be a lioness.

That reminded me. "Did Lou come back with you?"

"She must be in the apartment downstairs." Liza looked at Jacob and then to me.

"Best let me go in first, no point in spooking Gregor," I said, after checking on the cover. I felt elated and in control. I underestimated my abilities sometimes.

Chapter Forty-One

ANTHONY

An apparently oblivious Louise walked in and draped her jacket over a chair.

She visibly jumped as Gregor greeted her. "Ah, Miss Weston, you are here for the handover, yes?" He put his gun away and approached her.

"Gregor, I told you over the telephone, we gave the blessed cover to your people. I personally arranged delivery. Why you found it necessary to kidnap my brother, I will never understand."

"Your girl went to fetch it now."

"My girl? Which girl?"

"Yes, your girl, Connie, is it?"

"Is she here? Why am I surprised? With my brother half dead in a chair, she couldn't be far away."

"Hey, sis, chill, leave her alone." The boy sat up, rubbing the side of his head.

Con marched in, smiling. "Here we are, all present and correct."

Louise's head darted around. "What is that, Constance?"

"Gregor's missionary envelope, the one he bought in 1981. The cover you are keeping safe for him."

George, now reanimated, but again missing a mule, stretched his arm out as Con approached. "Here we are, Gregor. This is what we agreed. Such a rarity. So many others wanted this amazing piece. We reserved it for you. Please, Connie dear, hand the missionary cover to our greatest friend here."

"Enough of this madhouse." Gregor snatched the plastic sleeve and delicately extracted and scrutinized the amazing piece. He nodded, sniffed, and left without a further word.

We all stared at each other for a few seconds. Louise erupted into a volcanic rage, demanding to speak to Liza, before firing off a barrage of text messages to her. George and the slipper-mouthed Pomeranian danced around the room, the latter leading.

The boy seemed woozy as he came to the door with us. Con suggested he ask a doctor to check him over. He gave her a light peck on the cheek. Was their passion fading?

"Will you be joining us later, Sam?" Con's expression was like that of a hopeful lapdog at the dinner table. Sickened, I comforted myself with the belief that her rather desperate approach would fail long term.

Ⓐ

As soon as we got back to my suite at the Chelsea, I ordered up a celebratory bottle of Veuve Clicquot before examining Con's photos.

"These are sharp and clear. We now have everything we need. The map is by far the most important part of the document. The rest may prove useful when we find the location."

"If we find it." Con was still skeptical. What the heck did I need to do to persuade her?

A knock on the door announced the champagne's arrival. I gave the guy a twenty, which I was keen for Con to witness—my need for approval, I suppose.

"Cheers." She held up her flute.

"Yes, a British 'cheers' on American Independence Day." I touched her glass with mine and smiled. I sensed something starting between us, but then the boy arrived and killed it. He immediately excused himself, needing the bathroom. On his return, I noticed he'd overdone his cologne—or more accurately, my cologne. Con shared a little wave in front of her nose when the boy wasn't looking. I lived for those moments.

Sam ordered up another bottle, along with copious snacks and treats, which he was presumably charging to my room.

"So, Sam, are you free to join me hunting treasure in Hawaii? Her ladyship may need to be convinced."

"I will indeed join you, sir." The champagne appeared to have put him into an uncharacteristically mellow state.

"Count me in, guys. I'm coming along." Con radiated joie de vivre through a haze of bubbles.

I set my glass on the side table. "I'll complete the arrangements." I viewed the costs involved as an investment to secure my and Con's future together. Was I so besotted by this woman that I couldn't see the many risks involved? *Very likely.*

"Let's go to the fireworks." The boy sucked the last dregs from his flute.

While the liquor might have played its part in making me feel positive, I was now sure that their love affair would be little more than the proverbial flash in the pan. The treasure could be the catalyst. With a million dollars, the boy would be off like a rocket.

After Con had gotten over him, she and I could travel the world together. Maybe even settle down someplace and have a couple of kids.

Chapter Forty-Two

CONNIE

Wednesday, July 5, 2000

The sun found its way through the gaps in the curtains and burned into my eyelids. As I moved out of range, my Nokia started up, but I couldn't focus on its tiny screen.

"Hello." The flavor of car exhaust in my mouth suggested smoking—a definite bad sign. A splitting headache and croaky voice added to my regret. Today would definitely be alcohol free.

"Morning, how are you? No ill effects from last night's festivities?" Anthony's perkiness annoyed me. My memory was a little hazy on how I had gotten back to the hotel. No doubt, my protector had ensured Sam didn't take advantage of my situation—that was a shame.

"No, all fine, thanks." *Take painkiller* went straight to the top of my to-do list.

"I spoke to my guy in Honolulu last night when we got back."

"Wonderful . . ." I tried for more perkiness. Particularly as I was now really up for our trip. A few million from finding the treasure would allow Sam and me to enjoy a fantastic life together.

"Can I come down?"

"Yes, why not?" He had already hung up when I said, "But give me an hour, would you?"

Within five minutes, his jaunty knock went right through my throbbing head. Walking over to open the door, I spotted a half-full glass of champagne on the dressing table and took a sip. Ugh. No more booze.

I tried for an enthusiastic note. "Wow, you're on it, my man." Not sure I pulled it off, though.

"Hmm . . . Thanks, Con. Yes, this guy who was Billy's friend from way back owns an apartment we can use. Newly refurbished, but not rented out yet."

"Yes, sounds . . ." A wave of nausea hit me.

"Are you okay, Connie?"

"A slight headache. How are we getting to Hawaii?"

"Again, we're lucky. We have seats on the Continental flight out of Newark tomorrow morning."

"God, Anthony, you're on fire today."

"Thanks." He didn't appear worried about how much all this cost. He was obviously well set up and generous with it. I liked that—a lot.

He wouldn't sit with me on the bed. Instead, he settled himself in the armchair and started talking about his papers. I nodded every so often but was keener to find something for my throbbing head. A rummage through the bottom of the Burberry unearthed an unusual blue tablet with a wonky butterfly motif. I brought it out and blew off some bag fluff before swallowing it. Anthony appeared oblivious.

I stared at the clock, waiting for the pill to take effect. Where was Sam?

A knock on the door got me to my feet. As I opened it, a smiling woman from housekeeping offered to service the room. While I was rejecting her offer, Sam ambled up.

His face lit up when he spotted me. "Hey, Con, how's it going?"

"Sam, hi." Unable to hide my glee at seeing his handsomeness, I grabbed his arm and guided him in. He smelled delicious. Was I too old for him? No . . . yes, probably.

"Okay, so, I put together my stuff, including those twenties I discovered in Dan's locker."

"Right, then let me run you both through my findings," said Anthony. "The edited version, I promise."

Ma's medication had kicked in, and I held on tight to the bedcover as my kaleidoscope eyes began adding crazy sparkly diamonds to everything.

"Are you okay, Connie?" one of them said.

"Club soda, please." I drank it down and burped. "Pardon."

Sam came and sat next to me on the bed. My vision stabilized as I grabbed his hand. "Up at the apartment, Liza and Jacob are gone, and Lou is trying to find help caring for Dad."

"There's something dodgy about Jacob. I'm sure he's been nowhere near Scandinavia." My words flowed again, but with colors.

"Others may be pursuing the gold," Anthony said, changing the subject. "The inside of the envelope was open for all to see. A treasure map is always alluring, and it clearly stated Honolulu."

"So, Ant, when are we going, man?"

"Tomorrow. We're flying from Newark early."

"Is it okay if I stay with you guys tonight?" Sam started Dan's silver dollar performance in his hand.

Anthony looked at his papers in silence.

"Definitely, Sam." My grin was far too broad.

"Of course, yes," said Anthony. "You could take the couch in my junior suite? Or we could ask for a trundle—"

"Wow, a junior suite. I'm obviously paying my *junior* too much."

Anthony stared at the bed. "Or you can bunk down in here, if Connie—?"

"Yes, fine with me."

Sam took out his cell and headed into the bathroom, presumably to take a call. After less than a minute, he returned to tell us that his girlfriend, Jess, was kicking up a fuss about not seeing him.

The thought of some pussy whipper controlling my Sam sent me into a funk.

"Okay, guys, I better go." He headed out the door without even turning for a final goodbye. I needed more information, like how serious was the girlfriend?

"We'll catch up with him later," said Anthony, who appeared to be stifling a smirk. "Let's assume he's in for tomorrow. I'll text him the details, and we can meet him at the airport if necessary."

"He might be back this evening." I stopped myself from saying, "No girlfriend ticket."

Anthony tapped his chin. "I hadn't realized she was still on the scene. He'll need all his charm to escape with us."

"Oh, right." This was getting worse.

He moved toward the door. "I have to leave now, too."

"I'm meeting Josie in the Ballfields Cafe in the park at one, if you're interested in joining us." I was returning the once lovely linen jacket.

"Thanks, but I'm tied up for most of the day."

"I'll enjoy some alone time then, until my lunch." What the hell was Anthony up to? He told us that he'd already sorted out the arrangements for our trip. Did he have a forgotten girlfriend, too?

Things had looked to be coming together nicely. I decided to remain positive and assume Sam would want a slice of a multimillion-dollar horde. Yes, the three of us would soon be hunting treasure in beautiful Hawaii.

Scanning the room, I caught sight of a stray bottle of something tasty.

Chapter Forty-Three

ANTHONY

Needing an urgent meeting with Louise Weston, I made my way up to the Dakota. I had been dismissed by email too many times. For Pete's sake, the last response I'd gotten from her had informed me that the boy was my new boss.

Her father's decline had resulted in the print shop accounts going unpaid. Not only had I covered these debts myself to keep things running, but the family also owed me three months' salary. The reserves I had built up from George's special payments were almost exhausted, and the impending Hawaiian excursion needed funding.

Walt opened the door as I approached the front office. "Mr. Anthony, good morning."

"Good morning, Walter, is Louise Weston at home?"

After a call to the apartment, I was admitted.

No one met me at the open door. "Hello . . . Hello, Louise, it's me, Anthony." The place smelled fresher.

George appeared from the study. "Ah, yes, Anthony, you're a little late for our meeting." Wearing a crisp white business shirt and tie above his pajama pants, he invited me in, before sitting down at his desk.

I stood behind the too-low chair opposite. "Um . . . Is Louise at home?"

"Sit down, my boy. Did you bump into Evie on your way up? She hasn't been in for her morning briefing yet."

"Evie? Evie Williams? Connie's mom?"

"Yes, who else?"

George still seemed confused. Was Louise continuing with Jacob's regimen of medication? Perhaps I should say something to her?

"She lives in London now. In England."

"No, no. She was here. Ask Connie. Where is Connie? Please send her in."

"Connie will be at the Ballfields Cafe at one. Shall I ask her to come over?"

"No, no need. I'll be in the park later."

"Perhaps it would be worth asking your daughter to contact Mrs. Williams directly. She might be able to persuade her." It suddenly occurred to me that if Connie's mom was in New York, Connie might stay on.

"I wonder why Evie left us. Did you upset her, Anthony? I'll give her a salary raise."

"Talking of salaries—"

"Oh, don't worry, my boy. I'm back at the helm now. You can rely on me."

"Thank you, I'll look forward—"

"Yes, yes, sounds like everything is under control. Bye-bye." With that, he got up and left the room briskly.

Through the open door, I spotted Louise coming around the corner from the kitchen with Josie.

"Oh, here you are, Anthony," she said. "Did you see my father?"

"Yes, but he's gone off to do something."

"Well, he's evading his new caregiver. She was trying to dress him. Anyway, what can I do for you?"

Josie kissed Louise on the cheek, then nodded in my direction before leaving us.

"Well, I've settled some accounts at the print shop myself to keep things running, and also my salary hasn't been—"

"Let me stop you there. You know how things are now. Liza and that Jacob have both abandoned me. Why don't you put it all in an email?"

"I already have."

"Well, please be patient. Anyway, you should be addressing these issues to my brother now."

Perhaps I should have opted for a share of the cash Jacob had been planning to extract from the family. At least enough to pay back the debt the Westons owed me. A successful treasure hunt would solve all of my financial problems. I had a number of credit cards in reserve, and it was time to go all in.

"Anthony, could you do me a favor? Would you go up to the attic apartment and secure it for me?"

I doubted she'd been up there in years. "Yes, of course."

After reminding her of my unanswered emails, I made my way upstairs.

The door to the tiny apartment was open and everything a mess. I was hoping to find a clue as to where Jacob was hiding the bag that contained the printing plates and Winston's letter. I wouldn't be free from his control until they were back in my possession.

Running my eye over a bunch of papers, I came across a letter addressed to Jason Jackson. Jacob's real name, perhaps? Also on the top of a pile of correspondence was a Post-it Note with a familiar flight number and time.

Dammit, he and Liza had likely already arrived in Honolulu.

Chapter Forty-Four

CONNIE

A light breeze rustled the leaves of the trees above me while, all around, kids and adults hit and chased balls. Josie caught up to me as I arrived at the entrance to the Ballfields Cafe. We double kissed. She was in for just one, but European doubles had become my standard. I handed her the bag containing you-know-what.

"Clinique Happy," she said, unzipping it.

"Yes, well done. Thanks for lending . . . er . . . Let's sit down."

We took an empty table and scanned the plastic-coated menu. As we placed our order, a familiar figure came out of the foliage.

"George, are you okay?" I guided him to the spare seat.

The surprised server backed away.

George wore a white shirt with a perfectly knotted tie, but also what looked like candy-striped pajama pants.

"Oh, thank you, Connie, you managed to make our meeting," George said, checking out the menu.

"Josie, I better take Mr. Weston home."

"Can I help?" She picked up and hugged her bagged jacket.

"No, thanks. I'll check in with you later." I held out my hand. "Now, George, let's go home."

"No, Connie. I need us to go up to the bench."

"Can't it wait until—"

"No, my dear, I'm afraid it can't. We need to go now before they find me."

I called the front desk at the Dakota. Walt answered.

"It's Connie. I'm in the park with Mr. Weston. Um . . . senior . . . George."

"Oh, my, Miss Connie, yes. Miss Louise thought he might be on his way to the print shop."

"He insists we take a walk, but I'll bring him back within the hour."

"Understood, Miss Connie. I will relay the information to all concerned. Everyone will be relieved. Goodbye, for now."

I hung up and slipped my arm through George's. We set off on the twenty-minute stroll up to the Shakespeare Garden. He was happy, chatting about the various trees, birds, and squirrels as we made our way.

When we arrived, George went over and sat at the far end of the Whisper Bench. He gestured for me to sit on the other side. He held tight to the sidearm and put his ear to the stone back.

I whispered into the granite. "George, are you listening?"

"Yes, I am, Connie."

"How can I help?"

"Jacob opened the safe, and some important stuff is missing. We are in trouble. Anthony needs to be careful. I didn't keep my promise to him to destroy the evidence. Jacob took everything. My daughter Liza is not to be trusted. Everything is in my little book. The apartment is—"

The flow was interrupted when a couple came and sat in the middle of the bench.

What did George mean about Anthony needing to be careful? I had seen him uncomfortable in situations with Lou and evasive when I quizzed him about stuff connected to Jacob. If the family had some hold over Anthony, it would account for a lot. Though I found it difficult to believe that he would be involved in anything dodgy.

George started to walk away, so I rushed over and retook his arm.

"Oh, Connie my dear, how lovely. Are you enjoying the park, too? We should be heading home. Your mom will be wondering where we are. How about some tea?"

We chitchatted all the way back. He wouldn't say anything more about his worries. Was George faking his memory difficulties? If so, how could he keep it up day after day, and why? I hoped Lou had arranged for a more appropriate caregiver.

When we arrived at the Dakota, I delivered George up to the apartment.

"Connie, my dear," said George, "we should have that tea I promised you. Will your mother be joining us?"

Lou was waiting at the door and took charge of her father. She signaled for me to follow them in.

A miserable-looking middle-aged woman greeted us in the hallway. She wore a uniform white coat and black pumps. "Sir, please don't walk out when I am trying to dress you." She must have been deep into George's walk-in closet when he made a run for it.

"I managed to find someone from an agency to cover for Jacob." Lou glanced over at the woman. "But Daddy hasn't taken to her."

George came over and grasped my forearm. "Connie, my dear, let's have our tea. I'll instruct Polly."

The caregiver woman fought to change his pants as he walked off into the kitchen.

Lou led me into the living room, and we sat down.

"Connie, this is all such a mess. Rosa had agreed to release Sam immediately once they received the cover, so I dispatched Jacob to deliver it. I can't believe what he and Liza did."

"We were worried after getting a weird text from George's cell," I said.

"Jacob's doing, but I presume Liza was wrapped up in this, too. They're both gone, left with suitcases."

I drew a sharp breath through my teeth. "Yes, an awful betrayal."

"Have you seen anything of my brother today?"

"He's visiting his girlfriend, Jess, is it?"

"Oh, God, her. Yes, she'll keep him in order. She's been away in Europe with her parents on some church thing."

"Have they been dating long?"

"About six months. You might remember her mother, Sonia? She used to babysit us sometimes when Mom and Dad went to dinner with Grandpa Billy and Grammy."

"Vaguely—she kept trying to make us read the Bible. Oh yes, and she was too smart to fall for any of our tricks for staying up to watch *M*A*S*H*."

"Well, Sonia and Reverend Rhymes had a daughter, Jessica—now about the same age as the twins."

Knowing her pedigree was interesting, but it didn't help me. I fired off a quick text to remind Sam of the massive horde of treasure awaiting us in Hawaii.

The caregiver woman appeared at the door. "Excuse me, ma'am, Mr. Weston's disappeared again."

The woman marched out of the room and put her coat on. "I'm leaving, too. Nobody explained the situation. Good day to you, ma'am, and to you, ma'am."

Walt called to say George had turned up down there.

A small audience was already gathered at the front desk when we arrived.

"Well, did you hear him?" George asked no one in particular.

Walt responded in a kindly tone. "Who would that be, sir?"

"John Lennon. He's been playing that damn song over and over. I can't think of its title."

"John Lennon died twenty years ago." Worth mentioning, I thought.

"Oh, Connie, dear, I know. I'm not completely mad . . . It was his ghost."

"Wow, imagine," I said.

"Of course, well done, Connie." George winked. "What am I doing down here? The cocktail hour is upon us."

On that note, I decided to leave them and headed back to the Chelsea.

Before I reached the Seventy-Second Street station, my cell buzzed with a reply to my text. It just read *Butt out, Con—whatever that's short for? Sam has a girlfriend.* Shit, no. So, controlling Jess was monitoring his cell. Why had I signed off with the three kisses?

Barely holding back tears, I paced back and forth outside the station while I composed a text message to Anthony: *Suspect Sam is not able to come with us. Reschedule?*

When I arrived back at the Chelsea, I went straight into the bathroom to check on my puffy eyes. As I dabbed around them, my cell beeped and rattled. Anthony's reply popped up on the tiny screen: *Just spoke to Sam, and he says he wouldn't miss it. Will you join us?*

I sniffed, smiled broadly, then laughed before responding with: *Thanks. Yes, of course, see you bright and early tomorrow.*

The whole George thing concerned me. What was his broken promise to Anthony? What had Jacob taken from the safe? Where were Liza and Jacob? Was Jacob still out to get me? On a more positive note, Lou now seemed friendly.

The trip to Hawaii with the guys would help me get my Sam plan back on track, and I could work out just how serious this girlfriend was. And there was the possibility of all that gold, too—this trip could change my life.

Part Two

Chapter Forty-Five

ANTHONY

Manhattan
Thursday, July 6, 2000

Con's carry-on bag was swinging from one wheel to the other as she
dragged it rapidly across the lobby. Rushing to help, I caught a whiff of
her delicious perfume.

"Sorry, Anthony. My packing took too long. I just need to check
out." Her face looked more radiant than ever from hurrying.

"No problem, we have plenty of time." We did, but I preferred a
healthy cushion. I liked that she worried about keeping me waiting.
Telling the front desk that I would be retaining my suite provoked an
approving nod from Con. Earlier, I'd arranged with the concierge to
store my stuff and planned to cancel the room when I had a moment
alone at the airport. All my remaining credit would be needed for our
trip. My financial situation would be rectified instantly with a share of
some treasure. This whole Hawaiian adventure was a massive gamble,
but necessary if I wanted any chance at a life with Con.

I needed to be brave now.

In our cab to Newark, I snuck a glance over at Con every so often. She was likely thinking about the boy. I still wasn't sure he would arrive in time for the flight, if at all. I would need to persuade her to board without him if necessary.

As we arrived outside the terminal, I pulled out my cell. "A text from Sam." I paid the driver and extracted the luggage before pretending to read a message. "He's going to join us in Honolulu." Mean of me, perhaps, but I wanted to test the waters.

"Join us in Honolulu? It's not like we're day tripping to Coney Island." She stomped over to the window and pulled out her cell.

I sensed an impending bailout. "He told me no way would he miss our trip."

"Hell, what is he up to?" She sounded like Louise.

I needed to get us beyond security. "Let's go through. I can run over my latest findings with you."

"Sounds fun." Even with her head down, I saw the end of an eye roll. "Sorry, I'm still tired."

"You can sleep on the flight."

"Now what I need is the ladies' room."

"I'll wait here for you." I took the opportunity to telephone the Chelsea. I was finishing my call as Con rejoined me.

"Anybody interesting?"

"Sam's in a cab. He should be with us soon."

A massive grin broke out on Con's face. "Plenty of time." She examined and shook her watch. "Is there? What about Jess?"

"He must have squared the trip with her."

"Probably a row. Let's go to the departure lounge, and you can run me through everything. Thanks for working so hard on this."

Con kept looking behind us as we crossed the concourse. "Okay, let's sit here." I indicated a couple of chairs next to the gate. "I can take you through where we should begin in Honolulu." After a short time, I could see she was looking everywhere but at me. "I'll wait until the three of us are together."

"Sorry, yes, thank you."

The final call came for the flight. We picked up our bags and prepared to board. I hoped we'd reached the point of no return and headed toward the gate without looking back, closing my ears to Con's protests.

"Hey, guys, are you going without me?"

The gate attendant gestured at the sauntering Sam. The guy almost closed the doors in his face when Sam gestured back with the finger. I decided that the boy coming along could be to my advantage. Con's infatuation would surely fall off fast when confronted with his immaturity.

Chapter Forty-Six

CONNIE

In flight from Newark to Honolulu

A sarcastic announcement about a delay caused by late-boarding passengers greeted us as we shimmied down the aisle with our carry-ons. Checking around in my tote, I found my Ray-Bans and slipped them on. While I was in there, something therapeutic fell into my hand. The green-and-white capsule took some swallowing without liquid.

We sat in a row of three. Sam bagged the window. Anthony kindly offered me the aisle, but I declined.

Sam, totally unaware of the current mood of the cabin, tried to flirt with the stewardess. She was unmoved by his plea for pre-takeoff refreshments. Years of passenger abuse and the low-grade air had clearly left her immune even to his charms. A middle-aged steward farther up the aisle appeared more enamored. Together we enjoyed a crafty peep at Sam's exposed midriff as he wrestled his blue North Face duffel into an overhead bin.

Anthony had his nose in a small notebook like the one George had pushed into my hand. "Our accommodation should be comfortable, with two bedrooms and a sofa bed in the lounge."

"Sounds wonderful—thanks for all your work." I smiled and stayed hopeful about the sleeping arrangements. Sam had already proven he was attracted to me, and I was sure we would make love again on this trip. From my experience with overly enthusiastic younger guys, I could help him hold out a little longer.

"As soon as we can, we should go along to the church and mission museum—the place where they drew up the agreement, by all accounts." Anthony was, no doubt, testing our current level of interest.

Sam sat up and leaned across me. "So, bring me up to speed, guys."

"What have you done to your hand, Sam?" My finger hovered above a midsize Band-Aid on the side of his hand.

"Only a couple of scratches. So, Ant, what do I need to know? Just the important stuff, man."

Anthony kicked off his sneakers, relaxed into his seat, and continued. "Well, the map suggests that what we're looking for is either in the church or mission museum."

Sam stuck out his chin. "Well, this is an easy one."

I cut him some slack for his needlessly sarcastic tone. The awful Jessica had played a part in his moodiness, no doubt. As he leaned away and then back in again, I inhaled deeply.

"I assume there will be further instructions. The map shows where James Joy's soul would be prayed for. Most probably a sophisticated confidence trick perpetrated by the Reverend Goodwife."

"Yeah, and he skedaddled with the loot one hundred and fifty years back?" Sam suggested.

Anthony pondered. "Well, yes, I would agree with you."

"So why the fuck are we headed to Honolulu?"

"Hang on, Sam—Anthony said 'would agree.'"

Anthony nodded and shot me a smile. "Goodwife and his good lady wife died in an accident soon after the agreement was signed. That occurred a couple of days after James left for San Francisco, never to return or, indeed, ever heard from again. I believe the gold is still to be discovered—by us."

"Hmm, over to you, Ant, my man. We're with you every step of the way." Sam's mood was now jollier—perhaps connected to his downing of a large whiskey and Canada Dry with another on the way. All courtesy of the ogling steward, who Sam chatted up on the way back from the lavatory.

Sam looked and smelled sexier than ever today, a little stubbly and just on the right side of unbathed. He slept for most of the flight. His head rested against my shoulder for a short while somewhere above the Pacific. I almost thrust my hand into his gorgeous hair. My imagination worked on the rest, to the point where I needed to excuse myself.

Ⓐ

Landing in Honolulu made the ghosts of possibilities swirl in my head again. In a different life, where the A to Rockaway had spared Dan, we'd have been living here. Our child or, more likely, children would have grown up in this beautiful place. Anthony, of course, handed me his freshly laundered handkerchief in advance of our arrival. Sam, of course, remained oblivious.

As we stood, waiting for a cab in the warm, fragrant afternoon air, a sense of unworried anticipation started to wrap around me. Thousands of miles away from my old life and Ma's problems, I was ready to begin an exciting and hopefully profitable adventure with my husband's brother. Perhaps it was a trick of the light or jet lag, but for a moment, when I looked over at Sam, I saw Dan and began to cry.

Chapter Forty-Seven

ANTHONY

Honolulu

We walked into the apartment, dropped our bags, and stared at the fabulous vista from the floor-to-ceiling window. The panoramic view of the whole Waikiki shore from Diamond Head to Honolulu itself left me lost for words. Even the boy appeared to be gaping. Billy's old contact, Chuck Wilson, had gone above and beyond my expectations. The aroma of fresh paint confirmed the place had been recently refreshed and refurbished, as promised—a brand-new Apple Mac on the side table a bonus.

"So is everyone happy with their rooms?"

Con put her hand on my shoulder until our eyes met. "Thanks for arranging everything. The place is perfect. I feel like I'm on vacation."

"Well done, Ant, man. I'm sleeping in the lounge, but not until you guys decide to go to your huge comfortable beds, but yeah, the couch is fine for me, thanks very much."

"I did offer you the bedroom."

"Fair, old Ant. You're the man. I need cigarettes. Guess you didn't arrange a supply for your boss? An oversight, my man, but I'll forgive you this once."

"There should be some on the counter by the sink. I requested Camels; hope they suit."

"Well, I need a light now." He headed for the door, knocking a cigarette out of the pack.

The moment he left the apartment to go inhale his Camel, Con and I sat back and exhaled our tension. Jet-lagged, we stayed in our own thoughts. I was relieved and elated that the accommodations impressed her. The boy's petulance was clearly annoying even Con, which was a bonus. I just needed to deliver on the gold. He would likely go his own way with his share. Con plainly wanted to change her life, so when Sam disappeared, or she tired of him, I would be there to step in. I needed to broach the difficult subject of my part in her husband's death. There would be a mountain to climb, but the treasure would hopefully make it easier. Or was I being naive?

A frantic ringing of the doorbell heralded Sam's return, his mood now lifted by an encounter in the elevator lobby. "Guys, guess what? I got us invited to a pool party. This evening, and in the building, would you believe?"

"Wow, trust you," Con said. "We've only been here a couple of hours, and you've scored us a party."

"So, you two up for it? Tonight?" He wanted commitment. "Hey, come on, Ant, man, let's take a night off."

"We're in the middle of a treasure hunt, Sam."

"If he wants some 'me' time, we should let him go." Con was a little too eager to see me home alone. For a moment, the mountain climbed higher.

"Ant, don't be so hasty. You might get lucky tonight. You should come along, man."

"Put me down for it," Con said.

The boy turned and beamed at Con. "You'll be pleased you did. Let's put Ant as a maybe for now."

I was anxious to get the hunt underway before this whole trip turned into some sort of spring-break vacation. "Guys, if you're okay with it, I suggest we pay a visit to the Kawaiaha'o Church, the place where James Joy and the Reverend Goodwife sealed the deal."

"Hey, we should chill today, man, and rest up for the pool party later. Catch a few rays. Drink a few beers. We can make an early start tomorrow. What do you think, Con? We can hit the world-famous Waikiki beach. How does that sound? Down a few cold ones and hang out. The treasure has been hidden for one hundred and fifty-odd years. Another day won't make much difference." Sam had rarely been so eloquent.

"Yes, why don't we?" Con said. "I'm up for a couple of hours at the beach."

"Why don't you two go then? I want to get started. I can meet you later."

"Let's grab a few rays of Hawaiian sunshine for that oh-so-pale face of yours. Let's color you up for this evening, Ant."

"I guess you guys didn't spot who else was on our flight, in first class?"

"The pope?" Sam suggested.

"No, Gregor and his sidekick, Rosa."

"Shit, are they following us?" Con now looked engaged.

"They have the original copy of the map, remember? The cover had been opened up a few times. The map would be plain to see. It mentions Honolulu and talks about the amount of gold. He may also have an inkling Jacob and Liza viewed it."

"Are they here, too?" Con drew up a dining chair and sat opposite me.

"They arrived yesterday."

"Why are you only telling us about this now?" She moved in closer to inspect the map.

"Jesus Christ, Ant. This is turning into a race."

"Like the movie *It's a Mad, Mad, Mad,*"—Con counted on her fingers—"*Mad World.*"

"Oh yes, I love that movie—Phil Silvers, Mickey Rooney, and so many more." I watched it many times as a kid.

"Mickey who?" The boy appeared not to be on the same wavelength as Con and me.

I was determined not to be sent off on a tangent. "We have a couple more pages of the document than anyone else. In fact, we're missing only one page. I think it could be either at the church or the mission museum."

"Surely not after all this time." Sam took a cigarette from his pack.

"There must be a chance, though. A museum's job is to hold on to that sort of stuff." Con sounded like she was finally getting interested in our quest. "So am I right in thinking that the missing page contains the signatures of the people involved in the contract?"

"Absolutely, Connie."

"Wow, Con, teacher's pet, or what?"

"Any clue about where Jacob and Liza are staying?" Con asked.

"My contact told me they got a cab from the airport last night to the Royal Grove Hotel, the bright-pink building we passed on the way in. And Gregor will almost certainly be at the Hawaii Prince. My guy is checking."

"Anthony, how do you know all this stuff?" Con leaned in. She smelled so fresh. "Who is this contact of yours?"

"A longtime friend of Billy's. He handled the business the print shop had with the military here and can sort out anything we need. He's the same guy who helped Billy find the apartment for you in 1980. Dan would have met him when he visited."

Con flinched at the mention of this, and I immediately regretted the unnecessary detail.

"Sorry, Connie, I didn't mean to . . ."

She blinked and took a deep breath. "Wow, so is anybody else here?"

"My sister Lou and Dad, perhaps." Sam, with a still-unlit cigarette bobbing up and down in his lips, continued. "Or your mom, Con, with Walt riding shotgun?"

"You're funny." Con hid her eye roll from the boy, but I saw it.

Weirdly, his joke contained some truth, as Chuck Wilson was Walt's father. Billy had been instrumental in getting Walt his position at the Dakota, something that Chuck was eternally grateful for. Young Walt had gotten involved with the daughter of some local bigwig who had threatened something nasty. Chuck wanted him well away from harm.

"On a more practical note, I called the Royal Grove earlier, and they told me Mr. and Mrs. Weston-Jakobson arrived ten minutes before. I told the clerk we were arranging a surprise for the couple's anniversary and asked him to send me a text message if they went out again."

"Well done, Ant, man. I guess let's postpone the lovely frosty beers and Hawaiian sunshine in favor of the dusty old church."

"I agree," said Con. "Let's go now. Can we walk from here?"

"No, a little too far, but we have the use of a car—should be in the garage below."

"Of course it is." Con beamed—I loved that smile. I loved her.

"Some more excellent planning, Ant." The boy managed only a sneer as he finally ignited his Camel.

Chapter Forty-Eight

CONNIE

Our Apple Mac not only gave us directions but also told us that Kawaiaha'o Church, known as Hawaii's Westminster Abbey, was built of coral slabs from reefs surrounding the island.

We managed to park our stylish silver Mercedes C-Class outside the gate. The Kauikeaouli clock struck five as we walked up the path. Inside the church, a middle-aged woman was arranging flowers. Her hairstyle was Barbra Streisand in *Funny Girl*—a tad on the young side for her. She checked us out with a couple of sideways glances.

Anthony picked up a leaflet from the display. "Our map doesn't relate to the church directly. It must be one of the three buildings on the grounds, either the Frame House, the Chamberlain House, or the Printing Office."

"Yeah, dude, let's investigate." Sam looked relaxed in his ecru linen shorts, Stüssy tee, and some Birkenstocks I hadn't seen him in before.

Anthony examined the leaflet. "They're the museums. Damn, they're closed."

"Ant, bad planning, bud."

"I guess we can come back in the morning." I attempted to keep things light.

Sam looked at his empty wrist. "Time for those beers."

"From what I can see, the building we want is the Printing Office," Anthony said as he walked over to the woman. "Excuse me, ma'am, is there anyone we can speak to about access to the museum?"

"I'm sorry, but the museum is closed for today," she said and continued arranging.

"Duh, we know." Sam gave her one of his sulky looks.

"Yes, I apologize, ma'am, my mistake. I thought it was open until five thirty. We've come all the way from New York and were wonder—"

"Jeepers, all the way from New York City. I went there once. What a mess, graffiti sprayed everywhere. Waiting for our flight back to sanity, we got the news about that Beatle being shot. No, the Big Apple ain't for me."

That evening I lost my unborn baby. When I imagined my child, I always visualized a boy. He would have grown up to be like Dan. My mind not only associated Sam with my husband but also now the son I never had. This confused the hell out of me.

Sam took his Camels from his pocket. "Guys, I'm going outside for some air."

I stared after him while my brain was still working on the confusion.

Anthony now had space to work his magic. "We were wondering, could someone possibly . . . ?"

"The Printing Office is the place you would like to visit?"

Nothing wrong with her hearing.

"Yes, please, a few minutes would be amazing. We want to check something out. We're working on a book titled *A History of the American Missionary*."

"Sounds like a riveting read." She had a pleasantly sarcastic tone.

"So it would be useful if we could . . . Then we can work on our draft this evening. My name is Anthony, and this is Connie. Our friend Sam is outside."

"He doesn't appear as interested."

"He's a boy," Anthony said.

I shot him a glare, but he wasn't looking.

"I have one like him at home. Well, you seem like nice folks. My name is Maureen, by the way."

"Good to meet you, Maureen." Anthony continued to charm.

"Let me find my keys. I'll meet you at the Printing Office in five minutes. You might like to make a donation on your way out?" She nodded toward a largish wooden box with a slot in the top and a huge poster above it: *Your church needs a new roof, urgently!*

"Yes, of course." Our leader pulled a folded twenty from his small wallet and deposited it.

Sam had a youngster around fourteen years old in tow when he rejoined us for the walk to the museum. The scrawny, sunburned waif was enjoying a cigarette, mooched from Sam, no doubt. He blew nifty smoke rings, one after another.

"Little dude, we'll catch you later. Say, Ant, my man, would you give my young compadre here a couple of *dólares?*"

Anthony dipped into his small wallet again and this time pulled out a five and I think tried to give it to Sam's new friend.

"No, sir, let me work, sir, if you please."

Anthony pushed the bill into the young man's raggedy shirt pocket. It was ancient but made from lovely linen. "Payment on account for when we need your help."

The teen beamed and nodded enthusiastically. Part of his right earlobe was missing. "Much thanking you, sir," he said in his peculiar accent. He tagged along with us and sang some weird ditty. "Bobby Shaftoe's gone to sea, silver buckles on his . . ."

As we arrived outside the Printing Office, Maureen marched up, her heels click clacking and with a massive key pointing forward in her hand.

I didn't spot the youth slipping behind Sam, but Maureen did. "Don't you be getting involved with the likes of that one. He's been hanging around here all day. Annoying visitors and begging for money."

"Please, my ladyship, I am no begging boy."

Oliver Twist sprang to mind.

She sniffed and shot him a look. "Hmm, well. He keeps saying he's waiting for someone to take him home. I'm sure he hasn't seen home for a long while." She tracked him all the while. "Those two who came in earlier weren't so friendly."

"Were they also from New York? Do you know?" I asked.

"Not sure, they didn't say much. A crafty-looking man in his midtwenties and an attractive girl who's the spitting image of your young friend." Maureen waved her key toward Sam. "I left them to it. They examined all three houses. The man kept going from one to the other, as though he'd lost something."

"Yes, they're also working on a study, a competing study." Anthony tried his best to make it sound believable.

She let us in.

"So the agreement was struck in here. The map refers specifically to this room." Anthony paced around. "The church is only mentioned because that was where the prayers and vigil were to be."

"Are you researching anything in particular?" Maureen asked.

"Uh, the saving of a soul." Anthony touched his fingertips together. "A contract to save a soul."

"Oh yes, we have one of those up on the wall." She nodded in the direction of a neatly framed document. "Yes, those two were so interested, I had to stop the man from pulling it off the wall. They took a lot of photos."

I ran my hand along the edge of an old, polished hardwood desk. "Lovely desk." It was hideous.

"Oh, yes. It's over a hundred and fifty years old. Commissioned by the Very Reverend Artemis Goodwife." She pointed out the script signature of the reverend on the agreement. "Most likely signed on this actual desk."

"And he preached, or whatever, here in the 1840s?" I was getting into it. I started to see what Anthony saw in all this.

"Oh, yes," said Maureen, "from February 1840 to January 1847. He died in a carriage accident, according to our records. His wife was killed, too. Not long after he signed the document. All sorts of dubious stuff came out after his death. He couldn't even save his own soul."

"Sounds fascinating," said Anthony. "Please, tell us more."

"No, not today. Take your pictures and let me lock up." Something made me think she knew more but didn't want to say. Why was she reticent?

Anthony photographed the framed page and took lots of photos of the desk from different angles. He felt around the top and legs as Maureen headed off to check the windows and doors.

"The secret drawer," said Anthony in a whisper, like he knew where to find it.

He touched a spot deep inside, and a drawer popped open just as Maureen reappeared in the room. Sam accidentally or on purpose knocked into a display, which sent a printing roller running across the floor.

"Careful," said Maureen, "these are artifacts. Please don't touch anything."

Anthony zipped the camera back in its case. "Maureen, thank you so much. I'm sure we'll meet again before we finish our work here."

"The museum is open Tuesday through Saturday from 10:00 a.m. to 4:00 p.m." Something she repeated many times during her day, no doubt.

We walked out of the Printing Office and through to the exit.

Sam's young friend joined us, holding a family-size bag of Lays. He offered the salty chips to Anthony first. Sam teased him by grabbing the bag and not returning it for a short while. The kid got quite upset. He kept saying, "We share," again and again.

My eyes were on Anthony's back pocket. "What did you find in the secret drawer?"

"A key wrapped in a piece of paper. I'll show you when we get back."

"The key to the treasure chest?" Sam asked.

Anthony winked. "Maybe."

I checked on the boy from the rear window of the car as we sped off. I could tell he wanted to follow—like a stray cat. He reminded me of my Simon. I had petted him in the park, and he followed without me noticing. He stayed outside our basement for a couple of weeks. Ma and I fed him up with prime cuts of roast chicken and whole milk. On a wet and windy night we let him in, and he became a part of the family. This kid looked to be out on his own like my beautiful Simon.

"Sam, did you find out anything from that boy?" I asked.

"No, Con, he's a bit young, even for you."

"That was uncalled for," said my protector. "Sam, apologize for that."

"Sorry, Con. Sorry, Ant. I was only joking, anyway." Sam rolled his eyes.

He needed to drink that long-promised ice-cold beer.

Chapter Forty-Nine

ANTHONY

We arrived back at the apartment with pizzas and beer. Sam all but abandoned his pepperoni once he sampled Con's pineapple pieces. He dealt out the ice-cold Bikini Blondes, supplying the refills as and when required.

After clearing up the boxes, I casually placed the key wrapped in a small piece of musty-smelling paper on the table and waited for them to notice.

Con came over. "Aha, that's what you discovered?"

Sam had been on his way over to the couch but reversed back to the table.

"A cabinetmaker's drawing in Burt's papers showed me how to access the sneaky little secret compartment in the desk."

"Anthony, the key. Tell us about the key." Con was bouncing on her chair. "Is it for the treasure chest?"

"Well, yes, I'm pretty sure it's for one of the padlocks the Reverend Goodwife and the seaman James Joy secured the strongbox with. It was wrapped in this piece of paper."

"Intriguing." Con came over for a closer look. "There are some crosses marked—a sort of floor plan, perhaps?"

"No, someone probably found the box already, years ago, and smashed the locks off."

"Oh, Sam, don't be so negative," said Con.

"If anybody had made a discovery on that scale in the intervening years, we would have come across a mention somewhere." I tried to close things on a positive note.

Con stayed with me at the table, and I took her through the papers in more detail. Sam did his best to distract her. After a cigarette on the balcony, he paraded through with his shirt off and lounged on the couch. Con licked her lips a couple of times and appeared mesmerized. She finally went off to the bathroom, but not before giving me a hug. I lived for those moments.

Sam glared at me, then stared after Con. "Don't forget, we have the party later."

"Don't forget we have the treasure to find and competition from two separate parties." Sometimes it felt like I was the only one taking this seriously.

Chapter Fifty

CONNIE

Around nine o'clock, the front pocket of Sam's 505s lit up after a buzz that startled him awake. While examining the text, he launched himself off the couch into the bathroom. Two minutes later, he was ready and looking hotter than ever.

As I stared at him, that something inside me stirred again. "Be with you in five," I said, heading for my bedroom.

"Ant, old man, are you with us?"

At the slightly open door, I hoped for a no from Anthony.

"Oh, I'll pass, if you guys don't mind?"

I did a small air punch. Great, Sam and I could enter the party together as a couple.

"Hey, Ant, you won't get laid unless you put yourself out there, dude."

"I'm not after a meaningless hookup."

"Whatever, dude, come for a few beers."

"All right, yes," he said. "I'll come for an hour."

Sam repeated the news flash outside the door. "Con, Ant's in."

"Great news." Shit, did he not want us to be seen together in public? Now, we'd look more like three friends hanging out.

Sam rechecked his cell. "Shandy is meeting us in the lobby."

Shandy, what the hell? A woman, no doubt. I needed to check her out and make a plan.

Sam dashed ahead to grab the elevator.

As we descended, the sound of pitter-pattering water from the fountains below us grew louder. Twin girls no more than sixteen years old with long bleached-blonde hair and overly made-up faces were there to greet us.

What the hell? They literally pounced on Sam.

"Howdy, Sammykins. Oh, you brought your mom and pop," said one. She gave each of us a funny giggle, before taking a deep breath through some pink gum clenched in her teeth. "I'm Shandy, but Sammykins knows that." She pushed a piece of fruit from her drink into his mouth and let her finger linger in there for too long. "This is my sister, Brandy. We're twins, always have been, right, Bran?"

"Sure are, Shan, for as long I can remember." Brandy's fluorescent teeth would be a hazard to oncoming traffic.

Wow, a pair of real smart cookies. I couldn't outcute them, but my brain could be useful. So long as I didn't soak it in liquor—which could be a problem. Why hadn't I made more headway with cutting back? Away from Ma, I had assumed it would be simple.

After some sharp elbowing through a throng of beachwear, we finally made it to the bar. Sam picked up and downed a Blue Hawaiian without missing a beat. He handed Anthony and me a couple of mai tais, before taking one for himself, together with a Bikini Blonde from a giant ice bucket. He raised his glass and bottle, for a sort of toast to us.

The twins were somehow trapped in his orbit. When he patted one of them on her little butt with his Bikini Blonde, they both squealed with delight. Sam's eyes jumped between their perky breasts. Perhaps he was trying to make me jealous—*mission accomplished, Sammykins.*

The music pumped up, and the chatter increased as more revelers joined the party.

The unlimited liquor began to take a toll. By the fourth mai tai, my body loosened, and I shimmied across to the dance floor. Sam spotted me and bounced over to perform a couple of expert moves in front of me. He grabbed my hips and gave me a huge kiss on the lips before bouncing off like a pedigree rabbit.

Two hours in, I realized Anthony had disappeared. Chugging on a Bikini Blonde, I caught sight of him chatting with a rather attractive woman about our age. She whispered in his ear and pecked his cheek. He beamed and whispered back. The sheer audacity of the woman. Why the hell was I jealous?

Anthony wound things up with his new friend as he spotted me approaching. "How's it going, Con? I'm calling it a night. Are you ready?"

"I'll meet you up there." My eyes scanned the dance floor. No sign of Sammykins or the twins.

"I'll leave the door unlocked. Enjoy the rest of your evening." God, Anthony was such a terrific guy. I should be going back upstairs with him. Why was I chasing the flaky one? Where *was* the flaky one?

"Anthony, thank you so much." I leaned across to kiss him, but he'd already gone.

He glanced back at the door and gave a little wave. My Sam-distracted, boozed-up brain failed to lift my waving arm.

Sam reappeared about five minutes later. Something had gone down. He picked up a Blue Hawaiian at the table and drank it down while holding on to a follow-up Bikini Blonde. The trailer-trash twins giggled behind him, each flexing a pinkie finger. Glaring, he turned to them and said something. Shan and Bran linked arms and sneered before stomping off, their pink ballet pumps squeaking in unison. Sam came over to join me.

"You okay, Sam?"

"You okay, Constance?" His smile twisted into something ugly.

"I'm leaving, how about you?"

"No, Con, let's have fun. Where's old Ant? Gone to bed early. The dude is a lightweight." He leered around the room.

I reached for his arm. "Come on, Sam."

"Don't tell me what to do, Jess. Fucking leave me alone, or I'll—"

"Are you okay?"

"I'm so sorry. I didn't mean to . . . Please forgive me—"

"I forgive you, Sam. Take my arm." We linked up, and I guided him to the door. He needed propping up as we moved toward the lobby. After leaning him up against the polished marble wall, I called the elevator. By the time it arrived, Sam had slipped down onto the gray terrazzo floor. He crawled into the car. I followed before the doors closed, and we were on our way.

As we reached our level, Sam perked up and stood unaided. "Con, you pooped on that party." He laughed, sniffed, and laughed again.

"What do you mean?" Even in my intoxicated state, a familiar sense of anxiety began to stir in my gut. Specifically, the feeling I got from handling Ma's Auntie Betty moments.

"You ruined the party for me." Sneering, he kept jabbing his index finger into my right shoulder as he spoke. "What . . . made . . . you . . . do . . . that . . . Constance?"

Acid swirled into my alcohol-filled tummy, and a wave of nausea broke at the back of my throat. I swallowed hard. Why was he so mean? "Come on, Sam, let's get you into bed." He followed me out of the elevator, then stopped and refused to move.

Grabbing his crotch, he said, "Oh yeah, this is what you want. This is what you're after. This is what they all want." He went to thrust and fell down.

"Please don't." My panic reflecting in the floor-to-ceiling mirror was not helping me. This was the man I loved so much? How could he be so cruel?

He edged up the wall to return to his feet. "Oh please, women of your age are so polite with your pleases and thank-yous."

I tried to ignore him but at the same time push him in the direction of the apartment. "Come on, almost home."

"Can't wait to pull my pants off, eh? Been there, done that."

Yes, Brandy and Shandy had shown their pinkie-fingered disappointment. I considered throwing that into the mix but thought better of it. "Will you be hooking up with those party girls again?"

"Hookers? No, Constance, I don't have to pay to fuck. Do you have to pay, eh? Bet you offer extras to your schoolboys. Straight As for extra effort in the sack? What was it like with my dead brother? Did he satisfy you like I do, huh?" He rubbed his nose. "What are you looking at?"

"I . . . nothing." I gasped in between words. "Please, can we . . . ?"

"Please, can we. Can we what, Constance?" He mocked my desperation, then lifted and drew back his arm. I had not expected his hand to connect with the left side of my face with quite so much force.

Stars flashed around my head. What the hell? "Oh, Sam, why did you . . . ?" My eyes started to tear up. How could this happen? Had I provoked him? Was this physical abuse? Yes, the bastard hit me on purpose. It occurred to me that I hardly knew him—was this the real Sam? It was all too confusing for me, in my intoxicated state.

"No point crying now, Constance, he's dead. You killed him twenty years ago. Do you want to kill me, too? Are you one of those black widows?" He made his fingers dance like the legs of a spider.

My God, stop it. The evening had turned from a bad dream into a full-blown nightmare. As I thought about my options, Anthony appeared at the apartment door.

My knight in shining armor galloped down to me.

Chapter Fifty-One

ANTHONY

I heard familiar voices outside the apartment, but Sam's words disgusted me. Such cruelty. How could Con put up with that onslaught? Wrenching on my jeans, I was still finding the head hole in my buttoned-up Henley shirt as I dashed along the corridor to where they were.

I focused my eyes on Con. "Are you guys okay?"

"Yes . . . we're fine, thanks." Con's hesitant voice and eye dabbing screamed otherwise.

"Your woman here just told me about her scoring system with her schoolkids." Sam's face contorted as he sniffed hard. Con shook her head a couple of times.

"Let's go back to the apartment to continue this." My first instinct was to punch the jerk, but I knew how to control my temper.

Sam put his hand on my shoulder and started swaying. "I need a drink. Ant, a beer for your boss, now."

"Let's go inside, and I'll get you one. Connie, please go ahead and prop the door open?"

Con dashed over and placed a chair under the handle before returning to help me. We both got our arms around Sam, who wriggled, squirmed, cursed, and muttered as we inched him toward the open door. Only days before, we'd rescued this scumbag from a fume-filled office.

Once in the apartment, he headed, unaided, to the refrigerator. He pulled out a Bikini Blonde and waved it at me to be opened. I obliged, and then prepared the sofa bed before steering him over. Sam dropped the bottle and slumped down onto the couch, kicking his sneakers off with far more effort than required. Incapable of releasing the button of his jeans, he gestured with his chin. Con shook her head and looked away. I removed them with a single pull. We both gaped, startled at his lack of underwear and the flurry of beverage napkins. I draped a sheet over the little embarrassment.

"Time for some rest, Con, important day tomorrow."

"Thanks, Anthony. Thank you for everything." She was blinking and looking at her hand.

"Are you okay?"

"Yes, I banged my eye getting Sam out of the elevator. It's a tad blurry. Be fine in the morning."

Con came in for a good-night hug and held me tight for longer than I expected.

"Thank you again." When she released me, she headed to her room without looking back.

I loved her more than ever.

Was this the end of her Sam obsession? If so, how would it affect the treasure hunt? In her emotional turmoil, could I be sure she wouldn't give up and want to go home? I was in a quandary. The gold now seemed almost close enough to touch, but I didn't want to lose Con in the process. Which was worth more to me?

Chapter Fifty-Two

CONNIE

Friday, July 7, 2000

Starting around six in the morning, my heart rate began to rise as each of the previous night's details dropped into my mind. My eye ached, but the bathroom mirror showed me nothing. It'd obviously been more of a slap than a punch. Showering and prepping allowed me time to think about my situation. I'd been verbally abused by my mother in her Auntie Betty moments too many times to count. And there was a guy, a couple of years back, who had shoved me quite hard when I decided to call it a night.

I still found myself hugely attracted to Sam, and he was the natural successor to my husband. An image of him on his bed after Anthony had removed his 505s pushed out the hurtful gibes and even the slapping. What occurred could be put down to a long, jet-lagged day, followed by the booze-filled evening and that awful Jessica nagging in his mind. The unfortunate encounter with the hillbilly twins had created a perfect storm.

Apart from all that, my body seemed to have an agenda of its own, perhaps connected to my fertility: *Constance, we need Sam.*

Standing in my bedroom doorway, I enjoyed the innocent boyish Sam wrapped up in his birds of Hawaii comforter. How had those hate-filled words come out of such a beautiful mouth?

"Morning, Con. You like what you see, eh?" He unwrapped his top half and turned from side to side, showing off his hairless, toned, muscly torso.

Last night's image reentered my mind. I caught my smile, reflecting in the window. "How are you this morning?" A spike of pain pierced my head. As my hand went up to rub my eye, an almost full Bikini Blonde on the side table tried to lure me over.

"Quite a night, eh? What time did we get to bed? On second thought, do you have any Advil? I'll need to be on it for Ant."

"Before midnight," I said, picking up the beer.

"No, I always dance until daybreak."

Trying to hide my painful eye roll, I examined and swirled the Bikini Blonde. After a quick sniff, I returned the lukewarm beverage to the table. Had he no memory of what happened? Did that make it okay? A dig in the tote rewarded me with some of Ma's hospital-grade painkillers. With a rush of joy, I grabbed an oval tablet imprinted *TV* for myself. A couple of regular-strength Tylenol from a jar on the counter would do for Sam. He was off my guest list for the good stuff.

Milk, butter, and preserves were all in the refrigerator, but we needed fresh bread and croissants. While in search of shoes, I heard the front door open.

"Wow, Anthony, I was about to—"

"I decided to enjoy the sunshine and grab breakfast. Coffee, anyone? You okay, Connie?" He stared at my eye and lifted his hand. "Is there something—"

Turning away, I rearranged some hair. "A slight hangover, perhaps."

The Hawaiian birds on Sam's comforter appeared in flight as he swooped onto the terrace for his morning Camel. Wow, what a beautiful man. How had he tanned so quickly? Would he remember Brandy and Shandy belittling his smallness? To be honest, that was his most disappointing feature. His brother was so much more impressive in that department.

Sam caught me checking him out again when he returned to the living room.

"Hey, Con, what are you thinking? You can't stop staring, can you, girl?" He did a twirl and a thrust.

A Hawaiian honeycreeper took to the air.

At least he called me a girl. I still grabbed at those straws. My insecurity about my age and waning attractiveness gnawed away at my self-confidence. Having a child, a Weston child, would lay all the ghosts to rest. It would also give me back what had been destroyed.

Anthony glanced up from his breakfast prep. "Sam, put it away. Grab a croissant while they're warm." He wagged a stub of pastry in a way that made me smile—our private joke.

"Okay, Dad, be right there. Oh, yeah, Con's like a sexy mom, a MILF."

"Sam, you need to watch what you say." My protector was straight on it.

"How do you mean, dude? You work for the Weston family, Anthony, uh . . . whatever your name is. Remember, we . . . well, you know." Sam looked ready to take it further, but Anthony hid behind his coffee cup.

Sam had struck that nerve again.

My cell lit up and buzzed: Ma calling.

I stood and headed for the terrace but, after a thought, turned. "Anthony, it's my mom. Have you spoken recently?"

"No, not since we left the city."

"Hey, Ma," I said, reaching for the tepid Bikini Blonde I'd flirted with earlier. "How are you doing?"

Anthony dashed over and switched the bottle for an ice-cold Mango Madness Snapple.

"Connie, love, I'm doing really well." Her tone was way up.

"Terrific news." As I put the Snapple down after a quick swig, my thumb went up in Anthony's direction, for some unknown reason.

"Yes, finally, the call has come. They need me as soon as possible. George is calling for me. My new passport is packed, and I'm on the eleven-twenty BA flight tomorrow. Louise is paying for everything, and in business class, Con—would you believe?"

"Wow, I'm pleased for you, Ma."

"Yes, Louise has been let down by the caregiver, and the children are gone. I understand you've taken up with the young brother. What about lovely Anthony?" She was her old self, flying to New York without a second thought.

"Er, yes, no, well, I'll fill you in later."

"I guess I'll be seeing you tomorrow."

"Ma, we've left the city for a few days. I'm with Anthony and Sam. We are taking a short vacation." I held my breath, waiting for a typical *Ma* reaction.

"You're out in the Hamptons, no doubt, how wonderful." Wow, she appeared to be her laid-back old self again. "Oh, yes, Gilbert and Tom are looking after Simon, in case you were worried. He popped upstairs earlier."

My beautiful cat stretched out on Gilbert's bomber came to mind as I rested my eyes on Sam. In my head, I was kissing his cute pink nose.

"Do you want a quick word with Anthony?"

"No, lovey, but give him a big kiss from me, would you? Thank him for taking care of you. Be careful of that Sam. He's trouble."

"Thanks for your advice. Call me tomorrow when you arrive. Bye, Ma."

Anthony, already checking through his notes and getting ready to brief us, nodded in my direction. "All okay?"

"She sends you a big kiss." I puckered up and blew.

Now smiling, Sam said, "Old Ant is popular today."

Anthony lifted his chunky Montblanc pen. "We should start preparing for another visit to the church."

"Fill us in on your latest findings, Professor," I said.

Cigarette in his mouth, Sam struck a match.

"Out on the terrace, please, if you don't mind," said Anthony.

"Yeah, yeah, I'm going."

Between slurps of cold coffee, Anthony summed up everything he'd learned.

Sam breezed in from the balcony. "Hey, you started without me."

"Anthony was going through what we know."

"I'll go to the bathroom, then."

By the time he rejoined us, Anthony had begun to talk about his plan for today. "Well, we have an advantage over Jacob and Liza with the key and the note."

"We're rich. Come on, Ant, tell us how to find this treasure chest. I wanna buy a condo here. Hell, I'm buying something on the shore."

I wondered if he imagined me in this new home by the sea.

An impassive Anthony continued, "The first thing we should check out is this number on the last page of the agreement." He showed us the photo of the framed page and zoomed in to the bottom right corner below the signature.

"Seven eighty-four," I said, "but what does that say before it?"

Sam leaned in to take a look. "It might be *plot*."

"Oh, yes, plot seven eighty-four."

"So, the treasure is buried in plot seven eighty-four." Sam stood up. "Let's go."

"Hang on a moment, I think the seven is a one. People wrote ones like sevens in those days." Our prof was on it, as ever.

"Confusing or what? Plot one eighty-four, is it a grave?" I suggested.

Anthony nodded and beamed.

The gold was getting more real by the minute. I started to think about how it would improve my life—so many possibilities. Sam and I could travel the world together, staying in the finest hotels. We would be careful not to spoil our kids, though. We could give Ma enough to set herself up properly. Though, perhaps, she was sorting herself out on that front, now she was headed back to the Dakota.

"Bring on the grave desecrating, guys."

"Well, let's go find it first." Anthony stood and shuffled his papers together. "Another visit to the church is called for as soon as possible."

"I'm ready, Ant. Let's go do some damage."

"You better put your pants on." A command I thought I would never give Sam. As he passed me, I inhaled, expecting the usual pleasant buzz, but his odor hovered only a whiff away from full-blown stank. "You should take a shower, too."

We were ready by 8:50 a.m. and full of anticipation for the day ahead. Anthony made sandwiches with the breakfast rolls. He packed them along with water, soft drinks, and three Bikini Blondes into a "Beaches of Hawaii" tote. Meanwhile, I sent in a reinforcing pharmaceutical to deal with some unpleasant head throbbing.

Chapter Fifty-Three

ANTHONY

The air-conditioning in our Mercedes clicked on within moments of us driving out of the garage. We made fast progress despite heavy traffic.

I parked in the same spot as the day before. "We're a little early. The museum doesn't open until ten, but we can go check out the records for burials. We may need to find the priest or whoever runs things."

"Oh, our little friend from yesterday is here." Con called him over. "We should find out his name."

"Didn't I say? His name is Jo," Sam said.

"Jo what?"

"Didn't ask."

The boy ran up to us, his face beaming. I opened the tote and offered him a sandwich. After being reassured they were all the same, he seized the closest and playfully grabbed one of the Bikini Blondes.

"Hey, careful, little dude, those babes are for the grown-ups," Sam said in a light tone.

Jo shrugged and handed the bottle back to me. I exchanged it for a Snapple Lemon Tea.

"What happened to your eye, Jo?" Con moved in to examine a nasty blue-black bruise. She pushed some hair over her own eye at the same time.

"I is fine. Thanking you, my lady."

He told us a man and a woman visited the church soon after we left yesterday. He said they "talked in foreign." With Maureen not around, he'd followed them as they looked through windows and tried doors. When he told them the museum had shut for the day, the man started to force the lock on the main entrance. Jo declared he was "telling the law," and the man grabbed and threatened him. He wriggled free but caught a punch to his eye in the scuffle.

"Could be Gregor making an appearance," I said. "We need to find the priest."

"Pastor man . . ." Jo struggled with his words. "He's in the wood house."

I touched his shoulder. "You keep away from those foreign-talking folks."

He nodded furiously with a solemn expression before shifting back to his usual grin. We left him to his Snapple and made our way to the mission houses.

Our competitors were circling.

Entering a damp and musty-smelling anteroom, we were invited to sit by the short, bald, neatly dressed, middle-aged reverend. He was a friendly type who took any opportunity to chuckle and kept glancing over at Sam. We told him about our research and mentioned plot 184 in the graveyard. He went away but soon returned and handed me a piece of paper. We thanked him and made our way out of the building.

The morning lacked a cooling breeze, so we decided to recline in some chilled executive German air while we planned our next move.

"The grave belongs to—" I began, as a Lincoln Town Car pulled up close by. I spotted Gregor and Rosa climbing out of the rear doors and charging over to the mission houses, followed by young Jo at a wary distance. I started to slide down in my seat and indicated to Con and Sam to do the same.

"Yeah, get down, guys. My sister and Jacob are coming up the road."

"I'm going to drive around the block." As I pulled out, they took our parking spot.

"Perhaps we should leave them for a while?" Con said. "What were you going to say about the grave?"

"Oh yes, the grave belongs to . . . Yes, it belongs to—"

"For fuck's sake, man." Sam snatched the paper. "John Stephens, whoever he is."

"John Stephens was one of the two survivors of the *Spec*, the ship that foundered with the gold on board."

"Time to buy some shovels," Sam said.

"Hmm, maybe we should pick up a metal detector, too." I'd been thinking along this track ever since we arrived.

"Will the thing work six feet under?" Sam asked.

"With that amount of gold, I'm sure it will. Guys, we're going to need to do the grave survey under cover of darkness."

"I guess the others will be onto it, too," Sam said, ever the pessimist.

"But we needed Anthony's considerable research." Con was so on my team.

"Did we really?" Sam glanced quizzically at her before sending a questioning look in my direction. "I thought we just read the number off of the picture."

Sadly, there was no denying Sam's observation. I started the car, and we set off to do our shopping. The competition was nipping at our heels. I hadn't realized until now how close we could be to losing out to Gregor, or heaven forbid, Jacob and Liza. The latter had surprised me with the swift progress they had made. If that happened, Con would be a lost cause and, perish the thought, I would need to ask Winston for work again. I wanted a new life with Con, away from forgery and chicanery. And without being controlled by a blackmailer. This was my chance—I deserved this.

Chapter Fifty-Four

CONNIE

We found a reasonably priced Garrett Treasure Ace 100 in a hardware store. A basic model, but Anthony was sure it would do the job. Back in the apartment, he showed off his professorship by putting on some snazzy eyeglasses before twiddling his apparatus.

"When do we head down to the graveyard, Ant? Come on, man. No way do I want Jacob and my sis to snatch our treasure."

"I guess it will need to be dark and deserted, maybe around 1:00 a.m. Does that work?"

"Can we assume the others are making similar plans for the early hours?" Sam was on it.

Anthony looked over the top of his eyeglasses, which had slipped down his elegant nose. "If they found the grave, they may well be planning to dig. But neither of those two couples is going to find things easily. Gregor will no doubt try to recruit some muscle."

"Jacob will think he can dig up the gold in ten minutes," Sam said. "He'll be there if they're onto it."

"We need to gather a little more intel while we wait for it to get dark." Anthony removed his glasses and stowed them in a neat leather case. "I gave Jo a few coins, and I asked him to call me at around two from the pay phone with an update on our rivals. I'm not sure the kid knew what I was saying, though."

"He'll have spent the cash on gum or chips. Anybody up for a frosty Bikini?" Sam's head was now in the refrigerator.

"Club soda for me." Even though I wanted to ask for a large glass of Zinfandel.

"So a wimpy seltzer for Mom. Pops, what about you?"

"I'll join you in a beer."

Sam paused for a moment. "Okay, so . . . Bikini Blonde for Pop, soda pop for Mom. Put some music on, Con."

There was a pleasing electronic clunk as I plugged a dangling input cable from the amplifier into the Rio's headphone socket. The waves from the start of John Lennon's "Beautiful Boy" soon broke from the Bang & Olufsen speakers. In my mind's eye, my beautiful husband strolled along a sandy beach toward me, as he always did when I played this song. This time, though, it was Sam's face that came into focus.

Sam covered his ears. "Yeah, no, anything else, Con?"

The beach disappeared.

Hmm . . . I scanned the available tracks of the six whole albums on the player. The guitar and harmonica of Neil Young's "Heart of Gold" started up.

"Great choice, Con."

"Glad you approve, sir." I smiled and was weirdly delighted to please him. Neil Young had been one of Dan's favorites, too.

Our son would have been at college by now. I had always imagined we would have called him William after dear Billy—a beautiful boy, the image of his gorgeous father. I glanced over at Sam and rested my eyes on him while he prepared the drinks. "I'll change my mind and take a Bikini Blonde, too, Sam, please."

He gave me his, and then he went to the fridge and grabbed another.

"My cell," Anthony said, picking it up. "Might be our agent on the ground. I'll put him on speaker."

"Who's there, please?" a man's voice asked. "Tell me now, please."

Anthony appeared rattled. "Hello, this is the Waikiki Surf Club, what you want?"

"Your boy can't help you today."

"You want to rent board? Yes? No? Sorry." He finished the call. "I have to go find Jo." He grabbed his keys and wallet and headed for the door.

"Shall we come along, too? Or—"

"Ant can handle it, Con."

"Yes, you guys wait here."

As Anthony disappeared through the door, Neil Young's "Old Man" started up.

Sam came over and put his arm around me. He set every nerve ending in my body tingling. Dan was the only other person to have ever made that happen.

"So, do you forgive me for last night? I am so sorry. Think I had a few too many Bikini Blondes."

Shandy and Brandy had been two of them. "Nothing to forgive," I lied with ease.

He moved up close. "You sure? I can't quite remember what happened. Ant told me I needed to apologize to you, but I was going to anyway." His smell was beyond awesome.

"No worries." I fibbed again.

"I want you, Con."

"Are you saying . . ." I wanted him to touch me, to be in his arms. *Hold me, Sam.*

"This is my bedroom, so." Unbuttoning the linen shirt he had, no doubt, borrowed from Anthony, he pushed his tanned torso toward me. He kicked off the classic Birkenstocks, which I had been admiring since I first spotted them yesterday. He released the button on his 505s and, following a thrust, unfortunately reminiscent of the previous evening, he treated me to a slow reveal of his Calvins. I fixed my eyes on his flat stomach as his lithe body quivered. It was plain to see he was ready. As I hurried to peel off my 501s, he pushed me onto his bed, which had been turned back into a sofa. He used his toes to remove my underwear as I shed my top.

"Con, you're so—"

"Oh, God, yes." My superconfused brain began flashing up cherished Dan moments.

"Yeah, oh, fuck . . . Look what you made me do." He was done, his eyes already searching for his clothes.

Another epic fail. Sam's beautiful wrapper promised so much.

We both heard the key go in the lock and shared an astonished stare before springing into action. I dashed for my bedroom, kicking my jeans and wiping off Sam as I went. From my open door, I watched Sam's three-second reset. He zipped himself up, slipped his arms through his shirt, and slumped back on the sofa with a Bikini Blonde in hand. His Calvins lay to the side, as exposed as his chest.

I climbed into a dress and smoothed myself down. Entering the living room, it occurred to me that I needed to put some underwear on. This thought distracted me from my disappointment.

Chapter Fifty-Five

ANTHONY

Driving out of the garage, I spotted Jo running up the road. He was checking out the buildings and scanning cars and pedestrians. Immediately, I stopped the car and opened the door; he dashed up and hugged me tightly. An immense feeling of calm came over me, and for the first time in my life, I imagined myself as a father—I liked the idea very much.

He climbed into the car and started pressing buttons on the dashboard and opening compartments.

Likewise, when we arrived back at the apartment, he ran around checking everything out. His eyes bulged at the panoramic view.

"Hey, guys, look who's here. The smart kid found us."

"Are you sure nobody followed you, little dude?" Sam buttoned up his shirt, then leaned over and tucked something under the couch. Something had occurred in here. I detected an odor. For Pete's sake, I was only gone ten minutes. I took a deep breath and regretted it—I needed to stay calm.

"No. Nobody never follow Jo."

"So, how did wily young Jo let our number fall into enemy hands?"

"Leave him alone—he's in shock. Gregor tried to break his arm. He emptied his pockets." I glared at Sam. My eyes rested on his shirt. Or my shirt, actually.

"Ant, hope you don't mind. I need to do some laundry. Since you didn't say anything earlier, I thought . . ."

"Well, yes, I guess that shirt does go well with the shoes you borrowed."

Con came over to join me. "Is Jo okay?"

"Yeah, how is poor little Jo? Should Mom and Pop change his diaper?" Sam's humor missed the mark.

The boy put his tongue out and gave Sam two fingers. The two fingers struck me as unusual.

Jo was eyeing Sam's beer and licking his lips. "Are you thirsty?"

"Please, sir, a one of them Snappers, please."

I found a Mango Madness behind a six-pack of Bikinis and removed the top for him. "Here you go, Jo."

He almost downed the whole bottle in one go, then burped twice before drawing his bare and bruised forearm across his lips.

"Lovely dress, Con." Why had she changed?—as if I didn't know.

She smiled and flourished a chocolate bar from the candy supply on the counter. "Would you like a Snickers, Jo?"

"Knickers?" He doubled up laughing.

Con looked worried. "Excuse me a moment, guys, I just need to . . ." She went off to her bedroom but soon returned, adjusting her dress.

"Where do you live, Jo?" Sam asked.

"In Lulu."

"Little dude, but where did you come from?"

He pointed out to sea. "Somewhere a long way off. Now from Lulu."

"He's trying to help us, and he's getting beat up. Jo, you should stay here for the time being," I said. "Would you like that? Do you need to tell anyone?"

"No one for Jo."

"Where will the little dude sleep? Not with me, that's for sure."

"Hmm, yes, Sam, you take my bedroom. I'll sleep out here and keep an eye on the boy." I lightly held Jo's shoulder. "Do you want to rest, or are you okay to tell us what happened at the mission today after we left?"

Jo proceeded to recount in his own unique way how Gregor and Rosa had gotten more and more annoyed. They couldn't figure things out. He went into detail regarding what Gregor had said.

Sam, in one of his moods again, puffed on his Camels out on the terrace, blowing smoke rings in through the door in Jo's direction every so often. Jo had obviously taught him something useful.

When Gregor realized Liza and Jacob were there, too, he got in a huge fight with Jacob. This, while Liza and Rosa talked calmly together. Gregor went off to find Maureen, but when he returned, he saw Jo.

"He surprise me—he did. He picks me up, look here." Those bruises were even more pronounced. "Turned me top to tail, upside downside, he did. He finds the paper with the writing. He tried to keep ahold of me, but I was off. I remember part of Lulu him said you is from." He nodded in Sam's direction. "So, I starts a running to tell you."

"We can be sure they know we're here." We had lost our advantage. It was all my fault. How could I have let this happen—everyone was relying on me.

"So, you didn't tell them anything, little dude?"

"No, nuthin'."

I held the boy's shoulders and looked into his eyes. "You're a good man, Jo."

Jo's wide grin animated his perfectly symmetrical face. He certainly wasn't from around here. He sounded more English than anything, so a boy who had spent a sizable chunk of his short life in England, perhaps.

Needing to keep everyone motivated, I went over my strategy for later. "I plan to run the metal detector over the surface of the grave while you guys wait in the car. If I discover the treasure, we'll all be digging. We have a long night ahead. Let's rest up now."

Sam couldn't relax and went to sit out on the balcony for some serious smoking. Jo joined Con on the sofa. They looked so adorable together, cuddled up. Con was stroking his hair but appeared to be in some sort of trance. I wondered what she was thinking.

Chapter Fifty-Six

CONNIE

My eyes found it hard to focus while a dense, swirling mist surrounded me. As the fog began to clear, a scene in a tavern opened up. A familiar-looking boy stood in the center of the room with an attractive, lean, and muscular blond-haired young man. He was a few years older than the boy, with youthful beardy fluff on his face. The boy was undoubtedly Jo, but fuller in the face and rosy cheeked.

To begin with, everything was like a paused video. Then someone pressed play, and my face and arms started to warm from the nearby fire.

Some sailors scraped chairs across the flagstones and gathered around a table to the left of me. They began to sing.

"Bobby Shaftoe's gone to sea, with silver buckles on his knee. He'll come back and marry me, and if he doesn't, I'll ram those silver buckles down his lying throat!"

Within moments, a couple of the sailors started arguing, then fighting. This drew a crowd from all corners of the smoke-filled tavern. They cheered and bet on their favorites. A no-nonsense woman arrived and, with a few words, which I couldn't make out, calmed it down.

I returned to the two young guys.

"Time for our celebrations," said the young man.

"We is rich," said Jo.

His companion put his finger to his lips. "Shut your mouth. That is our doings, for no one but ours."

Jo mimicked his shipmate's finger and asked, in a whisper, "Jim, we is sharing, right?"

"We talk about that later—enjoy the night. Have fun." He seized Jo. "Don't you go blabbing to your milady about where things is."

A couple of gaudily dressed girls approached the pair. They were twins and no doubt prostitutes. They groped and fondled the shipmates, trying to arouse them. Jo, not into it, pushed the one concentrating on him away, although she'd apparently found something to her liking. The young, blond-haired man's pleasure reached a new peak when the other twin joined her sister. The wenches poured strong liquor into his mouth between some bouts of frantic French kissing. Jo tried to pull him away, but his companion shoved him to the floor. The twins led Jim, now overwhelmed and with his trousers undone, off to a side staircase. Jo got up and followed. I did, too.

"You remember what we agreed." Jo's finger went to his lips.

Jim did the same and nodded but carried on with the women. They guided him up the short flight of stairs and through the open door, to a room on the upper level—no doubt ready and waiting for the likes of this young sailor. Jo followed them, still protesting. The door shut in his face. He leaned against the side wall, then slid down to a crouching position and focused on a woman in her late thirties. She rushed to his side and gathered him up. Shit, why did she look like me? After speaking a few words to him, she led him to the back of the tavern. They sat down in a red-velvet-curtained area, but my vantage point still allowed me to see.

Following a few exchanges, Jo snuggled up, put his head on her shoulder, and looked into her eyes. "My lady, I has a letter from my mum. Can I bring it to you for reading?"

"Yes, of course, you can, my love." She stroked his hair and kissed his forehead.

At that moment, the young man threw open the door of the upstairs room. The tavern patrons fell silent for a few seconds as he stumbled down the staircase. Regular service had already resumed when the twins reappeared. They were giggling and flexing their pinkie fingers.

Jo hugged the woman, got up, and rejoined his friend, who cuffed him hard around the head. Jim bought himself an ale, downed it, and headed for the door, closely followed by Jo. The older sailor swayed from side to side but managed to pick up and drink from a few more mugs he found on the way.

Outside, in the starless, moonless night, a lantern in the tavern window provided limited illumination to a sort of harbor. Close by, vessels of all shapes and sizes bobbed and creaked as their ropes tugged at the moorings. A general stink of dead fish filled the muggy air.

Once again, I found myself amid the action.

"You was listening to my doings with them women? Admit it?" said the blond shipmate, trying to grab hold of Jo.

"Was not no, I's speaking with my lady. Nowhere near your dirty doings."

"You speaking about our treasure to 'er ladyship."

"Was not." Jo's index finger went to his lips again.

"Just cos you can't do it"—Jim gripped his crotch and performed a short thrust—"you want to eavesdrop on mine. Right, true enough, innit?" He grabbed the boy around the neck. "'Tis true, innit?"

"Stop, leave him alone!" I was shouting, but they couldn't see or hear me.

"Stop, I begs you. 'Tis true, we is friends," said Jo in a half-strangled voice.

The young man released him and threw him to the ground with too much force. Jo didn't move. Jim started walking away, no doubt expecting the boy to jump up and go after him. He didn't.

He circled Jo. We both spotted the blood that had begun to pool under the boy's head. The young man panicked and ran away down the path.

"Please help—don't leave him. Help me!" As I desperately tried to find someone, Jim returned. He picked up the boy.

"Yes, you can save him. Take him into the tavern. Tell his friend. Find a doctor. Do something quickly!" Nobody took any notice of me.

He carried Jo to the water's edge and, after checking around, opened his arms and dropped him in.

"You can't do that. Somebody help him. Help me!"

Ⓐ

"Connie . . . Connie, you okay?" Anthony asked.

"Oh God, I was having a nightmare—it all seemed so real. Where's Jo?"

Anthony pointed. "He's over by the window."

Was my strange dream just my brain processing what we'd found out? Had my mind created the images of the shipmates celebrating the gold? Jo being there, and likely murdered, made it a bizarre experience. No dream I'd ever had was so vivid and believable.

Chapter Fifty-Seven

ANTHONY

In the warm, clear night, a half-moon provided some useful natural light. I parked in our usual spot outside the mission houses. The four of us sat quietly in the car, checking around for any sign of the competition. I had on my darkest North Face clothing, brought along especially for this type of activity. My plan was to climb over the wall into the churchyard and run the Garrett Treasure Ace over plot 184.

"Okay, I'm ready. You wait here in case we need a quick getaway. Con, you drive."

"Hey, Ant, man. Let me be your driver." Sam presented an endearing little-boy expression.

I glanced in Con's direction for permission.

"Fine by me."

"Me, too, cap'n," said Jo.

"Okay, Sam, but stay calm. If you need to move, text me, and I'll meet you two blocks over at the coffee shop. The Garrett will make short work of the grave. The shovels and pick are in the trunk, standing by." I stepped out of the car with the metal detector under my arm and headphones around my neck.

Moving the 'phones to my ears, I powered up the Garrett and climbed over the wall. A powerful fragrance of eucalyptus hit me immediately. My previous calculations about the plot's position paid off. I checked that the Treasure Ace was ready, testing it with my mom's wedding ring, which I always carried. The pointer shot across the dial, but there was no such response from any part of the grave. I made doubly sure of my location.

Before I could dwell on my utter disappointment, a text came in from Con warning me of our competitors and moving our meetup to the coffee shop.

Ⓐ

I didn't want to be seen walking along the road with a metal detector, so I deposited it into a dumpster at the 7-Eleven en route. I comforted myself with the fact that Gregor and company would likely have disrupted our retrieval of the treasure if it *had* been there.

The car was parked outside the shuttered coffee place. Under the streetlight, I noticed the rubber skid marks on the roadway.

The guys would be despondent. Still, thinking about it, we would've had difficulty claiming any rights to the gold if I had discovered it in the cemetery.

There was a sense of anticipation as I stepped into the passenger side. "Hey, guys, thanks for the tip-off."

"Ant, did we find the treasure?"

"Well, there's more to it."

Sam fixed me with a stare. "Simple question, man, did *you* find gold or not?"

"Unfortunately not."

"What a colossal waste of time, dude. We are so—"

Con tried to shush him. "When you say *more to it*—"

"The detector didn't find—"

"Where is the trusty Garrett?" Sam made a point of looking around me.

"I ditched it in a dumpster, but it did its job. Also, the grave had been dug recently. Not like in the last few days, but certainly this year."

"Typical—somebody has already found it." Sam banged his fists on the steering wheel.

"No, I don't think so. Possibly an official thing or maintenance?"

"Ant, dude, incomplete research here, man. Shoddy work, not like you at all, Professor."

"Yes, sorry, guys, I do feel a little responsible."

Sam stabbed the air with his finger. "Hey, no, Ant, totally responsible."

"Sam, wait," Con said, "we're in this together. We're a team."

"We is . . . ship . . ." Jo slid down in his seat.

"Jo isn't well, look." Con held him.

I took his pulse. "We need to get him to a hospital."

"Hey, which way to the ER?" Sam started the car and revved the engine.

"Okay, yes." They were relying on me again—I liked that.

Sam revved again. "I'm waiting, man."

"Along here and then the first left, then take the freeway. Off at the first ramp, right and right. How is he?"

"He's breathing, but he looks so pale." Con's voice began to wobble. "Come on, Sam, please, we can't let him . . ."

Sam parked in an ambulance bay. "Hurry, man. We don't want to lose the little dude." Sam's words remained with me as I dashed in to locate a physician. For Pete's sake, where were the doctors?

The nurse on duty wanted all sorts of irrelevant information, so I left her with my credit card and grabbed a passing white-coated guy by the arm. After confirming he was a doctor, we located a gurney and pushed it toward the entrance. We met Sam in the doorway, carrying Jo.

The physician examined the boy as he wheeled him quickly into the back.

I took a moment with Sam. "Look after Con. I'll text you."

"Thanks, man." He looked uncharacteristically anxious and hugged me tightly. I responded in kind. Jo was part of our family, and no way could we lose him. I took some deep breaths before heading inside.

Chapter Fifty-Eight

CONNIE

Five minutes after Anthony disappeared inside the hospital, Sam got out of the car, opened the back door, and carefully picked up Jo.

"Hey, wow, there's nothing to the little dude. He's so light."

In the entrance lobby, he met Anthony, who was rushing out with the doctor. Sam gently laid Jo on the gurney and squeezed his hand. Anthony lightly gripped Sam's shoulder, who responded by going in for a full-on hug. Anthony looked reluctant at first but then went for it. Their emotional connection hit me, and I teared up immediately.

Although I'd only known Jo for a short time, I felt a deep bond with him. He brought out maternal instincts I didn't think I had. I was ready to be a mother. The boy appeared to be affecting the guys, too.

"Ant says to leave him and for us to go back to the apartment. He's going to text us with updates."

A message came up on my cell moments after we got back.

Sam jumped up. "How's Jo?"

"No, my mom just landed at JFK. She says Lou sent a car for her." Ma had a focus again, and for once it was away from me. I didn't want to start up a whole texting thing with her, so I left it.

As Sam opened our second round of Bikini Blondes, Anthony's text arrived. Sam came over to me with my beer and rested his arm on my shoulder.

"Anthony says, 'Can't believe what happened. Getting a cab now.' Sounds weird."

"Typical Ant, keeping us in suspense."

Less than ten minutes later, a key turned in the lock. Sam dashed to the refrigerator, opened a beer, and handed it to Anthony as he came through the door.

"Thanks, Sam—just what I need."

"So, Ant, what does your text mean?"

"Well, they took one look at Jo and rushed him into the resuscitation area. As they gathered the team, a momentary power surge caused the lights to go out. The generator kicked in. Then when we checked the gurney, he was gone."

"Gone, dead?" I asked the obvious question.

"No, he completely disappeared. Nobody in the hospital saw him leave, but he was not on the premises."

We stayed up talking and drinking Bikini Blondes for another hour or so. The fact that Jo was nowhere to be found, we decided, was positive. I told the guys about my strange dream, or whatever it was. Sam started speculating about ghosts and spirits, which didn't impress Anthony at all. I kept mulling over my experience with Jo and couldn't help thinking it was relevant—like he was telling me something.

Ⓐ

My sleep was haunted by thoughts of Jo. Still on New York time, I got up early and headed for the living room. Anthony and Sam were dressed and sitting at the table.

Anthony stood up. "Coffee, Connie?"

"Please, let me. Anyone for a refill?"

"Come and sit with us." He patted the empty seat between them. "Would you prefer to return to the city?"

"No, we need to continue."

"Hell, yeah." Sam pumped his fist.

"We wanted to check with you." Anthony then began to summarize things in his usual way.

Sam yawned and wandered off for an alfresco Camel.

"A few of the graves were moved, according to this article." He referred me to the Mac's screen. "Ours looks to be one of them, but there's no mention of millions of dollars' worth of gold being discovered. This leads me to believe the treasure was never buried in the grave."

"Can you find anything about Reverend Goodwife? The guy who signed the soul contract?"

"You read my mind. Maureen told us he died along with his wife in a carriage accident a few days after he signed the contract." Anthony referred to his papers. "In fact, it was a boating incident on December thirty-first, 1846. They had started building a villa on the Big Island."

"Do you think that's where they stashed the loot?"

"Yes, there's a good chance. Maybe something for their retirement?"

"Perhaps they were sailing to, or from, the island when they went down."

Sam popped his head in from the terrace. "Let's hope they sank on their return trip, yeah?"

"Oh, yes, I see what you mean." Anthony had praise in his tone and didn't comment on the smoke pouring from Sam's mouth.

"Clever boy." As I smiled at Sam, he preened.

"If they managed to transport the coins to his house, then—"

"The treasure may be over there," Sam said, stubbing out his cigarette.

"What about the piece of paper?" I asked. "The one with the key?"

"It's a diagram of a room. I'm sure. A few places are marked."

"So the crafty old Rev broke open the chest and created easy-to-carry bags for the gold."

"Yes, makes sense," I said. "So, let's check out the Goodwifes' villa on the Big Island."

"We need to find a record of the property he owned," Anthony said. "That should give us the location. I can't find anything on the internet, so perhaps we should visit city hall. It's up near the hospital."

The mention of that place returned the discussion to our young friend.

"Let's swing by the mission on our way, in case Jo's turned up there." Anthony gathered his notes. "Oh, Connie, you should call your mom."

"Shit, yes." I dialed her cell.

"Hello."

"Ma, or should I say Mom? How's everything at the Dakota?"

"George, poor thing, is a tad confused, but I will be sorting out his meds and feeding him up." Her voice was bright and jolly. If George recovered, would she make a play for him? I wondered how Lou would feel about that. She might be grateful not to have to worry about her father's long-term-care needs.

Me, I needed a share of the multimillion-dollar treasure to give me options.

"Louise couldn't cope. George insisted I be sent for. Where are you, Con? Are you still vacationing?"

"Uh, yes, we'll be out of the city for a little longer. We'll be with you sometime next week." The three of us on a competitive hunt for buried treasure five thousand miles away in Hawaii struck me as something not to share until our return.

"Have you remembered to change your London flight?"

Shit. "Yes, I'm on it."

"Con, I'm needed at the Dakota again. After Jacob, the so-called caregiver, departed, it all came out. The caregiver was nothing of the sort, and the agency had no record of Jacob Jakobson. He left lots of stuff upstairs in Liza's room, including a letter addressed to a Jason Jackson. Con, he's the son of someone who used to work at the Dakota, would you believe? Do you remember the janitor who used to change light bulbs and do odd jobs around the apartments?

"As a kid, Jason and his brother, Jaden, occasionally came in with their parents, when they couldn't find a sitter. Aileen caught their father stealing back in 1980. She lost a treasured pearl-handled silver fruit knife given to her by her father. The next thing she saw was the guy using her lovely little knife to peel an apple."

The revelation caused an unpleasant gurgling in my stomach, which soon turned into nausea. I recalled my spree on that day. *Shit, I had no idea.*

"Yes, behind the front desk, with her knife, peeling an apple bold as you like." Mom would be relishing the detail. "A fruit knife, but—"

"Wow, shit . . . er . . . ." My brain scrambled around elsewhere. I couldn't believe there was now another aspect of that awful day to torment me.

"Anyway, he said someone must have put the thing into the garbage. You know how it works. They dismissed him on the spot when they found a load of stuff from the apartment in his locker. His wife lost her job, too. The guy turned to the booze and made life hell for the boys and their mom. He died of cirrhosis when Jason was ten. According to Walt, their mother got sick and passed the year after. For some reason, the boys got separated. Jason went to live with an aunt in Connecticut. His brother was adopted by a family who almost immediately returned to Scotland. Jason was likely after revenge."

My mind remained in a spin. "You arrived just in time, yes." Wow, the consequences of me not getting to my swag bag. I hadn't given it a moment's thought in twenty years. But did he really imagine that was all for the garbage?

"Well, George and I are about to eat lunch. Catch up later."

"Okay, then, bye." Even finding the button to hang up was hard for my tormented brain. What the hell had I caused? But I couldn't be blamed for forgetting to pick up a bag that day, of all days. My husband had been killed, and I'd had a miscarriage. It was all very unfortunate, but . . .

Anthony came over to me. "Are you okay, Connie? You've gone very pale."

"Um, yes, fine." I recovered some calm. "So Mom is doing well. Uh . . . She said Jacob is some sort of impostor. His name is Jason Jackson."

He was a dangerous person and threatening me just for getting involved with the family. I didn't want to think about what he might do if he discovered my part in his family's terrible downfall. Or did he somehow know already?

"Son of a sacked employee," Anthony said. "A son carrying his father's grudge."

How did he know that? I remembered that he had been cagey about something when I told him about Jacob threatening me—there was more to this. Once I'd gotten my brain together, I would start asking questions.

Anthony grabbed his keys. "Let's see what our rivals got up to last night." His face revealed that he'd already picked up on my suspicions.

Chapter Fifty-Nine

ANTHONY

Honolulu and the Big Island

Slotting the Mercedes into a tight spot between two cop cars outside the mission, it was apparent something had happened.

"I'll go check it out," Con said, opening the door.

"No, let's all go." Sam was like a dog, eager for his walk.

After leaving the car, we headed along South King Street. I spotted Maureen walking up the path to the church, and we followed her in. "Excuse me, ma'am. What's been going on in the churchyard?"

"Jeepers, yes, a lot. Someone went and dug up a grave last night."

"Why would they do that?"

"I can't imagine. There are some strange folks around. They caught a girl, likely the one that looks like you." She pointed to Sam with the large bunch of flowers she was carrying.

Sam failed to stifle laughter. "She'll be enjoying that, uh . . . not at all."

"Should we see if she's okay?" Though I couldn't suppress the feeling we'd got one up on the opposition.

"I guess we can check on the situation later and bail her out as a last resort." Con didn't seem that bothered, either.

"So you know the girl?" Maureen's radar was fully operational.

"Uh . . . yes, a passing acquaintance . . . a fellow New Yorker . . ." I coughed and checked my cell. "Anyway, thanks for all your help."

"Bye, now. Good luck with your book."

"Thanks. We're on our way to city hall," said Con.

"No, you'll find it closed today. Opens again on Monday morning at seven forty-five."

We left the church and drove around the area, deep in our own thoughts. I wondered what our competitors' next move would be—hopefully, they'd give up and go home.

Con broke the silence. "So, we need to find out more about the Reverend Goodwife. A library is bound to have a local history shelf."

"Is that open?"

"Well, Sam, hopefully, it is." Con pointed at the Starbucks across the road. "Let's ask in the coffee shop."

"Yeah, good idea, Con. A cappuccino, please. With an extra shot and a croissant."

"Ant, would you like anything?"

"Thanks, *Con.* Yes, please, a double espresso. I'll come and help you."

The coffee shop guy directed us to the state library, where we found a few books relating to missionaries. One went into considerable detail about the murky life of the Reverend Goodwife. He'd apparently employed many moneymaking schemes, few of which benefited the mission. His specialty had been saving souls, for a price. By 1846, he was nearing retirement and building himself a substantial property on the island of Hawaii, near Kailua Village.

"We should head over," I said. "Island-hopping flights are taking off all the time."

"I'm up for it. Let's go this afternoon," Con said.

"Not sure where we can stay, but I'm sure we can sort something on the way." I got to work with my cell. Three tickets for the 2:50 p.m. flight awaited us at the airport. We had time to return to the apartment and pack a bag. We planned to stay a couple of days, so we arranged to pick up a car there. Another credit card would now be approaching its limit. I didn't want to think about how this could go if I ran out of credit or, more importantly, the ramifications of not finding the treasure. My credit rating would be obliterated instantly. It could take me years to get back on track, and worst of all, *there would be no Con*. This was the biggest gamble of my life.

Driving past the church again, we spotted a familiar face. I pulled up a little ahead of Jo, who had yet to see us. As we all got out, he dashed up and hugged us all in turn, reserving the longest one for Con.

Sam crouched down. "What happened, little dude?"

"I remember waiting for you to do the detecting. Then next thing, I feel people trying to grab at me, then turning me over and over. I wake up in the churchyard with the law all around. They ask me questions. Then, I come looking for you."

I held his shoulder. "Jo, we are on our way to the Big Island. Would you like to come with us?"

He appeared puzzled but nodded vigorously.

Ⓐ

We arrived on the island at 3:45 p.m. and were in our rental car by four thirty, heading to Kailua Village. We found a guesthouse away from the main road in a quiet lane. Mrs. Hale, the owner of the three-story establishment, was from somewhere in England, from the sound of her. All her surfaces sparkled, her floors were waxed, and her antimacassars were without a trace of Macassar. A weird aroma of cooked ham pervaded the whole place.

Sam, Jo, and I shared the larger of the two bedrooms we had taken. A fair-sized Jack-and-Jill bathroom lay between our room and Con's.

Mrs. H., as we began to call her, prepared us a traditional island delicacy for supper: a sushi-type thing called Spam musubi. "People here understand what's possible with Spam."

The musubis tasted like wet blotting paper. But the dessert of Madeiran malassadas filled with haupia was terrific—basically, fried and sugared balls of fluffy dough containing a thick coconut goo.

According to Mrs. H., the military found it impossible to buy fresh meat in Honolulu, so they had imported Spam by the boatload—canned meat that lasted for years if left unopened. Lots of cans ended up in the shops, and migrant workers from Asia started incorporating the spiced ham into their recipes.

Mrs. H.'s knowledge of local history extended to the Reverend Goodwife, and she had an inkling of where his retirement villa might be.

She invited us to relax in her parlor while she busied herself with the clearing up. Jo wanted to stay in the kitchen, but she dispatched him with coffee and a Snapple. After handing out the mugs, he went and snuggled up to Con with his Snapple Apple.

Chapter Sixty

CONNIE

As before, following a quickly clearing mist, a scene unfolded in front of my eyes. The murderous young man from my previous dream stood, cap in hand, outside a familiar building. A distinguished-looking churchman opened the door and beckoned the youth into the Printing Office. I followed them in.

The church guy, presumably Reverend Goodwife, went over to his desk and picked up a document. "So, Mr. Joy, here is the agreement, please examine."

"No point, milord, I is no reader." Joy twisted his tatty blue cap back and forth.

"Well, no, of course you're not. The mission will pray for your soul on your death. This will be for six months, every morning and evening. You are getting excellent value for your donation, James, you can be sure."

"And my donation, as you calls it, does not rest with the mission until after I die, and the praying is done. Right, innit?"

"Exactly right, my boy. Your fifty thousand dollars in gold coin stays in this box." Goodwife tapped a sturdy container with his foot. He jiggled both padlocks on the strongbox with the toe of his rather dainty dress shoe. "You arrange for your key to be sent to us after your death, and we'll do the rest."

"Yes, I is leaving tomorrow for San Francisco. What if I changes my mind and want my gold?"

"The box will be here waiting for you. Just bring your key. The key is the important thing. Here is mine." He pulled it from somewhere under his vestment. "Both are needed."

Wow, this was all so clear. The gold coins were in the chest, and I was looking at the exact same key Anthony had found in the desk the reverend now sat behind.

"So my shipmate is in that box?" James nodded toward a small, cheap-looking casket lying on the print table.

"Yes, he was picked up in a net yesterday morning, drowned, apparently." Goodwife took the lid off the coffin in a single movement. "Will you take a peep? He was in the water for less than twelve hours, they reckon. His features are still intact, save for something chewed on his right earlobe."

The young man was reluctant to view his shipmate. I followed him over, and we both stared at the boy—at Jo, dead, in the casket. James Joy burst into tears and sank to his knees in front of the table. I broke down, too.

He put his hands together. "Pray for him, Reverend, please. I beg you."

"Yes, my boy, you can be sure. He will be buried here. I am allocating an exceptional plot that I was holding for a wealthy family." He showed Joy the grave on a plan. Goodwife picked up a pencil and wrote *plot 184* on the document.

"I feel so guilty, Reverend. I promised his mum I would be taking care of him. We survived the awful wreck. We was set fair." He was using his cap to wipe his face. He took a sniff, frowned, and pushed the stinky thing into his pocket.

A promise you failed to keep, James. You killed Jo. I wanted to tell the world.

"So you retrieved most of the gold?" The reverend raised an eyebrow and waited for confirmation.

"Yes, hush-hush-like. We gathered the coins up, together we did. We agreed to share. His part stays here 'cause I need it for my soul. You understand, don't you, sir?"

I wondered how sorry James Joy was. After all, this deal was to save his own skin—in his eyes, anyway.

"Yes, I understand, young man. I'm the soul of discretion, so to speak." He roared with laughter. "I won't be breathing a word. You did God's work, my son. You liberated the opium-tainted gold for the Lord. The mission will benefit in the future . . . the distant future. I'm sure your life will be a long and happy one. Your wealth will set you up in San Francisco. You're a man of substance now."

James appeared not to be listening to the clergyman's sermon. He continued down his own track. "Yes, took us six month, only for him to die in his accident outside the tavern like that. Or wherever it were. One minute he were with me, and next he were gone. I thought he had struck lucky with one of them saloon women. He was a favorite of that old one, Lady Constance is 'er name. Do you know her, milord?"

Goodwife nodded and then spluttered. "Not a place I frequent."

"Oh no, course not. Sorry, milord."

The clergyman tidied the papers on his desk and got up. "So you left him to it?"

"I did, milord, left 'im to his pleasures. He was a one."

"James Joy, you're a big fat liar," I shouted, but neither heard.

"My God, a fourteen-year-old."

"Yes, fourteen years old and a randy little bugger, he were."

Goodwife put his hands to his ears. "Please, Mr. Joy, curb your language."

"Sorry, Reverend."

"To seal the contract, we now both need to sign on this page." Goodwife brandished his pen before dipping the end in the inkwell and signing the document. His signature, ornate and bold, suited the man. "Now put your mark here, James, and we're done."

James Joy took the pen and had difficulty holding it. Then, with great concentration, he started to write. He spelled out the letters softly as he went. First, the nib ran out of ink, and then, after realizing he had to dip it, he dipped it too often. "May take a while to dry."

The reverend rolled a large blotter over both signatures and shook the document before returning it to the table. "All done. Your soul will be in excellent hands, James Joy."

"Thank you, sir. It's a weighty thing off of my mind."

The young man pulled the cap from his pocket and left the Printing Office with his head bowed. As the door shut behind him, a woman slid out of the shadows. She went to the window and watched the seaman walk up the path and onto the roadway.

Good riddance to him, I thought.

"Did you hear all that, my love?" Goodwife joined the woman and gave her a peck on the cheek she presented.

"I did, my husband. So I assume all is arranged for our friend the deacon to take particular care of young Mr. Joy during his passage?"

"Yes, my dear, indeed he will. The deacon is briefed. We can expect a little bonus for the mission when the ship returns in the new year. After our expenses, of course." He laughed, then started coughing.

"Control yourself, my husband."

"Sorry, my love."

No wonder Anthony couldn't find out anything about James Joy. He likely never made it to San Francisco, if this deacon carried out his instructions.

"What is our plan for the chest, in the meantime?" She kicked the side with a sturdy boot.

The reverend handed his wife a small ivory-inlaid ax. "Please do the honors, my love."

She broke off each lock with a sharp blow, opened the lid, and dipped a hand in. "Well, this will come in useful, my husband."

Wow, so the locks were *smashed off.*

"Our architect is amending the plans as we speak," said Goodwife. "That unique room, where you can indulge your little amusements, will now be a reality."

She went over, tugged her husband's arm behind his back, and put the lady ax to his throat. "I will ensure your little amusement is indulged, too."

He broke away and marched over to a shelf, dabbing a cut with an already bloodied handkerchief. He located and pulled down a stack of sturdy canvas bags, and they both started filling them with coins.

Right again, Sam.

"Don't fill them too full. We don't want to make them overheavy," she said.

"Yes, of course, my love."

"We need to move the gold to the island without delay," said Mrs. Goodwife as she tied up one of the bags with its thick cord. "We don't want that nosy bishop stumbling on any of this when he visits next week."

"You're right, as always." The reverend picked up a small envelope buried among the coins and put it into the bag, along with his handful, without appearing to notice it. "The builders will come here tonight and return to the island tomorrow. I warned them that we need to transport some special and weighty decorative pieces in tea chests. We'll need to go over there to unpack and secure the bags on the site. Some places under the floor will work perfectly." He showed his wife a familiar small sheet of paper containing a diagram.

"You always plan everything so meticulously, my husband."

He took a moment to puff out his chest and preen. "Thanks to you."

"What about the unfortunate boy in the box?" asked the reverend's wife, nodding in the direction of the small, lidless coffin.

"Yes, we'll bury him tomorrow at first light, in one eighty-four."

"Oh yes, plot one eighty-four, a piece of ground that could tell some tales." She moved over to the dead boy and lightly stroked his cheek. "Poor thing, what a life he could have had."

"Look here, my love." The reverend lifted the boy's linen shirt.

"Oh, my Lord, yes, what a monumental ... er ... life he could have enjoyed." She pulled a small bone-handled knife from somewhere in her nether garments and placed the hilt in the boy's fingers. "You may need this." She patted his hand.

"Plot one eighty-four served us well, but now we can plant a long-term resident. We'll forgo a ceremony—nobody's interested in the boy."

The reverend replaced the top in a single deft movement. "It'll be the last time we use that grave. We'll lay a stone and mark his name."

"The poor boy is going to be residing with many unsavory souls, my husband."

"He certainly is, my love. He'll find no rest in there."

Ⓐ

I awoke as Jo started getting very agitated. He made swiping actions with his hand and shouted to be left alone. I held him tight and stroked his hair. He woke up and looked at me before burying his face in my shirt.

Anthony would be appalled at the thought, but I was convinced that I'd experienced something supernatural. It was clear to me that Jo needed our help to finally rest in peace. It was almost certainly connected with the buried gold, which could be close by in what remained of the Goodwifes' villa.

"I understand, Jo," I said in a whisper.

He nodded, then headed off to bed.

Chapter Sixty-One

ANTHONY

The Big Island
Sunday, July 9, 2000

Around five in the morning, I took a short drive to where Mrs. H. had indicated the site of the Goodwife villa might be. Before returning, I checked out a parking spot hidden from the road and confirmed what was there. Con and I would share the moment of finding the treasure.

I tapped my usual knock softly on her door and cracked it open. "It's me, Con."

"Come in, Ant." She joined in the whispering. "What's the time?"

"Still early—around six thirty." I remained in the doorway. Her delicious smell permeated the room.

Patting the side of the bed, she asked me to sit. "So what's happening?"

I positioned myself a little farther away than invited and checked over the sheets for any evidence of a visit from my rival—nothing untoward.

"Jo had a weird night," I said.

"Poor boy, is he okay?"

"He woke me around two in the morning, shouting out. He appeared to be having some sort of nightmare. At one point he pleaded for his life. It sounded horrendous."

"Shit, how awful. Did he mention anything more about what happened when he disappeared?"

"No, he couldn't remember. He did recall being dragged out of the sea in a fishing net, though. Then having to defend himself in the churchyard with a small knife—another of his nightmares, most likely."

"Oh, yes . . . uh . . ." It felt like Con was going to launch into one of her ghost stories but thought better of it.

"Do you understand it?"

"Uh . . . No more than you. Have you been working on your stuff this morning?"

"My stuff, yes. I had a long conversation with Nancy last night. She—"

"Nancy?"

"Sorry, Mrs. Hale is more appropriate—our hostess."

"Oh, of course."

"Yes, she came up with the goods. She told me where she believes the Goodwife property is."

"Close by?"

"Yes, we could take a look now, if you like? Unless you would prefer a little more time to yourself?"

"Let's check it out, Ant, man. Shit, sorry, Anthony, I'll drop the 'man.'"

"Thanks."

"Let me throw on my jeans and a shirt."

"I'll leave a note for the guys. Come find me when you're set."

Ⓐ

Con joined me as I propped up a note on the nightstand next to Sam. A small black Pekingese was asleep above his head and sharing his pillow. I tiptoed over to Jo and tucked the sheet in around him. He responded with a murmur but continued to sleep. We then closed the door and made our way downstairs.

Mrs. H. shouted "good morning" as we descended. I answered in kind and told her that we would be back for breakfast.

We drove for less than ten minutes on the highway before turning off onto a dirt track for a quarter mile. After parking, I led Con to a scrubby patch of land where the remnants of a couple of walls were still visible, but little else. "Mrs. H. also mentioned that Goodwife swindled a local bigwig out of the site. Later, when the guy realized, he put a curse on the reverend and his whole family."

"None of that surprises me." Con sounded like she'd done some research of her own.

"So let's see if we can find"—I pushed through a gap in the bushes before returning, now from behind, which gave her a fright. "I need to grab something from the car."

"Wow, so you brought that along with you?"

"No, this is a new one—an upgrade on the old Garrett." I gave her a demonstration.

"Please keep an eye out while I check the ground, would you?" Moments later, an incessant beeping and flashing of lights heralded something exciting, as I moved the apparatus over an unremarkable piece of scrubland. "Jackpot, Con. The meter is showing a superstrong signal." I showed her the little dial pointer trying to move beyond its restraining pin.

"Shit, Ant." She put her arms around me. "You've only gone and found it."

I didn't want her to release me. I'd kept my promise—here was the treasure.

She pulled out her RDC-1. "I'll take some photos."

"We should go and tell the others, but let's play things down. Say we may have found something, but with an emphasis on the 'may.'"

"Shouldn't we dig it up now?"

"We'll come back tonight equipped with tools. It will take time to get it all out. Also, we'll need to find out if anybody has a claim to it. There are procedures to follow." I didn't want to celebrate right now, but my financial problems could soon be well and truly over.

Chapter Sixty-Two

CONNIE

Walking around their bed failed to raise the still-sleeping Sam and Jo, so I clomped over to the window and pulled back the curtains.

Sam stirred to life. "Hey, Con." He stretched and revealed some sexy midriff.

I stared.

He winked. "Mrs. Thing's Spam thing knocked me out. Weird dreams or what? You starred in one of them, Con." He winked again.

The black Pekingese lifted its head and blinked.

"Who's your friend, Sam?" The little dog avoided my petting attempts, preferring to rub its pretty little face against Sam's bare arm. A bitch, no doubt.

"The fur ball appeared in the night." He tickled her chin and ears. She went into ecstasy. A wave of jealousy rose inside me.

A brighter-eyed, fuller-cheeked Jo sat up and beamed.

"Hi, Jo, how are you today?" I asked, pleased to be distracted from my fixation.

"Yes, my lady, my bunks . . . bestest ever."

An Adidas sneaker appeared around the door as Anthony pushed his way in. "Coffee, anyone? Mrs. Hale sends her regards and asks if you would like her specially cooked breakfast?"

Sam tilted his head to one side. "Let me guess. *Spam?*"

"Yes, deep-fried in a light tempura batter, with eggs sunny-side up." Anthony tried to pet the Pekingese. It first shied away, then tried to bite his hand.

"I love the smell of Spam in the morning." Sam put two fingers in his open mouth. "Rolls and toast for me, thanks."

"So, no Spam, thank you, Sam." Anthony chuckled, and the dog yipped.

"What would you like, Jo?" I handed him a roll from the basket on Anthony's tray.

"Mmm, Spam, thank you, ma'am." He pushed half the roll into his small mouth after his word splurge.

"I'll let her know." Anthony left us and went downstairs. He returned a few minutes later with a tray of Spam.

Sam brushed a load of crumbs from his sheets and started nibbling on Jo's Spam. "Yeah, this is disgusting."

"Mine, no share." Jo lashed out with his fork.

Sam backed off. "So what's our plan for today, guys?"

"Well, Con and I went out earlier. We're almost sure . . ." Anthony paused, as he liked to do. "We found the Reverend Goodwife's building lot."

"You found his house?" Sam started out of bed without thinking, exposing his lower half.

Jo laughed and pointed at his predicament. "We got us bait for fishin'."

Thankfully, Sam missed Jo's wagging of his pinkie. Sam cuffed Jo on the back of the head, on his way to grabbing his jeans. As he slipped them on, he rewarded us with an eyeful of cute butt. Likely I was the only connoisseur, although I caught the dog sneaking a peek.

"Well, no," Anthony said, unfazed by Sam's peep show. "He never completed it, and he didn't own the land in the first place."

"A bit of a devious one, that Goodwife, huh?" Sam sniffed a T-shirt he found on the floor and pulled a face. "Ant, man, could I . . . ?" He waved the tee. "I need to do a wash."

"Yes, please help yourself. To cut to the chase, we have to explore this piece of land a little further. After dark would be best."

"Wow, fuck, we're rich. Is that what you're saying? All we need to do is to dig it up?"

Anthony used both his hands to mime a reduced volume.

As I was about to high-five Sam, Mrs. H.'s head appeared around the door. "You sound in high spirits today, my loves. Can I come in and collect your dirty dishes?"

"Oh yes, please, come in." Anthony helped her pick up the plates and cups.

"Me, Spam bestest, thank you, ma'am." Jo stood on his bed and made a small bow.

"Glad you enjoyed it, young sir." Mrs. H. performed a small curtsy and required Anthony's help to get to her feet.

Jo nodded and tried hard to say something else, but he gave up as Mrs. Hale's attention wandered away from him.

"So, Mrs. Hale, are you from England by any chance?" I asked.

"Yes, I lived in Cornwall before moving up to London. To near where this young fellow comes from, south of the river." She went over to Jo and ruffled his hair.

They could be mother and son, or grandmother and grandson, more like. Jo smiled and shrugged before going back to enjoying having his head stroked. My Simon came to mind.

"Yes, we talked in the night," said Mrs. H. "He came to visit me. Poor dear had nightmares. He kept calling me mum, mum this and mum that. He told me his boat sank and all sorts of other gobblygook. Him and a pal survived and sumert happened. Sounded terrible grue-some. I brought him back in here and put him to bed. Poor lamb can't remember any of it."

Jo smiled and bowed again. "Thanking you, Mum."

"Oh, that's where she is." The little dog lifted her head. "She must have slipped in here in the night. I hope she's been no trouble. I never seen her take to a guest before." Mrs. H. patted her knees. "Come on, Jess, your breakfast's downstairs."

"Away you go, Jess." Sam, with a look of horror on his face, shoved the dog off the bed. "Damn bit—"

Mrs. Hale loitered. She had an inkling we shared a secret and was the sort who liked to know others' secrets.

Five minutes later, the front door banged. We saw her from the window walking down to the road with a shopping bag under her arm. Likely Spam stocks had run low.

"Yes, we may have found the resting place for the gold," said Anthony. "I propose we visit the plot this evening and dig a test hole to confirm."

"Wow, Jo, we is rich." Sam apparently couldn't resist mocking him a little after all the attention he'd been getting.

Jo appeared worried, but after a few seconds started whooping it up, too. "We is rich."

"We need to keep this quiet. The landowner would have a strong claim." The wise old Ant had his hand, arm, and elbow in his thoughtful pose.

"Shh." Jo put a finger to his lips.

"So, if no one else knows . . . we can dig it up and not say anything."

"You think?" said Anthony in a loud whisper.

Sam pushed his chin out. "Yeah, why the hell not?"

"Let's check what we have first." I glanced around the group.

"Share fair, share fair." Jo was jumping on the bed again as he chanted.

"Yeah, we'll share the gold between us. We're millionaires, Jo." Sam moved out of Jo's view and switched to a whisper. "Not sure all should be in on this." He pointed sideways toward Jo.

"All will be fair," said Anthony, clenching both fists.

"Hey, no, Ant, man, yet to be decided."

Anthony broke the growing argument. "Let's go to Hilo on the other side of the island and buy some digging tools."

I smiled at my guys. "God, yes, shovels. We need picks and shovels."

We might all be extremely rich soon. I would need to reassess my expanded options very carefully. Sam's petulance and lack of maturity might prove difficult to stomach longer term. My new wealth could give me the independence I had never dreamed possible. I allowed myself a moment to bask in a new sense of freedom and possibilities.

Chapter Sixty-Three

ANTHONY

Lunching at Harrington's on Reeds Pond in Hilo, we kept to the non-Spam dishes, except for Jo, who still couldn't get enough. The trunk of our rental contained two shovels, a pick, gloves, and a couple of groundsheets. Not needing to rush back, I drove up the coast along to Pepe'ekeo for a scenic detour that took us into an area covered in tropical palms and waterfalls. My imminent wealth would give me so many possibilities. I would do a deal with Jason for the return of my property and then be free—freer than I had ever been. Maybe Con and I could move to Hawaii? When Jo hugged me, for a moment, I saw myself reflected in a shop window with a young boy at my side—a son. There was someone else there, too—surely it was Con.

We arrived back at the B and B around four. Mrs. H. appeared in the doorway as we walked from the car. The bright sunshine highlighted the fine lines on her face.

She held up an invisible cup between her fingers. "Cuppa tea, my loves?"

Sam and I both turned her down flat.

"Ooh, yes, Mum," said Jo.

"Me, too, please, Mrs. Hale," Con said, almost as enthusiastically.

"My cousin sends me a parcel of Yorkshire Tea every six months." She headed off to her kitchen.

After we settled ourselves in the parlor, she brought in a tray with the tea and a slice of carrot cake for each of us. Jo beamed every time he lifted the sugary drink to his mouth. He smiled at Mrs. H., and she nodded encouragement.

"All right, my dears." One of her wide grins took over her face. "I'll do something extra special for your suppers tonight. But now, my surfaces need attention." She mimed some vigorous scrubbing.

"Spam again?" Sam said, under his breath.

"Yes, it will feature. That is why we lives so long on these islands. Spam is our secret elixir."

"We'll look forward to that." I detected a hint of pungent cologne in the air—the cologne worn by Gregor. "Excuse me for asking, but did you have visitors while we were out?"

"Oh, yes," said Mrs. H. "An interested party came asking for accommodations. A man from somewhere foreign. He got nosy when I told him there was no vacancy. And I saw a middle-aged woman and a slippery-looking young man in a car on the lane."

"So you didn't mention anything about us?"

"Confidentiality, that is my watchword. I suggested they try Mrs. Kahale in the next town over."

"We appreciate that," I said. Chuck Wilson had texted me earlier to say the group had been spotted at the airport about to board a plane to the island. Some careful planning would be needed.

Mrs. H ruffled Jo's hair as she left the room.

"Fuck, they're here, and have apparently abandoned my sis."

His reaction to Jo's disappearing, and now what sounded like a genuine concern for Liza's plight, showed me that the guy had a caring side. I remembered the drug bust at a place on Amsterdam Avenue. Sam had insisted his infatuated sister had handed him the amphetamines she'd been holding for Jason when the cops searched them. He said nothing to the cops, even when his court appearance got splashed all over the newspapers and Columbia expelled him. The episode had soured Sam's relationship with his father, enabling Jason to inveigle his way further into the twins' lives. I was beginning to think the way he treated Con after that pool party was out of character.

Sam went to check the door in case Mrs. H. had strayed from her kitchen. "Yeah, so, do you think they know the treasure location?"

"They may be following us. We'll need to create a diversion this evening. Otherwise, we'll end up leading them straight to the gold."

"Fuck, yeah, a diversion." Sam started pacing around. "We should . . . hmm." He banged his palm on his forehead as if trying to free a thought. "Ant, dude, what's our plan?"

"Leave it to me. I'll brief you later."

Chapter Sixty-Four

CONNIE

Anthony popped out to talk to Mrs. Hale, and the rest of us went upstairs for a break. Sam seemed keen to join me in my room. In spite of a promise I had made to myself not to entertain another quickie fumble, I was soon on the bed with him on top of me. He finished in under five minutes and left me without a word. I ogled his bare butt and lithe, slim hips shimmying through the partly opened Jack-and-Jill door. *Shit, why did I let him do that?*

I hadn't physically enjoyed any of the sex with him, but he had at least been successful this time. My constant need to confirm my desirability was destroying me. These thoughts had haunted me over the past few years. My life needed to change now. Samuel Weston and others like him would never take advantage of me again—my flip-flopping was over. With my share of the treasure, I would forget ideas of living at the Dakota apartment and finally be free to do my own thing.

Ⓐ

Mrs. H.'s supper was as surprising as she had promised. Jo ate every morsel of his and most of mine. Sam, as usual, moaned on and on as he shoveled in his plateful.

We said goodbye to Mrs. H. that evening and climbed into the Honda Anthony had rented for us on this island.

Anthony started the engine. "Okay, guys, I didn't want to mention anything in front of Mrs. H., but yes, I've seen Gregor and company. Earlier, Mrs. H. told me she forgot to pick up the Spam, so I offered to go collect it from the store."

Sam mimed two fingers going down his throat again. "Hey, dude, no more Spam stories, please. Get to the point, Ant, man."

"Sam, take it easy," I said.

"You didn't say that when we—"

"I wish," I said, under my breath.

Anthony stared into the distance.

Sam theatrically cocked an ear. "What's that, Con?"

"Nothing."

Anthony spoke in a hushed voice. "A car was following me, so I took them for a ten-mile diversion and down an almost vertical hill to a bay on a dirt road. When they had difficulty getting up the slope, I managed to lose them and took the opportunity to return to the location to drop off our tools for later. They're wrapped in the ground-sheets and tucked out of sight in the undergrowth."

"Wow, you've been a busy . . . Ant." I couldn't resist it.

He smiled and continued on. "I made myself visible to them again outside the shop and got Mrs. H.'s order. I had to make two trips to the car to load up her supply of . . . you know what."

"So they never saw through your diversion?"

"Likely disappointed I was only carrying Spam."

"I can only imagine." Sam's face lit up with a cheeky grin.

"Mmm. Spam." Jo was in a reverie.

"So, we're on our way to the church hall for a showing of Barbra Streisand's huge hit. Anyone want to guess?" Anthony was up to his tricks again.

I couldn't think of one, and Sam and Jo were elsewhere in their thoughts. "We give up."

"*Hello, Dolly.*"

"Root canal surgery would be preferable."

"That's an old joke, Sam," I said.

He scowled. He was such a moody boy.

A pumped Anthony continued the briefing. "Ten minutes in, I'll leave and go to the restroom. Its side window opens to the yard at the back."

"So you cased the hall, too," I said. "Excellent work."

"When I got the tickets."

"Sam, a couple of minutes after I leave, you do the same. Check out the restroom before the movie—you'll understand what I mean about the window. We'll meet outside and walk across the field to the site. It's only five minutes away. It will be dark, so this could be useful." He passed Sam a pocket-size black Maglite, then he paused, on alert. "Someone is following us."

"We need to . . . uh . . . What's your plan, Ant?"

"Don't worry, I prepared for this eventuality. Our reserved seats are in a sold-out area and are exactly where we need to be for our early exit."

We parked on the road under a dim streetlight and made our way to the hall. Ms. Streisand was quite a draw.

This was some sort of community meeting place, and Sundays were reserved for movies. According to a chatty woman I met in the ladies' room, this was the third Streisand film in as many weeks. "I have my ticket for *Yentl* next week," she said. "Get yours quick, my dear; they reckon it'll be a sellout."

Two of our seats were occupied by an elderly gay couple. They were very apologetic when Anthony pointed out the seat numbers on their tickets. The 1950s metal chairs were all on the same level and fastened together with simple clips.

As the lights went down, Rosa entered alone. She headed toward the rear of the hall to where the only free seats remained, scanning the rows as she went. The type of seating and Rosa's distance away would mean she wouldn't be able to see the guys leaving.

As Barbra belted out "Just Leave Everything to Me," Anthony got up and left through the side door. As the number came to a close, Sam did the same. In doing so, his shapely butt lightly brushed against me. My new determination was being tested—I held firm.

While the movie played, the guys planned to confirm the gold's existence and prepare the ground for later. The intermission, ninety minutes in, surprised me. Where the hell were they? As the lights went up, Rosa stood, glanced over, and must have clocked that the guys weren't there. She dashed out the door and almost ran straight into Anthony and Sam. They arrived back with three Longboard beers and a rocky road ice cream for Jo. A relieved Rosa returned to her seat.

"Shit, perfect timing, Ant," I said.

Jo was straight on the ice cream.

"I spotted the intermission sign on the way out, so we adjusted accordingly."

Anthony dropped something the size of a half dollar into my palm. I looked down at a gold piece with an eagle on it. Shit, the actual treasure there in my hand. I wanted to high-five the team, but that would have to wait. The shiny coin was surprisingly heavy. "Check this out, Jo."

"Mine, my share." He handed me his rocky road and grabbed the coin. He put it in his mouth and refused to release it. Anthony dropped another into my palm.

"Jesus, so what's the score?" I couldn't stop moving the coin around in my hand. Dan's silver dollar came to mind.

"Thick leather satchels, still intact. Quite close to the surface." Sam, excited, started joshing with Jo.

"We didn't want to disturb the ground too much, so we grabbed a few samples and tidied up."

Rosa wandered along the far aisle. What was she up to? We dialed down our excitement and kept the coins out of sight. She returned to her seat as the lights dimmed.

Even Barbra's formidable talent couldn't hold my attention over the following hour. My fingers ran around the edge and over the faces of the coin during the entire second half. Wow, we had the treasure. How much would my share be? A million? More? Just as Anthony promised. Reliable old Ant. Rich, reliable, and eligible old Ant.

As soon as the titles began to roll, we dashed out. Poor Rosa couldn't keep up, and Gregor's car was moving when she jumped in. They blatantly followed us. We arrived at the house at 12:30 a.m. and went in without looking back.

Anthony glanced through the parlor window from the side of the curtain. "They're lingering outside. Let's lie low for a while and discuss how we're going to tackle the treasure in the morning. We'll have to lodge our claim before we do anything else."

"Great idea, Ant dude."

Hmm, I was sure Sam would want to go dig it up before daybreak. I retired to bed to dream about our good fortune and my plans for an independent future. From what Anthony had just told us about his latest estimate, we might get upward of two million each. What the hell, I was now "buy an apartment in Manhattan" rich. I would make sure that Mom was okay, but I had a feeling she had already mapped out her own future—with George at the Dakota.

Chapter Sixty-Five

ANTHONY

Monday, July 10, 2000

Sam and Jo had somehow disappeared in the night without me noticing. It was already eight in the morning when I knocked on Con's door.

Bleary-eyed, she opened the door a crack, then fully when she saw
it was me.

"Con, they're gone."

"Both of them? Shit, what the hell, Anthony, where are they?" She
stared at me for a second. "Have they gone to dig up the gold? They'll
mess everything up."

A noise came from the other room.

"It must be them." I didn't move.

She rushed to investigate, and I followed. There was a peculiar
metallic smell.

Jo flung his arms around Con in a frantic embrace. His clothes
were spattered with blood.

"Shit, what happened? Are you okay?" Con checked him over but found no wounds. "Where's this blood from, Jo?"

An anguished pleading gripped his face. "Please, my lady." He proffered a mildewed and bloodstained piece of paper. "Read for me, Mum."

Con kept on questioning him, but he refused to answer her and kept pointing at his letter. She wrapped her arm around him. He shut his eyes as Con read to him. "'My darling boy, we got your news about the terrible wrecking. Thanks to the Lord you was saved, my love. Your pa framed the newspaper you sent us, and he's nailed it up on the wall in the snug for you for when you gets back. We is missing you so much here at the Ship. Jack and your dearest pa sends bestest. Steers your course home to us soonest, my darling. Your always-loving Mum.'"

"Ah, thanks, Mum." Jo held Con tighter, and it looked like she was starting to drift off.

A loud banging on the front door broke the moment. We left Jo and stood at the top of the stairs as a sleepy Mrs. H. emerged from her room and headed down. The "butterflies of Hawaii" on her bathrobe fluttered as she descended. She glimpsed herself in the hallway mirror and did some rapid hair straightening as she passed. The opened door revealed two cops with hands ready on their sidearms. Mrs. H. took a step back but then ushered them in.

"Anthony, what the hell is happening?" Con was trying to catch my eye. "Where's Sam? Why is Jo covered in blood?"

Ignoring her, I ran halfway down the stairs and called them in. "He's upstairs."

Mrs. H. followed us up.

Con entered the room first. "Where's he gone?"

"Are you saying Samuel Weston was in here but has fled, ma'am?" asked one of the cops.

"No, we aren't sure where Sam is," Con said. "We think he may be injured. Our friend Jo came back covered in blood and—"

"Where is this man . . . Jo?" The cop's pen hovered above a notebook.

"He's more of a boy, fourteen years old. You can see the blood and his outline on the bed." Con pointed at the sheets and at her top.

"We have a warrant for the arrest of Samuel Weston."

"Why? What did he do?"

The cop appeared nonplussed by Con's line of questioning or being questioned at all. "He's wanted in connection with passing counterfeit currency. The Honolulu Police Department wants to interview him."

"No way. He's not a counterfeiter." Con looked to me for support. "Anthony, don't just stand there. Tell them, please. Now."

"What? No, can't be." For Pete's sake, he must've had some of Dan's old twenties. Things were unraveling everywhere.

A thoughtful Mrs. H. went downstairs and returned with a twenty-dollar bill. She said Sam had given it to her for some cigarettes.

The officer scrutinized the note. "Yeah, that's one of 'em. The forgeries are excellent, but because they're the old 1963 series design, we can easily spot them now. 'In God We Trust' is missing on the reverse. They think the forger left this out on purpose, as the bills are perfect otherwise."

My God, trust me to have made such a fundamental mistake. I had been focusing on the serial numbers and I ended up using the wrong reverse plate. "We can take you to where he might be." I needed to get them off this subject.

"We should arrange an ambulance, too," Con said. She was shaking.

The officer radioed in an update and, at the same time, arranged for the ambulance to meet us at the treasure site.

The cops would soon be all over the treasure, and it was me who had invited them. Our find was in serious jeopardy. How would I settle my debts? It was all such a mess. Con would never forgive me now.

Chapter Sixty-Six

CONNIE

We followed the police down to the treasure site. The ambulance arrived as we parked.

The long-hidden patch of dirt where Anthony and I had celebrated finding the gold only the day before was now all churned up and spoiled. A small pistol lay in among a few coins.

Coins that had once promised so many possibilities.

Whose blood was spattered all over them?

"Where's Sam?"

"Perhaps he's on the run with Jo," said Anthony.

What the hell. Why would he say that in front of the cops? And where was Jo?

A Toyota parked a little way along the road looked suspicious. "That white car? Has anybody checked it out yet?" Why was I doing the detecting? These cops appeared to be half asleep.

One did pick up on my suggestion, and through my fingers, I watched as he opened up the vehicle. To my relief, it was empty. One of the cops radioed in the license plate and received a reply saying the vehicle had been stolen the night before. I immediately thought of Jason.

We told the police everything we knew, and they informed us the gold would be secured for the landowner—our claim, most probably nonexistent. I stared at Anthony, but he wouldn't look at me. My amazing dream of an independent life gone—my Manhattan apartment in rubble. A wave of nausea surged up as Ma pushed her way into my head: *Your place is with your mother, Connie. We can look after each other.*

Surely we could salvage something? The mystery of Sam's disappearance added another major worry. My infatuation had waned, but I still felt connected to the guy.

Ⓐ

We returned to Mrs. H.'s, where she welcomed us with tea and the promise of Spam schnitzel for supper.

"What an awful unpleasantness," she said.

"Jo was likely involved in something bad," said Anthony.

What the hell. I frowned and shook my head.

"Ooh, no." Mrs. H. fiddled with the fraying hem of her housecoat. "I can't believe that, not that little lad, not a lad from my street, not young John."

"Jo?" An initial look of surprise faded, and Anthony nodded.

"Jo, short for John in this case," said Mrs. H. "He told me there being two Johns on his ship, they named him Jo, as he were the youngest. John Stephens be his full name, brought up in the Ship Inn at the end of my street in Southwark."

For some reason, none of this surprised me. "Do you know where he is now?" I asked.

"No, he told me he would be leaving once he got his letter read," Mrs. H. said.

"Well, I did that this morning." Why would he not say goodbye? Did we mean nothing to him?

Someone started banging on the front door. Mrs. H. went out to investigate.

Anthony got up and followed her. After a couple of minutes, I headed to the door, too, but met Mrs. H. in the hallway.

"What happened to Anthony?"

"He's gone off with a strange-looking woman."

"Did this woman say anything?"

"Yes, she said, 'If you vant to see your fraynd again, you come along viv me.'"

So he had gone off with Rosa, by the sound of it, no doubt to rescue Sam—a recurring theme. Why didn't he tell me? What was the matter with Anthony today? My team was who knows where, while I sat sipping tea with a seventy-year-old woman.

My helplessness depressed the hell out of me. It was like one of those never-ending Sunday afternoons in our basement in London. Shit, with my plans crumbling to dust, those afternoons looked set to return. I needed to shake this off. With money or not, I would take control of my life. There would be no more Bermondsey Sundays to endure.

"I'll make us a cuppa, my love. You can tell me all about it. Maybe, I can tell you sumert too?"

Ⓐ

We drank our tea, and Mrs. H. told me about a young woman and her daughter who had stayed at the B and B earlier in the year.

"Yes, she was very specific about the piece of land she wanted. The place everybody trampled on today. The land with them coins buried in it."

"So it was for sale?"

"Oh, yes, been on the market for a while. It was owned by one of them religious cults or some such that went broke. The site had no building permit, and they wanted rid—went for a song."

"Do you recall the woman's name?"

"Oh, yes, her name was Judy. Her surname is here, somewhere." She paged through the little book she kept in the embroidered front pocket of her chambray housecoat.

"Let me guess—Judy Robinson."

Mrs. H. shook her head.

"No, of course not, she would use Gibson, Judy Gibson?"

Mrs. H. nodded. "She will be a rich woman if she's the owner of the land now."

"Shit. Oh, please excuse my language, Mrs. Hale."

"Oh, yes, entirely called for in these circumstances."

"I'm phoning her, what's the time in the New York?"

"Must be around 10:00 p.m. You can call her from here." She passed me the telephone from the side table.

"You're a star, Mrs. H."

"Thank you, my dear."

I dialed. After a couple of rings, Judy picked up.

"Hello."

"Judy? It's Connie."

"Connie, hi, how are you?"

"Anthony, Sam, and I are in Hawaii. We're staying with Mrs. Hale. You remember her?"

"Wow, you've been busy. Send Nancy my love, would you?"

"Yes, she sends hers. Put my mind at rest, do you own the land?"

"Ah, yes, I completed the purchase soon after we met up. The Hawaii police called me earlier today, and I'm planning a trip next month to sort everything out."

"Oh. Wonderful news, Judy." I tried my best to sound pleased for her, but my true feelings leaked into my tone.

What the hell, she had bagged the damn treasure before I had even arrived in the state.

"So you worked out the clues from the envelope? Did Maureen at the church tell you about the Goodwifes' villa?" Judy sounded excited. So, Maureen *did* know more than she had told us. "I couldn't say anything to you before, because of the land—"

"Mrs. Hale mentioned that you and Wendy were here." I nodded to Mrs. H, who pretended only to be interested in her magazine.

"We had a lovely time. Spam for supper, is it, my love?" Judy laughed.

"Yes, of course." I glanced in Mrs. H.'s direction.

She nodded and smiled.

"So you checked out the property before you bought it?"

"Oh yes," said Dan's newly minted, multimillionaire stamp buddy.

"Well done, Judy. The cops took the coins into their safekeeping." I almost said *our coins*. What the hell, why weren't they?

"Good to know. Remember me to Anthony, would you?"

"Yes, will do. Bye."

Clever, Judy. What plans did she have for all her wealth? Was Anthony already on her list?

I took a deep breath. "So, wonderful news, Mrs. Hale. She owns the land."

Mrs. H. put down her magazine. "I'm pleased it worked out for her. Such a lovely woman, and her daughter is a little sweetheart. She's a stamp collector, you know. I gave her a bunch of old local ones I found under the lining of a drawer. Looked like nothing, just drab blue, with numbers on them. The little love picked them up with her stamp tweezers like they was worth millions."

Chapter Sixty-Seven

ANTHONY

Rosa, clearly not comfortable in the driver's seat, did some frantic looking around before we finally moved off.

"Please, Mr. Anthony, I need you to explain to Gregor. He is not hearing from me."

"Is Sam okay?"

"The boy is annoying. Gregor is worse because of the boy."

Rosa, a slow but careful driver, navigated the side roads without trouble. We arrived at a house similar to Mrs. H.'s after fifteen minutes.

"Here is the key to the front door," said Rosa. "The woman, uh . . . Mrs. Kahale is locked in the basement."

I made a mental note to release Mrs. K. before leaving. The place was almost a replica of our accommodation, with the same Spam-related aroma. "Where's Sam?"

"Follow me, please, Mr. Anthony. Boy is upstairs taped to a chair."

I followed Rosa up a steep flight of stairs, where family photographs adorned the walls. Likely taken in the 1970s, their color tones already faded to a tinted black and white.

"In here." She pointed into the doorway of a room that had its curtains drawn.

Sam was seated in what appeared to be a comfortable armchair, but with his arms and legs duct taped. It seemed like a whole roll of the stuff had been used.

He glanced around. "Hey, Ant. Great to see you, man."

"Are you okay?"

"Yeah, just a little tied up."

"Ha-ha, yes. Where's Gregor?"

"He's been a total nut job. He went on about the gold. When I told him he had left it all behind at the site, he started ranting. He sent Rosa back to deal with it, but what could she do? That's probably why she came and got you."

Gregor appeared in the doorway. "Anthony, good of you to join us. Rosa says you have intelligence on my gold. Coins that are rightfully mine, because their position was indicated on the map inside my cover. The cover that had been kept from me for so many years."

"Yes, highly frustrating for you, sir." I wanted to tell him that his map didn't show the treasure location, and the only reason he had found the coins was because he had followed me. I'd promised Con we would find the treasure, and we did. She likely wouldn't forgive me for losing it and, indeed, for the way I behaved this morning. There was so much I should have told her.

"Anthony, you don't know how angry I am." Gregor circled Sam, but his eyes remained on me. Blood was dripping from his sleeve onto the carpet. "Bring my gold to me now."

"It's in the hands of the Hawaii County Police Department and secured for the owner of the land, who is now aware of its existence." Something the cops had let slip, though they hadn't mentioned a name. I had an idea, though. Regardless of my unbearable disappointment and exasperation at this puffed-up buffoon, I needed to stay calm. I had to move Gregor out of the picture without any further problems.

"No, those coins are mine. Sort this out, or I shoot the boy." He pulled out his Smith & Wesson and waved it in Sam's face.

Sam's eyes followed the gun's gyrations. "Uh . . . Ant, please."

"The boy is annoying me. I will shoot him anyway."

I took a deep breath. "Sir, please, think what you've achieved. The return of your multimillion-dollar cover is a triumph. Also, that wound on your arm needs to be looked at."

Gregor put the gun to Sam's temple.

Sam closed his eyes. "Uh . . . Ant."

"Gregor, listen to me, the last thing you need now is to be involved in a battle for ownership of an unknown amount of gold. Also, you shot a US citizen this morning. He might be lying dead as we speak. You may well end up in jail for the rest of your life."

"Listen to Mr. Anthony," said Rosa.

"Yes, I need to leave this damn country. Please arrange this for me."

"You must release Sam now."

"Arrange things for me." Gregor pushed the pistol back into his shoulder holster. There was blood oozing through his shirt. He pointed at his injury. "Get this taken care of for me, too."

Chuck Wilson, as usual, asked few questions and got on with what I requested. He told me it would be expensive. Another line of credit would be necessary. I mentioned an amount to Rosa, but she just shook her head. I didn't want to get into an argument that might hinder their departure and send Gregor into another murderous rage. The more I helped everyone, the more debt I was accumulating.

Who would help me?

Within thirty minutes, Chuck got back to me to say an executive jet was on its way from Honolulu with a flight plan logged for Tahiti. All the documentation was in place, and *someone* would attend to Gregor's wound en route. There was currently no warrant out for Gregor or Rosa, so they could use their passports. I handed Rosa a note containing a breakdown of the costs and my bank details. She promised to speak with Gregor when they got home.

While they prepared for their departure, I headed down to the basement to placate Mrs. Kahale. I offered her compensation for the damage done upstairs, but the amazing woman wouldn't hear of it. She regaled me with her exploits with Mrs. H. when they were younger and new to the island. She agreed not to call the cops after I promised to tell Nancy all about the excitement she'd experienced. The delightful woman could've been Mrs. H.'s twin.

Gregor couldn't resist one last wave of his massive gun as I released Sam from his tape.

The Eastern Europeans needed chauffeuring to the airstrip. In the sedan, I took the wheel. Gregor sat in the front with me, with Sam and Rosa in the rear.

While I escorted them onto the plane, Sam hunkered down in the car. He perked up immediately on our drive back to Mrs. H.'s.

"Thanks, Ant. I owe you, man. That's twice you saved my life."

"You could repay me by not mentioning to Con what you saw earlier today."

"No problem, man. She probably wouldn't believe me. I'm not sure she likes me anymore. I'm hungry."

"For Spam?"

"Yeah, I've got a taste for the stuff now."

I'd lost us the treasure. My massive debt might necessitate me having to do all sorts of dubious work for Chuck as well as for Winston. Those credit card balances would need stabilizing—bankruptcy was imminent. Did I stand any chance at all with Con? No, of course not.

Chapter Sixty-Eight

CONNIE

While I was clearing away the tea things, young Jo popped into my mind. Something made me head to the front door and open it. There he was—fresh looking and without a trace of blood on his clothes. He reached for my hand.

His mouth opened and closed a couple of times as he got his words ready. "We was stopped this morning, my lady. I still need to show you sumert, before I can rest." He came close and put his arms around me. I held him like a mother would a precious son, and a familiar deep calmness took me over.

A dense swirling mist began to lift, and I focused on the scene in front of me. The hedge where we first discovered the gold was at my side. Although I accepted that our fortune was now gone, the treasure site started me off thinking about what we had lost.

Through the breaking dawn, I could make out Sam and Jo digging. Jo was presumably showing me what had happened earlier—I was immediately gripped. It took both of them to heave out a bag. Once the bag was out of the ground, Jo began to undo the top. The laces crumbled away as he pushed his eager fingers inside. He pulled out an envelope, which he kissed and then stuffed somewhere in the front of his pants. Sam smiled at him as they each dug out coins from the satchel. They laughed, hugged, and began dancing around the bag.

"We is rich." Jo paused and caught Sam in an intense stare. "We share?"

"Yeah, we share. You're my partner, little dude," said Sam.

Although they couldn't see me, I still found myself whooping and jigging with them and wishing the moment would never end. Jo suddenly grabbed hold of Sam and held him in a tight embrace. Sam momentarily appeared to go into a trance before shouting: *"Spam!"*

There was a screech of brakes followed by a car door slamming. Someone I couldn't at first make out stomped toward us.

"You're doing my job for me, thanks, guys."

"Go fuck right off, man," said Sam.

"Ours, not yours." Jo snarled and held his coins tighter.

Jason came forward and hit Jo across the back of the head. The force made him drop to his knees. He still managed to hold his gold, though. Sam stepped between them.

"You're a fucking bully." Sam lifted Jo to his feet and sheltered him behind his body. "Leave the little guy alone."

"Yeah, Sam. What the hell. Stop that bastard." I needed to shout encouragement regardless of whether they could hear.

Jo released his coins and checked on his envelope.

"You boys can help me move the bags to my car." Jason nodded toward the white Toyota. "I'll reverse it down."

"Fuck you."

"You picked the wrong side. Now, start piling up the gold here." Jason tapped his foot.

What did he mean by "wrong side"?

"Where are your Euro buddies today? And where's my sister?"

"Liza took the rap in Honolulu for a spot of grave robbing. They asked her to stay on for a while. Gregor and his woman are sleeping in late this morning. Some of your daddy's medications came in handy." He began laughing and found it hard to stop.

Sam's fists were tightly clenched. "You fucking . . . fuck."

"Ah, so you've finally decided to join us." Jason started talking to someone a short distance away.

"Well, well, what's going on here?" asked the man from the shadows.

"Ant, dude, you're just in time. Jacob, or should I say, Jason, is trying to take our gold."

My God, yes. Good old Ant to the rescue. How come he hadn't mentioned this? Was this true? *Is this what happened, Jo?* I tried to ask.

"Take our gold, eh? Isn't that what you were doing?"

"Hey, no, man. We're checking on the coins and having a look."

"We is . . ."

"I bet you is, Jo," said Anthony, but not in his usual pleasant tone. He sounded more like Jason. "The thing is, Jo, we're now going to play a different game. You can still help us, though. Do as Jason tells you, and no one will get hurt."

Shit. *What the hell, Anthony?* I couldn't believe it. Was he trying to spin Jason a line? Was he playing for the other side now? Or had he always been? Anthony often seemed to know more than he was letting on. He was a master at keeping things hidden. All that business with my mother.

But no, he was a good man, my protector. There had to be an explanation, for sure.

Jason pulled a small pistol from a shoulder holster and pointed it at Sam.

Jo took out his bone-handled knife from his shoe and ran toward Jason, yelling *"Lobcock!"*

Anthony grabbed Jo's hand and made him drop his knife. "Sorry, Jo, but I can't let you." Anthony kicked the weapon away.

The sound of screeching brakes jolted our attention over to a black sedan. A ferocious Gregor got out.

Gregor started an elephant-like charge toward Jason. "So you try to drug us, yes? You tried, but you fail. We are too smart for you, young man. We should have dumped you with your tart in Honolulu."

Sam's mouth opened and hesitated before shutting again.

Jason turned his aim from Sam and waved the pistol in Gregor's direction. "Don't come any closer! Stay right where you are."

Anthony took the opportunity to slip away. One minute he held Jo, the next Jo stood alone. What the hell was he up to?

Gregor moved forward. "You drop that puny peashooter, and I won't kill you." He pulled out a Smith & Wesson Magnum from under his jacket.

"No, you drop your . . ." Jason glanced at his own pistol and back at the massive gun pointing at him. He fired.

The bullet hit Gregor in his upper arm, but he appeared not to notice.

Without hesitating, Gregor sent a round straight into Jason's left side. He staggered and fell on Jo.

Sam rushed over, pushed him off, and returned Jo to his feet. "Hey, little dude, go find Con."

Jo picked up his knife and looked back with a worried expression, but Sam motioned with his hand to go.

Sam put his arms up and walked toward Gregor. "I don't have a weapon." He glanced at Jason as he passed him.

Gregor opened the trunk of the sedan and gestured with his Magnum for Sam to climb in. Sam obeyed without protesting. The car then sped off, leaving Jason on the ground.

Jo turned toward me and lifted his palm and waved. He put his knife back in his shoe and headed off in the direction of Mrs. Hale's as the scene faded.

Ⓐ

Mrs. H. was fanning me with a copy of the *Hawaii Tribune-Herald* when I awoke in her chair.

"You had a turn, my dear. You was babbling about young Jo." She handed me a cup of strong tea. "This'll help."

"Thank you. Yes, what happened to Jo?"

"I've not seen him. As I said, I think he's left us now, my love." Mrs. H. went off into her kitchen to attend to the frying pan. She returned, wiping her hands on a small gingham towel and bringing the aroma of Spam with her. "I'm cooking enough for the boys. They'll be with us as soon as it's done sizzling."

Was Sam being held by Gregor *again*? Where was Jason? Could I trust my protector? More and more questions poured into my brain. As I instinctually scanned the room for a bottle of something soothing, a car pulled up outside.

Chapter Sixty-Nine

ANTHONY

We pulled up outside our B and B in Gregor's sedan. The aroma of cooking Spam hit us as we made our way into the house.

"The schnitzel is on the table, boys." Mrs. H. popped her head around the parlor door. "Come in, you timed it perfect."

"Wonderful," I said.

"Yeah, can't wait." Sam licked his lips. "Mmm. Spam, lovely."

Con hugged us both, but with no enthusiasm.

Ⓐ

Later that evening, while Sam discussed recipes with Mrs. H. in her parlor, I joined Con in her room for a chat about the day's events. I didn't sit on the bed this time.

"Mrs. H. probably mentioned it was Gregor's sidekick at the door, earlier. Rosa told me that her boss had descended into a sort of madness. He couldn't bear the fact Jason had double-crossed him. He threatened to kill Sam unless we delivered the gold to him immediately."

"Why didn't you tell me where you were going?"

"Yes, I'm sorry. It was a spur-of-the-moment decision. Um . . . I didn't want to expose you to more danger."

"Hmm, right, yeah, thoughtful."

"Gregor soon calmed down when I told him there was little point in pursuing the gold because the coins were in a police vault. I convinced him that the return of the cover was his real victory and emphasized that he and Rosa needed to leave the States before the cops tracked them down. He also had a nasty bullet wound. My contact arranged a doctor and a plane to take them to Tahiti."

"Wow, this contact is amazingly useful. What exactly has been going on, Anthony?"

"So, anyway, Sam and I accompanied Rosa and Gregor to a small airstrip on the east side of the island. We put them on board and then came back here."

Con looked confused. "Anthony, there's something you aren't telling me. I need you to be honest with me, especially about your dealings with Jason."

"Nothing really to—"

The door opened, and Sam popped his head around. "You guys okay in here?"

"Hi, come on in. Connie and I have finished for the moment." *Well done, Sam.* I had so much to tell her, but I needed time to present it in the most palatable way.

"Hi, Con. I thought these might be useful." He brought in a small tray with three superchilled Longboard beers.

Con told us about Judy's purchase of the land.

Smart Judy Gibson was now very wealthy.

Why hadn't I been smarter?

Chapter Seventy

CONNIE

The mission dropped all charges against Liza, so we collected her from the Federal Detention Center on our short stopover in Honolulu. We filled her in on our Big Island adventure, and she said nothing when I told her about Jason's disappearance and probable injury. Anthony and his amazing contact somehow worked their magic on Sam's legal dilemma, and his counterfeiting charge went away.

While the twins rebonded over mai tais in the Barefoot Bar with the help of some fake IDs, Anthony asked me to join him in the Mercedes. He had something to show me. We drove along a lovely tree-lined road close to the mission and stopped outside a computer store. He led me through a yellow-painted side door, then up a narrow staircase into a light, spacious, and spotless apartment. A familiar fragrance from twenty years ago hung in the air. As we stood in the living room, I was drawn to an old sneakers box with the *VANS "OFF THE WALL"* logo, sitting on the round dining table.

"My God, this is Dan's stuff."

"Yes, please take a look." Anthony got out a freshly laundered handkerchief.

"Wow, what's it doing in this apartment?"

"You remember Dan came over to check out things, ready for your move?"

Nodding, I began to touch Dan's belongings. "Why would his stuff still be here?"

"You may recall me mentioning that my contact here was Billy's longtime friend? Well, he purchased the apartment on Billy's instructions as a surprise for you and Dan. Directed to prepare the place ready, and not receiving instructions to the contrary, he's maintained it ever since. Billy had apparently set up an account with a substantial balance to cover all ongoing expenses."

"Wow, it's been waiting here for nearly twenty years. Oh, wonderful, lovely Billy." His smiling face popped into my head. Oh, God. Dan and I would have been so happy here. All the thoughts were back. Now full strength and unspoiled by his younger brother.

Anthony slipped me his handkerchief and put his arm around my shoulders and held me. "Sorry about the strong aroma, but I couldn't resist opening the Hai Karate cologne bottle. The scent sort of escaped and engulfed the apartment. The window is open, but still . . ."

"Please don't worry. Yes, Dan loved that stuff, and the fragrance somehow completes the scene." Closing my eyes, I could imagine he had popped out for takeaway and would be back any moment. The tears started and wouldn't stop.

Anthony held me a little tighter.

"I came in earlier and checked around. Look, I'll go wait downstairs, no need to hurry." He released me from his embrace. "Pull the door shut when you're done."

"Thank you, this is so important to me." I opened the Hai Karate, inhaled, coughed, and smiled. A fancy ring box in with Dan's drawing stuff caught my eye. Inside sat the diamond solitaire ring he'd promised me.

The apartment had everything. All its fixtures and furnishings appeared unused. The bathroom with a spacious shower and fair-sized tub looked out onto a garden below. A small pile of linen was laid out, ready for making up the bed. The locked closet next to the refrigerator in the kitchenette drew my attention. Some searching produced the key from the back of a drawer in the sideboard.

Opening the door, I held my breath when I caught sight of the bright red Silver Cross stroller. Oh, my God. It contained a bunch of beautiful baby clothes. I carefully picked them up and imagined our baby in every one.

Perhaps thoughtful Anthony had placed all the baby stuff in here when he checked around the apartment.

After removing a tiny yellow baby onesie, I shut the door and returned the key. I lingered at the top of the stairs with the brushed cotton pressed to my cheek.

A baby gurgled in his cot.

A toddler hugged my leg. "Mommy . . ." His first word.

A boy fresh from school, clutching a painting of himself between Mom and Dad. "I love you, Mommy."

A petulant teen disappeared through the fast-closing front door. "You don't understand me."

A young man kissed me. Off to college in California to do pre-med. "See you at Thanksgiving. Love you, Mom."

Dan walked up and held me as we waved him goodbye.

We had raised our son. A glorious, handsome man, the image of his father.

Chapter Seventy-One

ANTHONY

Con remained in her own thoughts as I drove her to the Barefoot Bar. I needed to sort out an important matter before we headed to the airport for our overnight flight to New York.

I parked the car outside the bar and turned to her. "Connie, are you okay?"

"Uh . . . yes. Sorry, my mind was all over the place."

"I hope that wasn't too much? I thought—"

"No, I'm indebted to you." She put her hand on my arm and squeezed. "I can't tell you how important that was for me to see."

Letting out a sigh, I sat back in my seat. Sam and Liza were visible from the car. They appeared deep in conversation.

"Thanks again." She kissed my cheek before stepping out of the car.

My meeting was ten minutes away, in a less salubrious part of town. Once out of sight, I slammed my foot down on the accelerator.

Over an hour past the agreed time, I pushed my way in through the rear door of the deserted pool hall. The stagnant air was uncomfortably warm and fetid.

A sweaty man clutched his side and winced as he turned toward me. "Oh, Ant. Thank Jesus, I thought you'd abandoned me."

"Arrangements have been made for you to consult a doctor of sorts."

"I can't go on much longer like this, man."

"The car's outside. The place is five minutes away."

I ordered Jason to lie flat across the rear seat and covered him in a groundsheet. At the anonymous-looking office, I parked around the back, as instructed, and went inside to confirm all was ready.

Back in the Mercedes, I moved the sheet enough to expose Jason's stubbly face. "Time to keep your promise."

"In my wallet." He turned slightly, which caused him to wince.

I fished out his bloodstained leather wallet and tipped out a flat key and docket with the Manhattan Storage Company details.

After maneuvering him inside the office, I laid him down on the table. Jason stared at the various animal pictures on the wall and smiled.

"Ant, the envelope in my back pocket." He tentatively lifted his side. "I need you to send it to my brother. You'll find his address in a red notebook in my storage locker."

I removed the grubby envelope and slipped it into my jacket.

"No need to open it. It's a note to say that I won't be able to join him in London. We planned to do Europe and celebrate our birthdays together in December."

I watched the physician take a sip from a medicine bottle with an equine label before he approached his human patient.

Jason hadn't shared his post-recovery plans with me, but he promised to keep away from Con. Jason's promises were, of course, worthless, so I would need to keep an eye out for a few months, at least.

I needed to start looking after myself.

Aside from credit card debt, my account with Chuck Wilson stood north of fifty thousand dollars and would become due within days of returning to the city. A quiet word with his son might buy me extra time, but not more than a month for sure. There was no way I could run from this. I knew from my father's fate that people like Chuck Wilson didn't take kindly to being cheated.

Chapter Seventy-Two

CONNIE

In flight from Honolulu to Newark

Anthony had snagged us first-class tickets for the long flight home. The twins sat together, which suited me. We lifted glasses of champagne and toasted our reuniting, before settling back in the generous leather seats. Sam and Liza were still quite sober since the Barefoot Bar called out their IDs after the first drink.

Sam was glued to a book entitled *Hawai'i's Spam Cookbook* by Ann Kondo Corum. When he caught me looking, he stuffed the yellow paperback into his North Face. "Oh . . . Mrs. H. gave it to me. A present for Lou—as a joke."

The twins soon fell asleep. Anthony, on the other hand, appeared restless and keen to talk. "Connie, your opinion of me is going to change, for sure."

"You're scaring me. It can't be that bad." Although I had yet to confront him with what Jo had shown me.

Anthony covered his eyes and didn't respond to my attempt at a reassuring smile.

A cheerful steward offered me another glass of champagne, which I accepted.

Anthony sat up straight and began to talk. "Con, it might surprise you, but my dad was a highly skilled forger. Billy was unaware, but George used his skills regularly."

"Is your father still around?"

"No, he died in 1981, but before that, he disappeared for a few months in the previous year. That was when the Westons stepped in to help my stepmom and me financially. But when Mom began losing her mind and required full-time care in a home, I had to come up with my own plans to keep us afloat."

"Well, yes, of course."

"Helping Dan with the Apple computers gave me a little extra, but I needed to make some cash urgently. I dug out some of my dad's counterfeiting plates and banknote paper. One night, after everyone went home, I used one of the presses in the shop to run off a hundred or so twenty-dollar bills."

The alcohol, combined with the altitude, made my world all light and fluffy. "Wow, you literally made some cash." I smiled at my pun. Anthony missed it. Taking a mouthful of my refill, I found the quality had plunged from bubbly Gallic chic to gassy domestic sweet. I returned it to the glass.

Anthony looked away and sipped on his club soda. "Unknown to me at the time, and not until the cops pointed it out this week, I used the wrong reverse plate."

"So the bills Sam found in Dan's locker . . . but how—"

"I'm getting to that. Hope you're still okay hearing all this?"

"Yes, yes." Spotting an approaching steward, I hid my almost full glass behind a menu. "Please, may I try the Chardonnay. Oh, and some snacks."

When the steward returned with something cloudy and a tiny bowl of nuts, Anthony drained his glass. He then accepted the offer of a refill himself.

"So to continue"—he cleared his throat—"one evening in late November 1980, Dan walked in on me and spotted the bills rolling off the press. And, well, he wanted a cut."

"But surely . . ." Casting my mind back, in the week leading up to the accident, Dan was treating people to drinks and buying expensive sneakers. Also, those twenties Sam found in his locker . . .

"Dan gave me no option but to comply. His best buddy, Jack, spotted him splashing cash around the Chelsea. Next thing I knew, they both came to me with some cockamamie plan to ramp up production. One of Jack's close friends worked in the finance department at the hotel and planned to slip the bills into the takings. I wanted none of it." Anthony took a deep breath. "Then they stole the printing plates and blackmailed me—said they'd inform the FBI."

"What the hell, Anthony, how awful."

Sam stirred and wanted a sip of my drink. "Yuck, Con, what happened to the good stuff? I need a whiskey to take the tang away. Anybody else?"

"Gin and tonic, please," I said, to prevent a slide into Pinot Grigio.

"I'll take a beer—a Bud will do," Anthony said.

"Excuse me, miss." Sam got up, then pursued one of the hostesses, but her pace accelerated until she managed to lock herself in a bathroom. In the end, he went over and put our order in with a more accommodating guy in the galley.

Our refreshments arrived with the steward, who pouted and flirted with Sam for a short while. He gave him a tap on the knee before heading off. Sam took a couple of sips of his whiskey and fell asleep again.

"So, on the day of Dan's accident . . . Oh, Connie, I'm so sorry." Anthony put his head in his hands. Red-eyed, he continued, "On that day, I needed to show the pair . . . you understand . . . So, quite by chance, Jack was at the West Fourth Street station when I arrived there. I had no intention of harming him. You have to believe me."

Nodding for him to continue, I sipped my gin. What the hell was he telling me?

Anthony blinked his eyes. "Well, Jack was standing right on the edge of the platform—on the yellow line. I decided to show Dan how easily I could stage an accident."

He mopped his brow before staring at me. "I positioned myself behind Jack in such a way Dan would be able to see that, with a sharp shove, his buddy would be on the tracks. I'm sure Jack, himself, was totally unaware."

I couldn't speak for a moment and just stared up the aisle to the cockpit door.

"Connie, I didn't expect him to jump down from the platform and to cross the tracks."

"Shit, you made Dan do that. What the hell, you forced him onto the tracks. You killed my husband!"

"I only wanted to show them what I could do, if they didn't leave me alone." Anthony covered his face with both hands for a moment.

I said nothing.

"After Dan's death, Jack distanced himself from the Weston family. This isn't what you want to hear, but I'm positive he and Dan were lovers, and that was why Dan reacted in the way he did."

"What do you mean *lovers*?" I shook my head and refused to make eye contact with him. "They were best buddies since forever. They were very close, that's all."

Would Dan have crossed the tracks for me?

I hurried down to the bathroom and locked the door. Staring at myself in the small mirror, I ran through everything Anthony had told me. Was he really to blame for Dan's overreaction? Dan and Jack lovers? Was I blind? Why hadn't I seen it? We were married, for Christ's sake—moving to Hawaii. I dabbed my face with a fistful of tissues. What the hell, someone started knocking on the door. "Okay, okay. I'm almost done." I waited a couple more minutes before returning to my seat.

"Are you all right for me to continue?" Anthony seemed keen to get everything off his chest.

"There's more?"

"Sorry, I can stop if you like."

"No, no. Please go on."

"So, at some point, Dan had blabbed to his father what was happening at the print shop. Probably to protect him and Jack in case someone discovered us. Later, George himself used the stolen plates to blackmail me. To start with, he needed someone with the expertise to replicate a special document."

"The missionary cover?"

"Yes, it must have been. I made the arrangements with one of my father's contacts but didn't know what the item was. George kept me on to mind the print shop. I worked on counterfeiting commissions over the years to feed George's sales of historical letters and documents. He helped Louise to get a job at Dials, and then began to sell pieces through them—a New York auction house added legitimacy." Anthony stood up and stretched before hiding his face in his handkerchief.

"Are you okay?" I asked.

"Oh, Con." He blew his nose, returned his handkerchief to his pocket, and sat down. "I've been under their control for almost twenty years—like a prisoner." He swallowed hard and continued, "So when Jason, or Jacob, as I knew him then, approached me with a plan to rip off the Weston family and for me to get the printing plates back, I grabbed the chance. Connie, your arrival in the city complicated everything for me. It made me question my involvement with him. You know how I felt about you?"

I nodded, noting the past tense. Anthony had caused Dan's death, but Dan and Jack were blackmailing him. A desperate Anthony had tried to show them he wasn't going to put up with it anymore, only for Dan to overreact. Shit, my brain was spinning.

I didn't want to believe Dan and Jack were lovers, though. Why had Dan been prepared to leave Jack and join me in Hawaii? He had even set things up over there. I'd seen the beautiful home he created for us.

Anthony emptied his glass. "I didn't mention anything about our Hawaiian trip to Jason, but with Jason and Liza in Honolulu, it was impossible to avoid him."

"So, what happened to Jason?"

"Well, Gregor wounded him, but as you saw, he disappeared before the cops got there. It's unlikely we'll see him again."

How could he be so sure? If Jason was still alive, I felt certain he'd come after me.

Yes, Anthony had suffered a great deal, but his lashing out had destroyed my life with Dan. But did Dan love me more than he loved his best buddy? With some serious thinking to do, I went to sit in a vacant seat on my own and ordered strong black coffee. Now, I needed to stay out of the past and start considering my future.

Chapter Seventy-Three

ANTHONY

My confessions during the flight home resulted in a feeling of total relaxation. Something I'd missed for as long as I could remember. Although Con knew me better after our expedition, my involvement in her husband's death—however unwittingly—remained a massive obstacle to us getting together. At least Sam had failed to go the distance. Hopefully, Con would be staying in the city for a while now that her mom was here. It was time for a new strategy, but not until I'd sorted out my dire financial situation.

When I switched on my cell, a text from Judy popped up, asking me to contact her as soon as possible. I called her as we walked from the gate, and she asked me to come over to her apartment.

"Connie, you all return to the Dakota. I need to do some stuff and sort out my room at the Chelsea. I'll meet you later. Be great to catch up with your mom again."

"God, yes, my mom. Are you sure you wouldn't like to share a cab?"

"No, but, thank you."

I grabbed a cup of coffee, checked my address book for Judy's details, and headed to the taxis. I needed to stop off on the way.

At the Manhattan Storage Company, I found and opened Jason's box. I stared at the black PVC bag containing the printing plates and allowed myself a silent but triumphant fist pump.

The end of twenty years of blackmail gave me an incredible sense of calm. I was even able to forget my financial woes for a moment. I peeled off the barely sticky duct tape and put my hand inside. To my utter relief, Winston's incriminating letter was still there. I pulled it out and stuffed it into my jacket pocket.

No more "Anthony, I must insist you do that."

No more "Anthony, remember, I hold something of yours."

No more "Anthony, we own you."

Passing by a small office on my way out of the building, I spotted something useful. An obliging young man there agreed to deal with Winston's letter for me. I stayed and watched for the few seconds it took for the two sheets to be pulled into the crosscut shredder. The plates would be going into the Hudson later that evening.

"You look like you just discovered a million bucks," said the cab-driver when I returned.

"Almost," I said. "Almost."

Ⓐ

As I traveled to Brooklyn, my mind focused on my finances. Chuck was a stand-up guy, but for sure, he wouldn't tolerate being made to wait too long for his money.

The cab took the last of my cash. Lucky I had a MetroCard for my return. After Judy buzzed me in, I climbed the stairs to her apartment, all the time thinking of my last visit there with Con.

Judy was waiting for me at the open door with Wendy by her side. Tigger stood between them and slightly forward, as if on guard.

"Anthony, how lovely to see you. Come on in." She took my arm and escorted me into the living room.

We sat together on the sofa. Wendy brought over a couple of club sodas without being asked—a testament to her fine upbringing.

"So, it all worked out in the end—I'm so pleased for you." I envied Judy's good fortune but didn't harbor any animosity toward her. In fact, I admired her smart strategy.

"Well, you found and touched the gold, too. It must have been a terrible disappointment for you all."

"We had competition from the owner of the cover, not to mention Liza and her friend. The whole affair turned into a debacle."

Wendy went off to tend her stamps at a small dedicated table in front of the TV. It was set up with her albums, catalogs, a huge magnifying glass, and the all-important tweezers.

"Anthony, you defended my interests at a critical moment. I insist that you take a share of the find."

"That is incredibly generous, but no, I couldn't—that treasure is yours by right." All my financial worries would be over instantly. "Oh . . . but I did incur some expenses that will need to be paid in a few weeks. Perhaps I could . . . uh . . . borrow an amount to sort things out before I can access other funds?"

"Of course, let me know when and how much. I will make no demand for the return of the money. Dials is auctioning the coins early next month."

"That will be so helpful, thank you." At a stroke, the pressure was off.

Wendy got up and led Tigger off to the kitchen.

"I wondered if you and Connie . . . um . . . I detected a spark of something when you visited."

"Well, yes, to be honest, I was hopeful. But what with the Weston boy, and my involvement in her husband's accident—"

"How do you mean *involvement*? I was there. Dan and I saw what we both thought was a young child on the tracks. We were mistaken, of course. But that was why Dan jumped down—to save a doll. *He lost his life saving a fucking doll.* So unless you put that thing on the tracks, it had nothing to do with you."

Can that be true? My brain scrambled at the possibility. Hours after telling Con I was responsible for Dan's death, I learned this? Yes, I had also spotted that doll. Con had kicked it onto the tracks when she almost tripped on the thing. For Pete's sake, paradoxical, or what? Inadvertently, she was to blame for her husband's death.

I decided never to mention any of this to Con. It would destroy her. Judy promised not to say anything, either.

We changed the subject when Wendy returned. She brought over her favorite album and joined us on the sofa. Tigger settled down on my lap while Wendy showed off her Hawaiian stamps.

During our parting embrace, Judy held on a little longer and tighter than I expected.

"We plan to move to Hawaii later in the year. Promise me now you'll come to visit?"

"Yes, I will—*I certainly will.*"

Chapter Seventy-Four

CONNIE

Sam, Liza, and I arrived back at the Dakota around ten in the morning. Anthony said he would join us later.

I did a double take when the 1980 version of Mom greeted me at the door. No more the frumpy, gray-haired, middle-aged, wearing-sweatpants-from-an-English-supermarket couch potato. Now the Manhattan power blonde in an Alexander McQueen designer dress and flawless makeup stood before me. It amazed me that this version of my mother had lain dormant for so many years. I was so pleased to see her restored to her former self.

She'd already reestablished order and the delightful aroma of beeswax and linseed. What was left of Aileen's prized Waterford sat on its correct shelves in the corner cupboard with the door locked shut. The reliable ticktock of Billy's grandfather clock echoed again throughout the apartment. Its face was smiling ten past ten as I passed by. Pompom snoozed in his basket and was now restricted to the kitchen until his behavior improved.

John Allan's at Saks Fifth Avenue had spent the previous afternoon transforming George's hair and generally restoring him to his former self. Mom said once she took him off Jason's weird cocktail of meds, his mind began to return. George admitted to me that he recalled my visits to the apartment. Liza denied knowing anything about Jason's activities or past. I doubted that.

Mom, George, and I sat down at the dining table.

"So, lovey, you've told us nothing of your vacation." Mom poured me some freshly brewed coffee. "How's Anthony? Are you a couple?"

I managed a half smile.

Sam ambled in with some mail in his hand. Why had I been so besotted with this boy? Something had changed in me during the last few days of our trip. I was now ready to stand on my own two feet, even without the help of a multimillion-dollar fortune.

He placed a small package under his arm while he wrestled an envelope open and lifted the contents partway out.

Something caught my eye. "Is that a cashier's check?"

He smiled and stuffed the envelope into the back pocket of his grubby, now-too-small-for-him 505s. He then walked over and kissed my cheek. "Payment for my Nintendo game."

I wiped the spot with my palm.

"This is for you, Con." He made a show of presenting me with the brown paper-wrapped parcel with a New York postmark. "I won't watch you open it."

"Thanks." I shot him a glare, which he acknowledged with a nod. Once through the sticky tape and paper, a short note on top of a pocket-size notebook read: *Meant to give you this when you visited. Dan put it in my bag with the missionary cover. Love, Judy X*

"Everything all right, lovey?" Mom asked, shifting her chair for a better view.

"Fine." I flicked the edge of the pages, then I stood and pushed my chair back.

"Con, did you tell everyone about our Hawaiian treasure hunt yet? And the ghost?" Sam was in high spirits—maybe something to do with the cashier's check.

"Perhaps we should leave all that for later when Ant is here. He's so much better at detail than either of us." I made my excuses and hurried off to look at Dan's secrets.

Sitting on the bed in what was now Mom's room, I took a deep breath and opened the precious notebook. A loose, simple pencil sketch of me dropped out onto the table. I picked it up and smiled at my younger self. After that, every page I turned contained an explicit drawing of his friend. Jack sitting, in profile, and full face. Jack standing, from the back and full frontal. His age in some of the sketches proved to me they had been lovers forever.

Yes, Dan had stepped up to his responsibilities, but he was that sort of guy. Would he have been happy living with me in Hawaii, though? How could he be, with those feelings and far away from his true love?

Familiar and long-cherished memories of Dan started to pour into my brain. But now, every one of these treasured thoughts disintegrated before I could enjoy it. I tried, again and again, to conjure up even the most reliable ones. I climbed farther and farther under the bedclothes, unable to stop crying.

Part Three

Chapter Seventy-Five

CONNIE

Creative works of all kinds are my passion now. After spending the afternoon at the Whitney, I'm on my way to Lincoln Center. A play caught my eye, and Josie is meeting me in the foyer at five forty-five for pre-theater drinks and a Caesar salad. I gave up drinking alcohol more than twenty years ago, just after our return from Hawaii.

Today is the fortieth anniversary of Dan's death and, of course, the death of John Lennon. Both are impossible to separate in my mind.

The Fourteenth Street station is crammed full of people. They take up more space on cold days. A rumble gets louder and turns into a clatter as the Uptown C shoots along the platform, brakes screeching. The doors slam open, and commuters spill out backward. Most of them want to reboard. I refuse to be late, so I battle my way on, ignoring protests—in the way we New Yorkers do.

I'm in an armpit of a sweet-smelling youth until Forty-Second, then take a vacant seat. As we shudder to a stop in the station, a young guy bends down to look out the window. His handsome and familiar heart-shaped face reflects in the glass. Coincidence or what? It's Daniel, my son. What the hell is he doing on this train?

My eldest son, older than his brother by twenty minutes, arrived back from traveling with school friends in Asia and the Pacific last weekend, but he was planning to stay with his father out in Montauk until Friday—his plans had obviously changed. Daniel is the image of his father at that age. Now, more than ever, he also reminds me of my late husband.

Within a month of returning from Hawaii, some big-time morning barfing brought me total joy. Sam's immediate reaction was to deny it could be anything to do with him. He had no interest in me by then, anyway, and spent most of his time out of the apartment, splurging on clothes and friends. I assumed he was funding this new lifestyle from his Nintendo check.

One morning in March 2001, my assumption turned out to be wrong. We were at breakfast when George opened a letter from the mortgage company, demanding the first repayment. By March twenty-eighth, the day the twins were born, we realized what had happened. Sam disappeared, and later the same day, Liza shipped out, too. I've not seen nor spoken to Sam since. He hadn't seen either of his boys until Daniel tracked him down. They met up on a couple of occasions this year. Sam's other son, Bill, refuses to have anything to do with him.

My lovely boys changed my life. I spent the past twenty years with no unhealthy habits, no humiliating hookups, and no worries about aging. Just a happy and joyful family life. And my mom and I get on better now than we ever did before.

Daniel spots me, and his face lights up with a broad, Sam-like grin. He gives me a little wave and heads over.

We check each other out.

"Hi, Mom, you look well."

"This is a lovely surprise." The smell of stale tobacco smoke is unmistakable. I'll need to have a word. "I thought you were staying with your father?" His luxuriant hair is long. My hand goes up. "You've grown your hair."

He lets me get a brief touch before dipping his head away. "Dad has this girlfriend. She's my age and a waitress at his restaurant—totally gross."

From what Daniel told me after his last visit, Sam owns a highly successful lobster roll place on the road out to Montauk. Pictures of celebrities all over the walls, eating his signature dish: *Sam's Spam Wham*, a lobster-and-Spam fritter in pretzel bread, with a secret sauce. The recipe was no doubt inspired by that little yellow paperback he got all those years ago. Daniel had shown me photographs he'd taken of the newspaper clippings. One picture, in particular, caught my eye. Under an *East Hampton Star* headline, *Bestest ever meal at new lobster-Spam fusion restaurant*, was the unmistakable image of Jo. It was clear to me now that we each had our connection to that mysterious boy.

The train grinds to a halt. Daniel is checking around to see who's looking at us—he can't bear people listening in.

I message Josie and take a rain check.

We stand in silence. I am aware that, without the cover of the train's clattering and banging, everyone in the car will overhear us. Daniel will start to shush me.

The conductor's voice comes over the intercom. "Your train is delayed because of an ongoing police investigation." I know what that's code for and take a deep breath.

Chapter Seventy-Six

After ten minutes or so, the train moves off again, and Daniel reengages.

"This weird guy with tattoos showed up at the restaurant with a woman Dad said was my aunt Liza."

"Did you get the guy's name?"

"We weren't introduced. He knows Dad from way back. Oh, yeah, Dad called him Jay or Jase. He was after cash. So I decided to split before things got heavy."

After Sam had disappeared, it came out that he was more involved with Jason than anybody suspected. Anyone except Anthony, of course, who finally told all. Jason had hatched a plot to bankrupt and bring down the Weston family. He wanted revenge. Revenge for having to suffer a jobless, drunk, abusive father. Revenge for being split up from his brother.

I still break into a cold sweat when anybody uses Aileen's knife. The pearl-handled silver fruit knife that ended up in my grab bag of stuff for Hawaii and kicked off the whole dreadful Jason affair. Now and then, someone finds it. "Oh, Aileen's lovely silver fruit knife, we should use this more often. Such a sharp blade, perfect for tomatoes."

Daniel starts flipping a large silver coin.

"What's that in your hand?" I know, of course.

"Dad gave it to me. A 1921 peace dollar—pretty cool. The year Great-Grandpa Billy was born, according to Dad." He starts the thing off doing a familiar spin through his fingers. Daniel pauses his performance. "Hey, Mom, has Bill moved his stuff out of upstairs yet?"

"I don't think so—he's been busy."

"Doing what? We agreed to share the attic apartment. Six months each."

As the train slows, my son indicates for me to continue our conversation via our cells. I shake my head. He harrumphs, and I think of his father.

Anthony told me how Jason wheedled his way into Sam and Liza's lives. Liza liked her boyfriend's idea of squeezing cash out of her father. Sam was unwilling to join in with their plan at first, but one night, after a blazing row with his father over money, he went and signed up. The scheme lacked detail until George tripped over Pompom and twisted his ankle.

Liza suggested that a physiotherapist friend could give him a few free sessions. This friend was Jason Jackson from Queens, but in the guise of Jacob Jakobson from Copenhagen. He put George on high-strength meds, which messed up his brain to the extent the poor man appeared to be suffering from dementia.

Jason planned to remortgage the apartment with the help of a power of attorney forged by Anthony. All this had occurred while Aileen was away on a wellness retreat in the Catskills. Immediately on her return, she arranged for her son to consult a neurologist, recommended by her best friend, Mamie Van de Coot. A couple of days before the appointment, Aileen was found dead on her bathroom floor.

Everything was in place and the mortgage granted when the missionary business blew up. The finance company cut a cashier's check on July 6, 2000, and mailed it to Sam at the Dakota. The letter arrived and sat on the little table in the entrance hall used for the mail until we all returned from Hawaii. Anthony assumed Sam had called off the swindle after our adventure together. The temptation of the mortgage money, though, had proved too much for him.

My son seems tired of waiting for the train to pick up speed again. "So Mom, what's my bro been up to now?"

I mouth, "He has a girlfriend."

"*A what.*" People look over. He moves some hair to cover his increasing redness.

"I mean, she's more of a woman friend. You remember Jessica?"

Daniel looks disbelieving. "What. Didn't you tell us she used to go out with Dad?"

Chapter Seventy-Seven

We stand in silence, waiting for the train to start moving again. Daniel is glued to his cell while I stare at him and think how well my life turned out.

A message comes through from him. He's asking me for more details about Bill and Jessica. I reply, saying he should talk to his brother about it.

I wonder if Jess started up their relationship as a way to get back at me for "seducing Sam," as she once said. Who knows? Who cares? Just in case, I arranged for Amazon to deliver a gift box of condoms directly to Bill.

The doors close, and we finally leave Columbus Circle station.

"Uncle Ant sends his love," Daniel says.

"God, yes, how is old Uncle Ant? I forgot you were visiting Hawaii."

Mom told me Anthony went there to live, and he and Judy had a child together—a boy they called Joseph. I'm not sure if they were ever married. Mom thinks not. Anthony wrote a couple of books on Hawaiian treasure and an unusual ghost story featuring you-know-who. We received a letter from him this time last year to say Judy had lost her long battle with breast cancer. Mom responded—in the way one does.

"He looks younger than Dad does."

"I should go visit."

Faithful Anthony had stuck around and become even more atten-
tive after Sam had abandoned me. I gained an understanding of what
he'd gone through. In the end, though, he gave up on me and moved
out of the city. After my continued lack of interest, who could blame
him? My biggest regret in my life was treating Anthony so badly.

We heard that Judy received nearly $12 million from the auction of
her coins and immediately moved to Hawaii with her daughter. Later,
Mom mentioned that Judy sent Mrs. H. and Burt's niece, Mandy, a
quarter of a million apiece. She also offered Anthony a sizable sum
with the idea he might split the cash with me, and we could settle
down together. She said that Judy made a large donation to a church in
Honolulu—enough for a new roof. Clever Maureen.

We sold our Bermondsey basement to Gilbert and Tom. My dear
Simon was so well settled with them that I gave up on any idea of bringing him over here. In late November 2016, Tom called to say Simon had
passed peacefully during the previous night. Both he and Gilbert had
kept vigil until the end. They buried him in the small garden at the rear
of the property, wrapped in one of Gilbert's cashmere bombers.

The cash I received from the sale of the apartment in Honolulu,
which dear Billy had put in Dan's and my names, was useful during the
twins' early years. I also made an investment in the family print business for my boys and bought a couple thousand Apple shares.

I can't remember the last time Mom and I argued. We haven't seen
Auntie Betty in twenty years, and we're both grateful for that.

George and Mom got hitched in 2005. He wanted to marry earlier,
but Mom, disgusted by the way he had treated Anthony, refused until
he dropped all his dodgy dealings. With Mom's help, they built San
Remo into New York's leading digital on-demand print shop. Shortly
after they married, Mom asked her new husband to take Pompom for
a walk, as he and the dog were getting in the way of her big spring-
cleaning. Pompom slipped his leash and dashed across Central Park
West, with George in hot pursuit. The outside mirror of a Downtown
M10 bus knocked George off his feet, and the wheels of the same bus
did in the dog. A dazed George carried Pompom's remains back to the
Dakota, where he told dear Walt to "deal with it."

Daniel puts his iPhone away in his jeans pocket and comes over to
stand close to me.

"It's good to have you back," I say in a whisper.

He looks around the car. "Yeah."

We arrive at the Seventy-Second Street station, and I am glad to be leaving the train.

Chapter Seventy-Eight

Nobody is at the front desk in the Dakota. The elevator takes us up.

George's British bulldog, Lennon, rushes to greet us, his tongue lolling out.

My son rubs the dog's flanks with both his hands. Lennon goes into ecstasy.

Lou now lives up the road at the Beresford with Josie. When my boys were growing up, she and Josie helped me enormously, and we shared so much together. Lou continued to work at Dials until her retirement a year or two back. She was prompted to step away by the reappearance of the missionary cover, offered for sale by the beneficiaries of the estate of Gregor Ionesco. Over the past twenty years, Lou and I wrote half a dozen stage plays together. We sold a screenplay to Netflix a couple of months back for a tidy sum. We have a development meeting with them next week.

The apartment door is wide open, and a shouty voice is coming from inside. We walk into the living room with Lennon lolloping on our tail. The corner cupboard door is hanging open. A tall, dark-haired man is standing with a woman who looks like Liza, only skankier. She is arguing with her father while Jason drinks Mountain Dew from a Waterford Crystal highball tumbler.

Liza turns. "Oh, Constance, come in and join the family. Yes, and your other darling boy." She reminds me of her older sister, back in the day.

"Tape them both up." Jason points to a roll of blue duct tape with his pistol. "Hey, Dan, who thought we would meet again so soon? Come over here and say hello to your brother. Don't try anything."

"What the hell? How dare you barge in here and terrorize us." I hold Liza's upper arm for a moment until she shrugs me off.

Jason is limping and clasping his side like an old man. An ugly sneer is a permanent feature on his alcoholic face.

Daniel tries to resist as Liza binds his hands with the tape. Jason points the gun at his head, and he complies. "Go sit with your brother, like a good little boy."

Bill acknowledges his brother with a nod. They are identical, but Daniel appears thinner and duskier after his travels. He tans well, like his father. I see him mouth. "Jessica, what the hell." Bill reddens.

"To bring you up to speed, we're here for what's mine." Liza's lined face twists into a snarl. "About time I got something from this fucking family."

"We have unfinished business." Jason wants the safe open and shoves George toward his study. Liza walks over and pulls a matching pistol from her oversized black Coco Chanel flap bag. The gold clasp is showing some green.

I'm now boiling with rage. I want them out of my home and away from my boys.

My mom isn't around. She was going to try to get a ticket for the play. My iPhone reports a missed call from her.

"You better give that to me, Constance." Liza shows me her "gimme" hand.

I pass her my cell, and she slips it on a shelf in the corner cupboard where two others are lying. She tapes my wrists as I desperately run ideas through my brain. I will not allow this to happen.

Jason returns to the room, stuffing his pockets with cash—the bills are mostly twenties. He throws Liza a cloth bag. "Check in there, doll. They're the real deal this time."

Liza dips her hand in and pulls out Mom's jewelry. She stuffs it back in and puts the bag in the wonky front pocket of her dodgy Chanel. Jason starts to screw a silencer to the muzzle of his Smith & Wesson.

"Move into the study, guys, and line up against the far wall by the clock." Jason guides the way by flicking his gun.

The grandfather clock acknowledges us by striking six.

George closes his eyes and is whispering something. No way am I going to allow these two desperadoes to destroy everything we have here.

Jason puts his ugly mug close up to the faces of Daniel and Bill in turn. "Two pretty boys, Connie. Double what you wished for. Aren't you the lucky one?" He punches Daniel in the stomach, and Bill kicks out. Jason grabs the roll from Liza and runs the tape around the twins' lower legs.

"Leave my boys alone, they're nothing to do with any of this. Take your revenge on me. It was my fault your father got dismissed—nobody else's." How can this be happening? I scan the room—I pray my brain is still working on something.

"The whole Weston clan needs to pay. Any last thoughts, guys, before I finally take my revenge on this godforsaken family?" Jason is laughing.

"Jase. Are you sure about this?" Liza asks.

"Liza, we're your family. What you did is all in the past. Please talk some sense into him."

"Jase, aren't we just here for stuff?" She stares over at him.

"Tell you what, Connie, I'll kill you last, so you can watch your beautiful young sons die."

George starts shouting. Jason goes over and cracks the old man over the head with his gun. Lennon takes offense at his master's treatment and attacks Jason's leg. He responds by kicking the dog's head— Lennon falls silent.

Aileen's pearl-handled silver fruit knife is sitting open on an apple-peel-strewn plate next to George's MacBook. With all my strength, I manage to fracture the single layer of duct tape on my left wrist. *Amateur-hour taping, Liza.*

As I reach over for Aileen's pride and joy, something deep within me is building.

I'm hiding the wee knife between the palms of my hands. I stare over at Jason, and I am shouting too, now. "You can't do this to my family, you fucking animal."

"Well, keep watching, bitch." Jason puts the pistol to Bill's right temple.

I scream and charge at him with the fruit knife before plunging it into his lower torso again and again. The gun goes off, but I can't tell if Bill is okay. The gun fires again. A searing pain tears through my chest. Blood is dripping on the parquet. Blood all over. My legs weaken and start to buckle. With all my remaining strength, I lunge forward and plunge the knife into the back of Jason's neck.

As I sink to the floor, Walt is coming in through the study door, pulling tape from his own wrists. Jason is clutching at the pearl-handled knife as he staggers around but doesn't seem able to remove it. He clips the corner cupboard, shaking the Waterford, before exiting the apartment. Liza stays in the room and is lost.

The comforting fragrance of Aqua Velva fills my nose. Walt is cradling my head and shouting out orders. My blood is all over his pristine white shirt. Liza is calling 911. What has happened? Where are my boys? I start to lose consciousness.

Epilogue

A dense, swirling mist surrounds me. I am unable to move but feel a complete calmness. The fog begins to clear, and a whole scene opens up in front of me. It's the West Fourth Street station. The A to Rockaway hasn't fully arrived at the platform. Everything is silent. A boy no more than fourteen years old is walking toward me. "Hey, Jo, what are you doing here?"

He is carrying something. As he gets closer, a ginger-and-white cat raises its head. Oh, my darling Simon. He has gray patches around his whiskers. Jo lifts him up and kisses the cat's head before placing him into my arms. Simon is purring. I start to cry and bury my head in his fur.

"Hey, Con, long time no see," says a voice I've not heard in forty years. "I hope you haven't been flaunting my Walkman on the train."

I look up through Simon's fur. I am full-on bawling. Standing in front of me is my Dan, my husband. Young and good-looking. He puts his arms around me. Jo comes up and joins us. The opening chords and harmonica of Billy Joel's "Piano Man" start up. A handsome guy with coal-black hair, milk-fair skin, and soul-piercing blue eyes stands a short distance away. Jack is looking serious. I beckon him over. A deep and lasting affection envelops us all. The mist descends again, but total calmness remains with me.

Ⓐ

Somebody switches off the music. Sunlight is making my closed eyelids glow red. There is a clinical odor.

"Shit, she's waking up. Con, can you hear me?"

"She's blinking—I'll go get the doctor."

My eyes start working. I notice that blurry patch in my vision. "My God, Sam. Is that you? What the hell are you doing here?"

"You got shot protecting our sons."

"Shit, yes. Where are they? Are my boys okay?"

"Our sons are both fine, everyone is fine. Dad took a knock to the head, but you know how resilient he is. Your mom worked her magic."

"So I'm not dead?"

"Yeah, no, you were out for a week, though. We've all come to check on you."

My sons take turns to make a fuss. Mom arrives with George, and she comes over. While I'm full-on weeping again, I spot Sam handing his father what looks like a cashier's check and hear him whisper, "Everything I took, Dad. With all the interest."

Mom strokes my arm. "Lovey, we thought we had lost you."

They leave as a doctor starts to examine me.

Someone is lurking in the doorway. "Anthony, is that you?"

"Con, hi."

Oh, my God, he hasn't changed at all. I start to think of everything he's been through. He's come all this way. My protector grins the broadest of grins when I catch his eye, and he licks his lips.

I call him over—my arms are open.

Acknowledgments

Special thanks to all at Girl Friday Productions, who did such a fantastic job. I was so lucky to be in the expert hands of Bethany Davis, who guided me through the publishing process and kept everything on track. My words were improved immeasurably by Faith Black Ross and Scott Calamar.

I also want to mention the incredible Mary Kole, who helped me so much during the latter stages of my manuscript drafts. And, indeed, for recommending GFP.

Finally, I would like to thank the UK's Open University for taking me into the world of creative writing.

SWH

Author Bio

S W Hessel writes in London, England. Little more is known about the author.

CPSIA information can be obtained
at www.ICGtesting.com
Printed in the USA
LVHW090955291220
675128LV00016B/824